LAST SEEN IN
MASSILIA

STEVEN SAYLOR

LAST SEEN IN MASSILIA

ST. MARTIN'S MINOTAUR

NEW YORK

www.minotaurbooks.com

PRODUCTION EDITOR: DAVID STANFORD BURR

Library of Congress Cataloging-in-Publication Data

Saylor, Steven.
    Last seen in Massilia / by Steven Saylor.—1st ed.
        p. cm.
    ISBN 0-312-20928-2
    1. Gordianus the Finder (Fictitious character)—Fiction. 2. Rome—History—Civil War, 49–45 B.C.—Fiction. 3. Marseille (France)—Fiction. 4. Missing persons—Fiction. I. Title.

PS3569.A96 L37 2000
813'.54—dc21

                                                                                    00-031744

First Edition: October 2000

10   9   8   7   6   5   4   3   2   1

For my sister, Gwyn,
THIS BOOK

Ubi tu es qui colere mores Massiliensis postulas?
Nunc tu si uis subigitare me, probast occasio.
                    —Plautus, *Casina* (963–964)

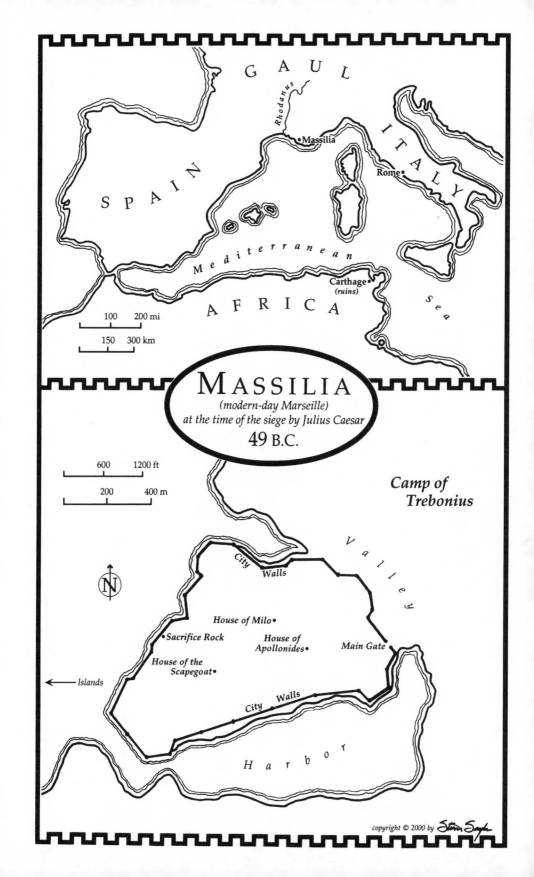

G A U L

Rhodanus

• Massilia

S P A I N

I T A L Y

Rome •

M e d i t e r r a n e a n

Carthage •
(ruins)

A F R I C A

S e a

100   200 mi

150   300 km

MASSILIA
(modern-day Marseille)
at the time of the siege by Julius Caesar
49 B.C.

600   1200 ft

200   400 m

Camp of
Trebonius

V a l l e y

City
Walls

N

House of Milo •

• Sacrifice Rock

House of
Apollonides •

Main Gate

House of the
Scapegoat •

← Islands

City   Walls

H a r b o r

I

"Madness!" I muttered. "Davus, I knew it was a mistake to leave the road. Shortcut indeed!"

"But, father-in-law, you heard what the man at the tavern said. The road to Massilia isn't safe. The Massilians are all shut up inside the city, under siege. And Caesar's troops are too busy laying the siege to bother with patrolling the road. Gaulish bandits are running wild, waylaying anyone who dares to take the road."

"A Gaulish bandit might not be entirely unwelcome at the moment. At least he might give us directions." I studied the bewildering prospect around us. Gradually we had made our way into a long, narrow valley, the cliffs on either side rising in imperceptible degrees around us like stone giants slowly lifting their heads, and now we found ourselves surrounded on all sides by sheer walls of pale limestone. A stream, almost dry at the end of a long, dry summer, trickled through the narrow defile, its rocky banks shaded by small trees. Our horses delicately picked their way around jagged rocks and gnarled tree roots as thick as a man's arm. It was slow going.

Early that morning we had set out from the tavern. We had taken the tavernkeeper's advice to abandon the flat, wide, finely wrought Roman road almost at once. As long as we used the sun to stay on a southerly course and moved in a generally downhill direction toward the sea, we couldn't possibly miss Massilia, the tavernkeeper had said, especially with so many of Caesar's troops camped before it. Now, as the sun began to drop behind the western cliffs of the valley, I was beginning to think the fellow had played a nasty joke on us.

Shadows deepened among the boulders. Tree roots, wildly splayed over the stony ground, seemed to quicken and quiver in the dim light. Again and again, from the corner of my eye I imagined thick clumps of snakes writhing amid the rocks. The horses appeared to suffer the same delusion. Repeatedly they snorted and shied and tested their hooves against the knotted roots.

Not knowing how we had entered the valley, I was equally uncertain how to get out of it. I tried to reassure myself. The sun had disappeared behind the cliffs to our right, so we had to be traveling south. We were following the direction of the stream, which meant we were probably headed seaward. South and seaward, just as the tavernkeeper had advised. But where in Hades were we? Where was Massilia, with Caesar's army camped before it? And how could we exit this hall of stone?

A band of lurid sunlight lit up the highest reaches of the eastern cliffs to our left, turning the chalk-white stone blood-red. The glare was blinding. When I lowered my eyes, the deepening shadows around us seemed even darker. The bubbling water in the stream looked black.

A warm breeze sighed through the valley. Sounds and sights became deceptive, uncertain; in the stirring of the leaves I heard men moaning, snakes hissing. Strange phantoms appeared among the rocks—twisted faces, tormented bodies, impossible freaks—then as suddenly vanished back into the stone. Despite the warm breeze, I shivered.

Riding behind me, Davus whistled a tune that a wandering Gaulish singer had performed at the tavern the previous night. Not for the first time in the twenty-odd days since we left Rome, I wondered if my imperturbable son-in-law was truly fearless, or if he simply lacked imagination.

Suddenly I gave a start. I must have pulled on the reins and expelled a noise of alarm, for my horse stopped short and Davus drew his short sword. "Father-in-law, what is it?"

I blinked. "Nothing. . . ."

"But, father-in-law—"

"It was nothing, surely . . ." I gazed into the murk of boulders and low branches. Amid the fleeting phantoms, I thought I had seen a face, a real face, with eyes that gazed back—eyes that I recognized.

"Father-in-law, what did you see?"

"I *thought* I saw . . . a man."

Davus peered into the gloom. "A bandit?"

"No. A man I once knew. But that would be . . . impossible."

"Who was it?"

"His name was Catilina."

"The rebel? But he lost his head ages ago, when I was a boy."

"Not so long ago—thirteen years." I sighed. "But you're right, Catilina was killed in battle. I saw his head myself . . . mounted on a spike outside the tent of the general who defeated him."

"Well, then, it couldn't have been Catilina you saw, could it?" There was the slightest quaver of doubt in Davus's voice.

"Of course not. A trick of the light . . . the shadow of some leaves on a stone . . . an old man's imagination." I cleared my throat. "Catilina has been much in my thoughts these last few days, as we've drawn closer to Massilia. You see, when he decided to flee from his enemies in Rome, this was where Catilina intended to come—to Massilia, I mean. Massilia is the end of the world—the end of the road for Roman exiles, anyway—a safe port for all the bitter losers and failed schemers who've seen their hopes destroyed in Rome. At Massilia they find a welcome—provided they arrive with enough gold to pay their way in. But not Catilina. In the end, he chose not to flee. He stood his ground and fought. And so he lost his head." I shivered. "I hate this place! All barren rock and stunted trees."

Davus shrugged. "I don't know. I think it's rather pretty."

I gave my horse a kick and moved on.

By some magic of the hour, the gloom around us seemed not to deepen but to stay as it was, growing neither lighter nor darker. We had entered a twilight world where phantoms whispered and flitted among the trees.

Behind me, most unnerving of all, Davus whistled, oblivious of the phantoms around us. We were like two sleepers dreaming different dreams.

"Look, father-in-law, up ahead! It looks like a temple of some sort. . . ."

So it was. Abruptly we left the maze of boulders. The stream curved away to our left. The stone cliff to our right opened in a great semicircular curve, like a vast limestone amphitheater. A thin waterfall trickled from the overhanging summit. The wall was riven with springs. Ferns and moss grew out of the stone.

The ground before us was flat. At some time long ago the space had been cleared and made into a vineyard. Tottering posts marked regular rows spaced well apart, but the vines, thick with leaves and heavy with dark grapes, were now madly overgrown in a wild tangle.

Surrounding this vineyard was a peculiar-looking fence. As we drew closer, I saw that it was made of bones—not animal bones but the bones of men, arm bones and leg bones nailed together and driven into the earth. Some of the bones had rotted and crumbled, turning dark brown or almost black. Others were bleached white and perfectly intact. Two limestone pylons marked a gateway in the fence. The pylons were carved with reliefs depicting battle scenes. The victors wore armor and crested helmets in the style of Greek seafarers; the vanquished were Gauls in leather britches and winged helmets. Beyond the gateway, broken paving stones choked with weeds led to a small, round temple with a domed roof at the center of the vineyard. I was transfixed by the strangeness of our surroundings. The gloom around us lifted a bit. The little temple seemed faintly to glow, as if the pale marble blushed in the twilight.

Behind me Davus sucked in a breath. "Father-in-law, I know this place!"

"How, Davus? From a dream?"

"No, from the tavern last night. This must be the place he sang about!"

"Who?"

"The traveling singer. After you went to sleep, I stayed up to listen. He sang about this place."

"How did the song go?"

"A long time ago, some Greeks sailed past Italy and Sicily and arrived in these parts on the southern coast of Gaul. They founded a city and they called it Massilia. The Gauls welcomed them at first, but then there was trouble—battles—a war. One of those battles happened in a narrow valley, where the Massilians trapped the Gauls and slaughtered them by the thousands. The blood that drained from the bodies made the soil so rich that grapevines sprang up overnight. The Massilians used the bones of the dead to build a fence around the vineyard. And the Gauls still sing a song about it. That's the tune I've been whistling all day. And here we are!"

"And the temple?"

"I don't know about that. Built by the Massilians, I suppose."

"Shall we have a look? Perhaps an offering to the local deity will help us find a way out of this accursed place."

We dismounted and tied our horses to iron rings in the pylons, then walked up the broken pathway. The vines shivered, animated by a warm gust of wind. The sky overhead was underwater blue, streaked with coral tints of pink and yellow. We came to the steps of the temple and gazed up. Sculptures in relief decorated the entablatures that girdled the roof, but the paint on the marble was so faded that it was impossible to discern the images. We mounted the steps. A bronze door stood ajar on frozen hinges. I turned sideways and slipped inside. Davus, on account of his size, had to squeeze through.

Despite small apertures near the ceiling, the light was very dim. The encircling walls faded into darkness. I had a sense of having entered a murky space with no perceptible boundaries. My eyes were drawn to a pedestal in the center of the room. There was something on the pedestal, a vague, unfamiliar shape. I took a step closer, straining my eyes.

A hand gripped my shoulder. I heard the slither of steel drawn from a scabbard. I started, then felt warm breath in my ear. It was only Davus.

"What is it on the pedestal?" he whispered. "A man? Or—?"

I shared his confusion. The amorphous form atop the pedestal could hardly be the upright figure of a god. It might have been a man squatting on all fours, watching us. It might have been a Gorgon. My imagination ran riot.

A burst of sound suddenly echoed through the temple—a sputtering, tittering, hissing noise.

The sound came from the doorway behind us. I turned about. Because of the light beyond, I saw only a silhouette. For a moment I imagined a two-headed monster with spiky limbs was barking at us through the open doorway. Then I realized that the barking was suppressed laughter, and the two heads belonged to two men—two soldiers to judge from their dully glinting helmets and mail shirts and the drawn swords in their fists. They were squeezed together into the breech, clutching each other and giggling.

Davus stepped before me, clutching his sword. I pulled him back.

One of soldiers spoke. "Pretty, isn't she—the thing on the pedestal?"

"Who—?" I began to say. "What—?"

"Listen to that, Marcus, the old one speaks Latin!" said the soldier. "You're not a Gaul then? Or some Massilian who's slipped the noose?"

I took a deep breath and drew myself up. "I'm a Roman citizen. My name is Gordianus."

The soldiers stopped their tittering and disengaged from one another. "And the big fellow—your slave?"

"Davus is my son-in-law. Who are you?"

One soldier put his shoulder to the door and pushed it open another foot. The screech from the hinges set my teeth on edge. His companion, who did all the talking, crossed his arms. "We're soldiers of Caesar. We ask the questions. Do you need to know more than that, citizen Gordianus?"

"That depends. Knowing your names might prove useful the next time I speak to Gaius Julius."

It was hard to see their faces, but from the ensuing silence I knew I had stumped them. Did I really know their imperator well enough to call him by his first name? I might be bluffing— or not. In a world turned upside-down by civil war, it was hard to know how to judge a stranger met in a strange place—and surely there were few places stranger than this.

The soldier cleared his throat. "Well, citizen Gordianus, the first thing to do is to have that son-in-law of yours put his weapon away."

I nodded to Davus, who grudgingly sheathed his sword. "He didn't draw it against you," I said. I glanced over my shoulder at the thing on the pedestal. In the greater light from the doorway, its shape was more defined, but still puzzling.

"Oh, her!" said the soldier. "Never fear, it's only Artemis."

I frowned and studied the thing. "Artemis is the goddess of the hunt and of wild places. She carries a bow and runs with a stag. She's beautiful."

"Then the Massilians have a strange idea of beauty," said the soldier, "because this *is* the Temple of Artemis, and that . . .

whatever it is . . . on the pedestal is the goddess herself. Would you believe they brought that thing all the way from Ionia when they migrated here five hundred years ago? That was even before Romulus and Remus suckled the she-wolf, or so the Massilians claim."

"Are you saying a Greek sculpted this? I can hardly believe that."

"Sculpt? Did I say sculpt? Nobody *made* that thing. It fell from the sky, trailing fire and smoke—so the Massilians say. Their priests declared it was Artemis. Well, if you look at it from a certain angle you can sort of see . . ." He shook his head. "Anyway, Artemis is who the Massilians worship above all the other gods. And this is *the* Artemis that belongs to them alone. They carve wooden copies of that thing, miniatures, and keep them in their houses, just like a Roman might keep a statue of Hermes or Apollo."

Peering at the thing on the pedestal, tilting my head, I discerned a form that might possibly be perceived as female. I could see pendulous breasts—several more than two—and a swollen belly. There was no refinement, no artifice. The image was crude, basic, primal. "How do you know all this?" I asked.

The soldier puffed out his chest. "We know, my comrade Marcus and me, because we two are stationed to guard this place. While the siege is on, our job is to keep this temple and the surrounding grove safe from bandits and looters—though what anybody would take I can't imagine, and you can see for yourself how the Massilians have let the place go to ruin. But once the siege is over, Caesar doesn't want Pompey or anybody else to be able to say he was disrespectful of the local shrines and temples. Caesar honors all the gods—even rocks that fall from the sky."

I peered at the soldier's ugly face. "You're an impious fellow, aren't you?"

He grinned. "I pray when I need to. To Mars before a battle. To Venus when I throw the dice. Otherwise, I don't imagine the gods take much notice of me."

I dared to touch the thing on the pedestal. It was made of dark, mottled stone, shiny and impermeable in some places and in other places riddled with fine pores. Riding through the valley, I had seen phantom shapes, illusions of light and shadow, but none had been as strange as this.

"It has a name, that sky rock," offered the soldier. "But you have to be a Greek to be able to pronounce it. Impossible for a Roman—"

"*Xoanon.*" The voice came from somewhere within the temple. The strange word—if word it was, and not a cough or a sneeze—boomed and echoed in the small space. The soldiers were as startled as I was. They clutched their helmets, rolled their eyes, and rattled their swords.

A cowled figure stepped from the shadows. He must have been there when Davus and I entered, but in the dimness we both had failed to see him.

He spoke in a gruff, hoarse whisper. "The skystone is called a *xoanon*, and *xoanon* is what the Massilians call the images of Artemis they carve from wood."

The soldiers exhibited sudden relief. "Only you!" said the one who did the talking. "I thought—I didn't know what to think! You gave us a start."

"Who are you?" I asked. The man's face was hidden by the cowl. "Are you the priest of this temple?"

"Priest?" The soldier laughed. "Whoever saw a priest dressed in such rags?" The cowled figure, without answering, stepped past him and out the door. The soldier pointed to his head and made a gesture to indicate that the man was mad. He lowered his voice. "We nicknamed him 'Rabidus.' Not that the fellow's dangerous, just not right in the head."

"Does he live here?"

"Who can say? Showed up in camp not long after Caesar began the siege. Word came down from on high that we were to leave him alone. Comes and goes as he pleases. Disappears for a while, then pops up again. A soothsayer, they call him, though

9

he doesn't say much. As strange as they come, but harmless as far as I can tell."

"Is he Massilian?"

"Could be. Or could be a Gaul. Or a Roman, for all I know; speaks Latin. He certainly knows a thing or two about local matters, as you've just seen demonstrated. What's that he called the lump on the pedestal?" The soldier tried to duplicate the word without success. "Anyway, why don't you and your son-in-law step out of the temple. It's getting so you can't see your hand in front of your face in here."

We followed the soldiers onto the porch and descended the steps. The soothsayer stood outside the gate, where there were now five horses tied to the pylons.

"So, Gordianus of Rome, what's your business in being here?" asked the soldier.

"My immediate business is to find a way out of this valley."

He laughed. "Easy enough. Marcus and I will escort you out. In fact, we'll escort you all the way to my commander's tent. You being on a first-name basis with 'Gaius Julius,' maybe you'll feel more comfortable explaining yourself to an officer." He looked at me sidelong. "Whoever you are, I don't mind saying I'm glad you turned up today. It's slow out here, so far away from the action. You two are the first visitors we've had to the temple. Are you sure you're not looters? Or spies? Only joking!"

We readied our horses. The soldiers did likewise. The soothsayer conferred with them for a moment. The soldier called to us over his shoulder. "Rabidus says he wants to ride alongside us for a while. You don't mind, do you?"

I watched the cowled figure mount his swayback nag and shrugged.

The soldiers led the way to a narrow cleft in the stone wall. The opening was impossible to see unless viewed straight on. I doubted that Davus and I would ever have found it by ourselves, even in broad daylight. A rocky path led between sheer lime-stone walls so close I could have touched both sides with outstretched arms. The passage was deep in shadow, almost as dim as the interior of the temple. My horse began to jerk in protest at being ridden over rough, unfamiliar ground in near darkness. At last a vertical slash of pale light appeared ahead of us. The path descended, dropping like a staircase.

We emerged from the fissure as abruptly as we had entered it. Behind us rose a sheer cliff of limestone. Before us was a dense forest, brooding and dark.

"How can we ride through that wilderness at night?" I asked Davus in a hushed voice. "These woods must go on for miles!"

A voice startled me. It was the soothsayer. I had thought he was ahead with the soldiers, but suddenly he was alongside me. "Nothing in this place is what it appears to be," he whispered hoarsely. "Nothing!"

Before I could answer, the soldiers doubled back, edging out the soothsayer and hemming Davus and me in on either side like sheep to be herded. Did they really think we might try to escape into that deep, dark wood?

But the forest was not as vast as it appeared to be. We rode through the enveloping gloom for only a moment, then suddenly emerged into a vast clearing. The last glow of twilight illuminated a landscape of endless tree stumps. The forest had been razed.

The soldier saw my confusion and laughed. "Caesar's doing!" he said. "When the Massilians refused to open their gates to him, he took one look at those thick city walls and decided an attack by sea might be advisable. Only problem: no ships! So Caesar decided to build a navy overnight. But to build ships you need big trees—cypresses, ash trees, oaks. Not many such trees in this rocky land; that's why the Massilians declared this forest sacred and never touched it, not for all the hundreds of years they've been here. Gods lived in this wood, so they said, gods who'd been here since long before the Massilians came, gods so old and hidden in the gloom that even the Gauls had no names for them. The place was rank and wild, powdery beneath your feet from so much rotted heartwood over the years, with cobwebs the size of houses up in the branches. The Massilians built altars, sacrificed sheep and goats to the unknown gods of the forest. They never touched the trees for fear of some horrible, divine retribution.

"But that didn't stop Caesar. Oh, no! 'Cut down those trees,' he ordered, 'and build me my ships!' But the men he ordered to do the cutting got spooked. They froze up, couldn't bring down their axes. Stood staring at each other, quivering like schoolboys. Men who'd burned cities, slaughtered Gauls by the thousands, scared Pompey himself out of Italy—afraid to attack a forest. Caesar was furious! He grabbed a double-headed ax from one of the men, pushed the fellow out of the way, and started hacking at the biggest oak in sight. Wood chips flew through the air! The old oak creaked and groaned! Caesar didn't stop until the tree came crashing down. Everyone fell to chopping after that. Afraid Caesar might come after *them* with that ax!" The soldier laughed.

I nodded. My horse seemed glad to be away from narrow, rocky places. He had no trouble picking his way between tree stumps. "But if this wood was sacred . . . I thought you said Caesar was making a point of respecting the Massilians' holy places."

The soldier snorted. "When it suits him!"

"He has no fear of sacrilege?"

"Was it sacrilege to cut down an old forest full of spiders and mulch? I wouldn't know. Maybe the soothsayer can tell us. What do you say, Rabidus?"

The soothsayer was keeping to himself, riding a little ways off. He turned his hooded head toward the soldier and spoke in a hoarse, strained voice. "I know why the Roman has come here."

"What?" The soldier was taken aback, but recovered with a grin. "Well, tell me then! You'll save us the trouble of torturing him to find out. Only joking! Go on, soothsayer, speak up."

"He's come to look for his son."

The strange voice emerging from the faceless hood chilled my blood. Wings fluttered in my chest. Involuntarily, I whispered the name of my son: "Meto!"

The soothsayer reined his horse and turned about. "Tell the Roman to go home. He has no business here. There's nothing he can do to help his son." He rode off at a slow pace in the direction from which we had come, back toward the last redoubt of the forest.

The soldier grimaced and shivered like a dog shaking off water. "There's a weird one. Not sad to see the back of him!"

Davus tugged at my sleeve. "Father-in-law, the fellow really is a soothsayer! How else could he have known—"

I hissed at Davus to silence him. For a mad moment I considered turning back to pursue the hooded figure, to see what else he could tell me. But I knew that the soldiers, for all their joking, would never have allowed it. For the moment, we were their prisoners.

We ascended a small hill. At the summit the soldier halted and pointed straight ahead at a distant hilltop ablaze with campfires. "You see that? There's Caesar's camp. And beyond that lies Massilia, with her back against the sea. She'll open her gates to us, sooner or later. Because Caesar says so!"

I looked behind us. A sea of tree stumps shone white beneath the rising moon. The soothsayer had vanished into the night.

II

"Says his name is Gordianus. Claims to be a Roman citizen. Calls the imperator 'Gaius Julius,' as if he knows him. Says he won't say more, except to Trebonius himself. What do you think, sir?"

The soldier had passed me on to his centurion; the centurion had passed me on to his cohort commander; the cohort commander was now conferring with the next officer above him. It was suppertime in the camp. From where I stood, just inside the officer's tent, I could peer out the flap to see a line of men queued up with metal bowls in their hands, shuffling forward at a steady rate. A torch was mounted on a pole at the nearest intersection in the grid of pathways between tents; the light shone on weary, smiling faces of men happy to have reached the end of the day, though some were practically asleep on their feet. Many were smudged with dirt, and some looked as if they had been rolling in mud. Soldiering during a siege means endless digging: trenches, latrines, tunnels beneath the enemy's walls.

From somewhere toward the far end of the queue I heard the

dull, repetitious knocking of a wooden spoon against metal bowls. I caught whiffs of a stew of some sort. Did I smell pork? Davus and I had eaten only a handful of bread since we'd left the tavern that morning. Beside me, I heard Davus's stomach growl.

From his folding chair, the officer perused us grudgingly. We were keeping him from his own supper in the officers' mess. "Really, cohort commander, couldn't this have waited until morning?"

"But, sir, what shall I do with these two in the meantime? Treat them like honored guests? Or prisoners? Or release them and send them out of camp? Granted, the older one looks pretty harmless, but the big one he calls his son-in-law—"

"You must be as stupid as you look, cohort commander, though that hardly seems possible, if you're going to base your treatment of loiterers and trespassers on the basis of how they look. That's a sure way of getting a knife in the back from some Massilian spy."

"I'm not a Massilian spy," I said. My stomach growled to punctuate the assertion.

"Of course not," snapped the officer. "You're a Roman citizen named Gordianus—or so you say. Why were you loitering at the Temple of Artemis?"

"We were headed for Massilia. We lost our way."

"Why did you leave the road?"

"The tavernkeeper told us that brigands rule that stretch of road. We attempted a shortcut."

"Why were you headed for Massilia in the first place? Do you have family there, or business connections? Or is it someone in the camp you're seeking?"

I bowed my head.

The cohort commander threw up his hands. "This is where he clams up, sir. He's hiding something, clearly."

The officer cocked his head. "Wait a moment. Gordianus—

I've heard the name before. Cohort commander, you're dismissed."

"Excuse me, sir?"

"Go. Now, before the cooks spoon all the good bits out of that swill they're slopping tonight."

The cohort commander saluted and left, casting a last, suspicious look at me.

The officer rose from his folding chair. "I don't know about you two, but I'm starving. Follow me."

"Where are we going?" I said.

"You said you wanted to speak to Caesar himself, didn't you? And failing that, to the officer in charge of the siege? Come along, then. Gaius Trebonius never misses supper in his tent." He clapped his hands and rubbed them together. "If I'm lucky, he'll invite me to join him."

The officer was not lucky. No sooner had he announced who I was and stated the circumstances than Trebonius, who sat chewing on a shank of pork, summarily dismissed him. The officer cast a last lingering glance not at me, but at the pork shank.

Like Marc Antony, Trebonius was part of that younger generation who had attached themselves to the comet tail of Caesar's career early on, and were now determined to ride it to glory or disaster. In the political arena, Trebonius had carried water for Caesar when he was a tribune, helping to extend Caesar's command in Gaul beyond constitutional limits. In the military arena, he had served as one of Caesar's lieutenants in Gaul, helping to crush the natives. Now that civil war had begun, he had once again cast his lot with Caesar. If his appetite was anything to judge by, he suffered no nagging regrets; the pork shank in his fist was gnawed to the bone.

I recognized him in a vague way from having glimpsed him on the rare instances when I had visited my son Meto in Caesar's camps. I suddenly remembered an occasion in Ravenna when Meto told me in passing that Trebonius kept a dossier of Cicero's witticisms, which he published for his friends. Trebonius had a sense of humor, then; or at least he appreciated irony.

He peered at me curiously. There was no reason he should have recognized my face, but he did know my name. "You're Meto's father," he said, pulling a string of pork from his teeth.

"Yes."

"Don't look like him. Ah, but Meto was adopted, wasn't he?"

I nodded.

"And this one?"

"My son-in-law."

"Looks big enough."

"I feel safer when I travel with him."

"Tell him to step outside the tent."

I nodded. Davus frowned. "But, father-in-law—"

"Perhaps these men could accompany Davus to the officers' mess," I suggested, referring to the soldiers who sat and stood about the tent, eating their supper. "That way we won't have to listen to his stomach growling outside the tent."

"A good idea," said Trebonius. "Everybody out!"

No one questioned the order. A few moments later, Trebonius and I were alone.

"I had hoped to find Caesar still here," I said.

Trebonius shook his head. "Left months ago. Has more important things to do than sit here and starve out a bunch of Greeks. Didn't you get the news in Rome?"

"The gossip in the Forum isn't always reliable."

"Caesar was here at the outset, yes. He politely asked the Massilians to open their gates. They hemmed and hawed. Caesar demanded they open the gates. They refused. Caesar laid the groundwork for the siege—conferred with engineers on a strategy for bringing down the walls, oversaw the shipbuilding, instructed the officers, addressed the ranks. Then he hurried on. Urgent business in Spain." Trebonius smiled grimly. "But as soon as he disposes of Pompey's legions there, he'll be back— and I shall have the privilege of presenting Massilia to him, cracked open like an egg."

"Back in Rome I heard that the Massilians simply wanted to remain neutral."

"A lie. When Pompey sailed east toward Greece, his confederate, Lucius Domitius Ahenobarbus, sailed here. Domitius arrived before Caesar did. He convinced the Massilians to side with Pompey and close their gates to Caesar. They were fools to listen to him."

I raised an eyebrow. "Summer has come and almost gone. The gates of Massilia are still shut and the walls, I presume, are still standing."

Trebonius ground his jaw. "Not for much longer. But you haven't come all this way to ask about military operations. You'd like to see Caesar, would you? So would we all. You'll have to settle for me in his stead. What do you want, Gordianus?"

The tent was empty. There was no one but Trebonius to hear. "My son, Meto."

His face stiffened. "Your son betrayed Caesar. He plotted to kill him even before Caesar crossed the Rubicon with his troops. It all came out after Pompey fled Italy and Caesar took Rome. That's the last we've seen of him. If your son came to Massilia, he came on his own. If he's inside the city, you can't possibly reach him until the walls come down. And when that happens, if we find Meto, he shall be arrested, to be dealt with by Caesar himself."

Did he believe what he was saying? Did he not know the truth of the matter? Even I had been fooled for a while into believing that Meto had betrayed Caesar—Meto, who fought for Caesar in Gaul, transcribed the great man's memoirs, and shared his tent. But the truth was far more complicated. Meto's betrayal had been an elaborately constructed sham, a ruse meant to trick Caesar's opponents into trusting Meto and taking him into their ranks. Meto had not betrayed Caesar; Meto was Caesar's spy.

That was why I had hoped to find Caesar. Caesar himself had concocted the scheme to fake Meto's betrayal. With Caesar alone I could have spoken freely. But how much did Trebonius know? If Caesar had kept him in ignorance, then I would never be able to convince him of the truth. Indeed, it might be dangerous to do so—dangerous to Meto, if he still lived. . . .

Trebonius's flat tone and the steely look in his eyes betrayed no double meaning. As far as I could tell, when he spoke of Meto's betrayal, he spoke what he believed to be the truth. But was he only doing so because he thought I was ignorant of the facts? Were we playing a game of shadow puppets, each aware of the truth but wary of revealing it to the other?

I tried to draw him out. "Trebonius, before Meto left Rome, I saw him, spoke to him. Despite appearances, I don't believe he's a traitor to Caesar. I *know* he's not. And surely, knowing Meto as you do—knowing Caesar—you must know that as well. Don't you?"

He shook his head curtly. His expression grew sterner. "Listen, Gordianus, your son was my friend. His defection was a knife, not just in Caesar's back, but in mine—and in the back of every man who's fought with Caesar. Even so, strangely enough, I can't say I bear a grudge against him. These are terrible times. Families are torn apart—brother against brother, husband against wife, even son against father. It's a wretched business. Meto made a choice—the wrong choice—but for all I know, there was honor behind it. He's my enemy now, but I don't hate him. As for you, I don't blame you for what your son has done. You're free to go. But if you've come here to collude with Meto against Caesar, I'll deal with you as harshly as I would with any traitor. I'll see you crucified."

So much for trying to draw him out. If Trebonius knew the truth, he was not going to reveal himself to me.

He attacked the few scraps of flesh that still remained on the pork shank, then went on. "My advice to you, Gordianus, is to get a good night's sleep, then turn around and head straight back to Rome. If you hear from Meto, tell him that Caesar will have his head. If you hear nothing, wait for news. The waiting is hard, I know, but you'll learn of Meto's fate sooner or later. You know the Etruscan saying: 'Once grieving starts it never ends, so there's no point in grieving an hour earlier than you must.' "

I cleared my throat. "That's the problem, you see. The day before I left Rome I received a message from someone inside Massilia. The message said . . . that Meto had been killed. That's why I've come all this way, to find out—whether my son is still alive . . . or not."

Trebonius sat back. "Who sent you this message?"

"It was unsigned."

"How did it come to you?"

"It was left on the doorstep of my house on the Palatine."

"Did you bring it with you?"

"Yes." I reached into the pouch that hung from my belt and pulled out a small wooden cylinder. With my little finger I extracted a rolled scrap of parchment. Trebonius snatched it from me as he might a dispatch from a messenger.

He read aloud. " 'Gordianus: I send you sad news from Massilia. Your son Meto is dead. Forgive my bluntness. I write in haste. Know that Meto died loyal to his cause, in the service of Rome. His was a hero's death. He was a brave young man, and, though not in battle, he died bravely here in Massilia.' " Trebonius handed the message back to me. "This arrived anonymously, you say?"

"Yes."

"Then you don't even know that it came from Massilia. It might be a hoax perpetrated on you by someone in Rome."

"Perhaps. But is it *possible* that the message could have come from Massilia?"

"Could a Massilian ship have slipped through our blockade, you mean? Officially, no."

"But in reality?"

"There may have been a few . . . occurrences . . . especially at night. The Massilians are expert sailors, and the local winds favor sailing out of the harbor by night. Caesar's ships are moored behind the big islands just outside the harbor, but a small ship might have slipped by them in the dark. But what of it? What if the message did come from Massilia? Why is it unsigned if the writer tells the truth?"

"I don't know. Since the day Caesar crossed the Rubicon, everyone wears a mask. Intrigues and deceptions . . . secrecy for secrecy's sake . . ."

"If Meto is dead, the writer should have sent you some tangible memento—Meto's citizen's ring, at least."

"Perhaps Meto drowned and his body was lost. Perhaps he died by—" In my imagination I pictured flames and blanched at the thought. "Don't you think I've gone over this a thousand times in my own mind, Trebonius? It's the first thing I think of when I wake, the last thing I think of before I sleep. Who sent this message, why, from where, and is it true or not? What's become of my son?" I stared at Trebonius, letting the misery show on my face. Surely, if he knew whether Meto was alive or dead, he would tell me at least that much to alleviate a father's suffering. But his grim countenance was as changeless as a statue's.

"I see your dilemma," he said. "A nasty business—uncertainty. I sympathize. But I can't help you. On the one hand, if Meto is alive and in Massilia, he's cast his lot with Domitius and become a traitor to Caesar. You can't get into the city to see him, and I wouldn't allow it if you could. You'll have to wait until the Massilians surrender, or until we pull the walls down. Then, if we find Meto . . . do you really want to be here when that happens, to witness his fate as a traitor? On the other hand, if Meto is already dead, there's still no way you can get into Massilia and find out how it happened or who sent that message. Look, I'll promise you this: When we take Massilia, if there's news of Meto, I'll let you know what I find out. If Meto himself is taken, I'll let you know what Caesar decides to do with him. I can promise no more than that. There, your task is accomplished. You can go back to Rome now, knowing that you've done all that any father could. I'll see that you have a place to sleep tonight. You'll leave in the morning." These last words had the unmistakable ring of an order.

He studied the fleshless bone in his fist. "But where are my manners? You must be starving, Gordianus. Go, join your son-in-law in the officers' mess. The stew's not as bad as it looks, really."

I left the tent and followed my nose to the mess. Despite the growling in my belly, I had lost my appetite.

III

We were given cots in an officers' tent not far from the commander's own. If Trebonius truly believed Meto to be a traitor, he was a generous man to give such hospitality to a traitor's father. More likely, he preferred to keep me close at hand so that he could be sure I left camp the next day.

Long after the others in the tent were sleeping, with Davus gently snoring nearby, I remained awake. I may have dozed once or twice, but it was hard to tell whether the images in my head were dreams or waking fantasies. I saw the canyon where we had lost our way that afternoon, the fence made of bones, the dark temple and the squat, primeval skystone of Artemis, the razed forest, the soothsayer who knew my reason for coming. . . .

What sort of place had I come to? The next day, if Trebonius had his way, we would be off again before I had a chance to find out.

Finally I threw off my coverlet and quietly stepped out of the tent. The full moon had begun to set, casting long, black shadows. The torches that lit the pathways between tents burned low. I paced aimlessly, moving gradually uphill, until I found myself in a clearing close by Trebonius's tent. This was the crest of the hill, with a view of the city.

In the darkness, I imagined Massilia to be a great dorsal-finned behemoth that had pulled herself out of the sea and collapsed face down, then been ringed about by walls of limestone. The jagged crest along her spine was a ridge of hills. The encircling walls gleamed blue in the moonlight. Impenetrable shadows lurked in the bends of the towers. Torches, mere dots of orange flame, flickered at regular intervals along the battlements. On either side of the city, outside her walls, two bays opened into the sea beyond; the larger inlet on the left was the main harbor. The still face of the water was black, except where moonlight burnished it silver. The islands beyond the city, behind which Caesar's ships lay moored, were lumpy gray silhouettes.

Between the high place where I stood and the nearest stretch of wall lay a valley lost in shadows. Across the gulf of air, that stretch of wall seemed disconcertingly close; I could clearly see two Massilian sentries patrolling the battlements, torchlight causing their helmets to flicker. Behind them reared a dark hill, the crested head of my imagined sea monster.

Somewhere in the darkness encircled by those moonlit walls my son had died, swallowed up in the belly of that recumbent behemoth. Or else he still lived, pursuing a fate as shadowy as the night.

I heard footsteps and sensed a presence behind me. A sentry, I thought, come to send me back to my bed; but when I turned I saw that the man wore a sleeping tunic. He was quite short and had a neatly trimmed beard.

He stepped up to a spot on the crest of the hill not far off, crossed his arms, and studied the view. "Can't sleep either?" he remarked, not really looking at me.

"No."

"Neither can I. Too excited about tomorrow."

"Tomorrow?"

He turned his head, studied me for a moment, then frowned. "Do I know you?"

"I'm a visitor from Rome. Arrived earlier tonight."

"Ah. I thought you were one of Trebonius's officers. My mistake."

I studied him in return. I smiled. "But I know *you.*"

"Do you?" He peered at me. "It's the darkness. I can't—"

"We met at Brundisium a few months ago, in circumstances not dissimilar to this. Caesar was laying siege. Pompey was trapped in the city, desperate to sail away. Caesar was building extraordinary earthworks and breakwaters at the mouth of the harbor, trying to close it off and trap Pompey's ships inside. You pointed out the structures and explained the strategy to me, Engineer Vitruvius."

He clicked his teeth, furrowed his brow, then opened his eyes wide. "Of course! You arrived with Marc Antony, just before all Hades broke loose." He nodded. "Gordianus, isn't it? Yes, I remember. And you're—you're that fellow Meto's father."

"Yes."

There was a silence, uncomfortable on my part. Together we stared at the moonlit view.

"What do you know about my son?" I finally asked.

He shrugged. "Never had occasion to meet him. As an engineer, I've always dealt with others among Caesar's officers. Know him by sight, of course. Seen him riding alongside the imperator, taking notes while Caesar dictates. That's his function, I understand, assisting Caesar with letters and memoirs."

"What else do you know about Meto? There must be rumors."

He snorted. "I never listen to camp gossip. I'm an engineer and a builder. I believe in what I can see and measure. You can't build bridges by hearsay."

I nodded thoughtfully.

"Is he in camp, then—your son?" asked Vitruvius. "Come to

visit him, have you, all the way from Rome? But then, you traveled all the way from Rome to Brundisium to see him there, didn't you? The gods must have given you a harder backside for traveling than I've got!"

I kept my face a blank. Vitruvius didn't know, then. The tale of Meto's betrayal was confined to those higher up or closer to Caesar's immediate circle. I took a deep breath. "Trebonius tells me there's no way into Massilia," I said, casually dropping the siege commander's name.

The engineer raised an eyebrow. "It's a well-fortified city. The walls extend all the way around, one continuous circuit along the land, along the sea, and also along the sandy beach that fronts the harbor. The walls are made of massive limestone blocks, strengthened at intervals by bastion towers. Extremely well constructed; the blocks appear to be perfectly fitted and stacked, without cement or metal clamps. The lower courses have slits for shooting arrows. The upper battlements have platforms for machine-bows and torsion artillery. This isn't like laying siege to some Gaulish fort thrown together with logs, I can tell you that! We'll never ram our way in, never bring down the wall with catapults."

"But the walls can be breached, nonetheless?"

Vitruvius smiled. "How much do you know about laying sieges, Gordianus? That son of yours must have learned a thing or two campaigning with Caesar up north and editing his memoirs."

"My son and I usually talk of other things when we meet."

He nodded. "I'll tell you about sieges then. The main virtues of the besieger are patience and perseverance. If you can't crash or burn your way in, you must burrow like a termite. The sappers will have all the glory in this siege. They're the ones who dig, burrowing under the walls. Burrow far enough, and you've got a tunnel into the city. Burrow deep and wide enough, and a section of wall comes crashing down under its own weight."

"It sounds almost too simple."

"Far from it! It takes as much thoughtful engineering and hard labor to bring down a city as it does to build one. Take our situation here. Caesar chose this spot for a camp because it's high up. Not only can you see the city and the sea beyond, but you have a clear view of the siegeworks going on in the valley just below us. That's where the real action is. Right now it's too dark, the valley's all in shadow, but come dawn you'll be able to see what we've accomplished down there.

"The first step in any siege is to dig a contravallation—that's a deep trench parallel to the city walls protected by screens. That allows you to run men and equipment back and forth. Our contravallation runs all along that valley down there, from the harbor to our left, all the way over to the smaller inlet to our right, on the other side of the city. The contravallation also protects the camp from the city; prevents the enemy from pouring out of the gates and mounting a counterassault against us. At the same time, it hinders anyone beyond the camp from running fresh supplies into the city. That's important. Hunger is every man's weakness." He ticked his fingers, reciting a list. "Isolation, deprivation, desperation, starvation: no battering-ram can match the power of those.

"But to mount an assault, you need to wheel your towers and siege engines right up to the walls. If the ground isn't level— and it's certainly not level in that valley down there—you've got to make it so. That's why Caesar ordered the building of a massive embankment at a right angle to the wall, a sort of elevated causeway. It took a lot of leveling before we could lay the foundation; you'd think we were building an Egyptian pyramid from the amount of earth we've moved. The embankment is made mostly of logs, stacked up and up and up, each level perpendicular to the one below, with earth and rubble packed into the interstices to make it solid. Where it cuts across the deepest part of the valley, the embankment's eighty feet from top to bottom.

"All the time this digging and building has been going on,

the Massilians have kept firing on us from the walls, of course. Caesar's men are used to fighting Gauls, who've got nothing bigger than spears and arrows and slingshots. It's another game altogether with these Massilians. The hard fact is, though I hate to admit it, their artillery is superior to ours. Their catapults and ballistic engines shoot farther and shoot bigger. I'm talking about twelve-foot feathered javelins raining down on the men while they're trying to stack heavy logs! Our usual protections— movable shields and mantlets—were totally inadequate. We had to build lean-tos all along the embankment to protect the work- ers, stronger than any such structures we'd built before. That's what I love about military engineering—always a new problem to solve! We built the lean-tos from the stoutest wood we could find, armored them with pieces of timber a foot thick, and cov- ered everything with fireproof clay. Boulders roll off like hail- stones. Giant javelins bounce back as if they'd struck solid steel. Still, the racket inside those lean-tos, with missiles and stones crashing down, can certainly set your teeth on edge! I know; I spent my share of time down there overseeing the work.

"Once the embankment was almost done, we set about build- ing a siege tower mounted on rollers, with a battering-ram built into the lower platform. It's down there now, at this end of the embankment. Tomorrow it will sally forth across the causeway, and there's no way the Massilians will be able to stop it. The men on the upper platforms of the siege tower are protected by screens of hempen mats too thick for any missile to penetrate. Once the tower is flush against the wall, the men on the upper platforms can fire down on any Massilians who venture out of the city to try to stop the operation, while the men on the lower platform can swing the battering-ram at will. Do you know what sort of panic that causes in a besieged city—the *boom, boom, boom* of a battering-ram striking the walls? You'll be able to hear it for miles."

I peered down into the valley. Amid shades of gray and black I could make out the straight line of the embankment traversing the valley from a point just below us to the base of the city walls. I could also make out the hulking mass of the siege tower at the nearer end. "But I thought you said that catapults and battering-rams would never bring down the walls of Massilia."

"So I did." Vitruvius grinned. "I really should say no more."

I raised an eyebrow. "The battering-ram is only a diversion?"

He was too proud of the scheme to deny it. "As I said, the sappers will have all the glory. They've been furiously tunneling since the first day we made camp. They've created a whole network of tunnels, running all up and down the walls. The longest is over that way." He pointed to the left, in the general direction of the main city gate and the harbor beyond. "By all our calculations, the diggers will break through tomorrow. In the blink of an eye, we shall have an opening inside the city walls. Just behind the diggers, troops will be packed inside the tunnel, waiting to pour out of that hole in the ground like ants from a stirred anthill. From inside Massilia, they'll rush the main gate. The Massilians will have concentrated all the men they can muster elsewhere, at the point where the siege tower and the battering-ram are assaulting the wall. An attack on the gate, from *inside* the city, will take them completely by surprise. The gate will be ours; and once our men have opened it, Trebonius himself will lead the charge into the city. The siege will be over. The Massilians will have no choice but to surrender and plead for mercy."

"And will Trebonius give them mercy?"

"Caesar's orders were to take the city and hold it for him until he returns. He intends to dictate terms to the Massilians himself."

"So there'll be no massacre?"

"No. Unless the Massilians are mad enough to fight to the death. Unlikely—they're merchants at heart—but you never know. Or unless. . . ."

"Yes?"

"Unless our men get out of control." From the way his voice

dropped, I knew he had seen such occurrences before. Meto had told me of Gaulish cities sacked and pillaged by Roman soldiers run amok. It seemed unthinkable that such a thing could be done to the people of Massilia, Rome's ally for centuries. But this was war.

Vitruvius smiled. "So now you see why I can't sleep, waiting for tomorrow."

I nodded glumly. "I thought a walk and some fresh air might help, but now—I don't think I'll be able to sleep either."

Tomorrow, if Vitruvius was right, Massilia would be opened. Why, then, did Trebonius insist on sending me away? What did he know about Meto that I did not? Was he sparing me the sight of my son's execution? Or sparing me from discovering some even more horrible fate that had already overtaken Meto? My weary imagination spun out of control.

"I'll tell you what," said Vitruvius brightly. "I saw a couple of folding chairs over by Trebonius's tent. I'll fetch them. We can sit here together and wait for the sun to come up. Reminisce about the siege of Brundisium, or whatever. You must have fresh news from Rome. I can't imagine what it's like there now, with Caesar's friend Marc Antony left in charge. One big orgy, I should think. Stay here."

He went off to fetch the chairs and quickly returned, with a couple of blankets as well.

We talked about Caesar's chances of putting a quick end to his enemies in Spain; about Pompey's prospects of raising a formidable force in the East to challenge Caesar; about Antony's reputation for drunken carousing. Sober or not, Antony had maintained strict order. The mood in Rome, I assured Vitruvius, was far from orgiastic. Stunned by the tumult of the last few months and fearful of the future, the city held its breath and walked on tiptoes with round eyes, like a virgin in the wildwoods.

We talked about the famous Roman exiles who had taken up residence in Massilia over the years. Gaius Verres was the most notorious; as governor of Sicily his rapaciousness had reached such extremes that Cicero had successfully prosecuted him for malfeasance and sent Verres packing for Massilia, taking a fortune in plunder with him. The reactionary gang-leader Milo had fled to Massilia after being found guilty of murdering the radical gang-leader Clodius; what would be his fate if Caesar took the city? There were scores of such exiles in Massilia, including men who had been convicted of various political crimes under Pompey's campaign to "clean up" the Senate; some were no doubt as crooked as crone's teeth, but others had simply made the mistake of crossing Pompey and the anti-Caesarians who had ruled the Senate in recent years. Inside the walls of Massilia, there must even be some old followers of Catilina, rebels who had chosen flight and exile over falling in battle beside their leader.

I stared at the walls of Massilia and the dark, hulking behemoth of the city beyond and wondered if Verres and Milo and all the rest were sleeping. What was it like to be a Roman exile in Massilia with Rome's new master knocking at the gates? Some must be quivering with dread, others with jubilation.

Vitruvius told me more about the siege. The first major engagement had been a sea battle. A surprisingly small Massilian navy of seventeen ships had ventured out of the harbor. Caesar's twelve ships sailed from behind the islands to meet them. Massilians watched from the city walls, while Romans watched from the hill upon which we sat. "Not much of a navy," said Vitruvius, disparaging his own side. "Ships hastily thrown together with green wood, heavy in the water, manned by soldiers who'd never sailed before in their lives. They didn't even bother to try to outmaneuver the Massilians; they just rammed straight ahead, caught the enemy ships with grappling hooks, rushed on board, and fought hand-to-hand across the decks, as if they were attacking on dry land. The sea turned red with blood. You could see great patches of red from up here, bright crimson against the blue of the sea."

That battle went badly for the Massilians. Nine of their seventeen ships were sunk or captured; the rest fled back to the harbor. Only the powerful offshore wind, for which the southern coast of Gaul is famous, kept Caesar's ships from pursuing; with the wind against them, only experienced Massilian sailors were able to maneuver through the straits and into the harbor. But the battle confirmed the blockade. Massilia was cut off by both land and sea.

There might yet be another sea battle if Pompey managed to send naval reinforcements to the Massilians. But Vitruvius remained convinced that the conflict would be settled on land, not water, and sooner, not later. "Tomorrow," he whispered, as I drifted off to an uneasy slumber beneath my blanket, too weary despite my worries to stay awake a moment longer.

IV

In the hour before sunrise, I gradually woke. Night and sleep receded in imperceptible stages. A hazy, dreamlike vision infiltrated the waking world. Out of the grayness, the arena of battle described by Vitruvius emerged before me.

Huddled in my folding chair with the blanket wrapped around me and over my head like a cowl, I saw the milky white walls of Massilia tinged with a faint pink blush by the growing predawn light. The black behemoth beyond acquired depth and definition, became a ridge of hills with houses crowded close together along the slopes and temples and citadels crowning the hilltops. The sea beyond turned from black obsidian to blue lead. The islands outside the harbor acquired solidity and dimension.

In the valley below me, the contravallation that circled Massilia cut like a scar across the trampled earth. The embankment that Vitruvius had described rose like a great dam across the valley, and the movable siege tower loomed below us. I saw no sign of the tunnels Vitruvius had talked about, but toward my left, at a corner where the landward wall bent sharply back to run along the harbor, I saw the massive towers that flanked the main gate into Massilia. Somewhere in that vicinity, Caesar's men intended to dig their way to daylight.

Slowly but surely—as slowly and surely as these images manifested out of darkness—I came to a decision.

It seemed to me that in my younger days I had always been methodical and cautious, slow to take any step that might be irrevocable, fearful of making a mistake that might lead to the worst possible outcome. How ironic that in my years of hardearned wisdom I should become a creature of impulse, a taker of wild risks. Perhaps it was wisdom after all for a man to turn his back on fear and doubt and trust to the gods to keep him alive.

"Vitruvius?" I said.

He stirred in his chair, blinked, and cleared his throat. "Yes, Gordianus?"

"Where does the tunnel begin—the one that's to break through inside the city today?"

He cleared his throat again. He yawned. "Over to the left. Do you see that stand of oak trees down there, tucked in a hollow that curves into the hillside? Actually, you can just barely see the treetops. That's where the entrance of the tunnel is, almost directly across from the main gate but still hidden from the city walls. The sappers are probably down there already, relaying digging equipment, rechecking measurements. The soldiers who'll take part in the attack will start gathering in about an hour."

I nodded. "How will they be equipped?"

"Short swords, helmets, light armor. Nothing too heavy. They've got to stay light on their feet, as unencumbered as possible. We don't want them tripping or stabbing each other as they scramble through the tunnel, or weighed down with too much equipment when they need to climb out."

"Are they all from a particular cohort?"

"No. They're special duty volunteers culled from several cohorts. Not every man's fit for such a mission. You can't effectively train a man not to be afraid of the dark or not to panic in a tight, enclosed space. Put some men in a tunnel and it doesn't matter how brave they are, they wet themselves the instant they lose sight of daylight around the first bend. You don't want to be standing next to such a fellow in a crisis. Sappers thrive in tunnels, of course, but sappers are diggers, not fighters. So you've got to have fighting men who aren't afraid to step on a few earthworms. The volunteers who'll make the attack have been doing tunnel drills over the last few days. How to carry a lighted taper so it doesn't go out, how not to stampede your comrades if the tunnel goes black, memorizing signals to advance and retreat, and so on."

"Sounds complicated."

Vitruvius snorted. "Hardly. These fellows aren't engineers. They're simple men. They just needed a bit of drilling so they won't trip over their own feet in a tight spot."

I nodded thoughtfully. "I suppose any reasonably bright fellow could pick up what to do on the spot."

"Certainly. Any fool could. And if something did go horribly wrong, he'd die just as quickly as the ones who've been specially trained for the mission." He snuggled under his blanket, closed his eyes, and sighed.

A red glimmer appeared along the jagged horizon to the east. I shrugged off my blanket and told Vitruvius he would have to watch the sunrise alone. He didn't answer. I retreated to the sound of gentle snoring.

In the officers' tent I managed to wake Davus and pull him from his bed without rousing the others. Half-asleep and confused, he nodded as I explained to him my intention.

From Meto I knew how Caesar arranged his camps and where

stores of surplus equipment might be found. The tent I was looking for was just behind that of Trebonius, and unguarded. What penalty would the commander deem appropriate for two outsiders caught stealing weapons during a siege? I tried not to think about that as we searched in the dim light among dented helmets, nicked swords, and mismatched greaves.

"This one fits perfectly, father-in-law. And I can't find any damage at all."

I looked up to see Davus trying on a helmet. I shook my head. "No, Davus, you misunderstood. My fault for explaining while you were still half-asleep. *I* will be going through the tunnel, not you."

"But I'm coming with you, of course."

"There's no need. If Vitruvius is correct, the city will be open in a matter of hours. We can meet up again tomorrow, perhaps even tonight."

"And if the engineer is wrong? You know what Meto says: Things never go exactly the way they expect in a battle."

I ran my fingertip along a dull, rusty sword blade. "Davus, do you remember the scene the day before we left Rome? Your wife—my daughter—was very, very upset."

"No more than your wife! Bethesda was frantic. Those curses she uttered made my hair stand on end, and I don't even know Egyptian."

"Yes, Diana and Bethesda were both distraught. But the night before we left, I made my peace with Bethesda. She understood why I had to come here, why I couldn't sit idly in Rome wondering about Meto, not knowing for certain if he was alive or dead. Diana was another matter."

"She understood too, in the end."

"Did she? I can hear her now: 'Papa, what can you be thinking, taking Davus with you? Didn't you just trek all the way to Brundisium and back to fetch him from Pompey's clutches? Now you want to go off to yet another battlefield and put him back in harm's way.' She had a point."

"Father-in-law, you couldn't possibly have traveled here alone. A man your age—"

"And you made Diana see that. Congratulations, Davus—you wield more influence over my daughter than I ever did! But before we left, she made me promise that I wouldn't put you in danger if I could possibly avoid it."

"So . . . you're saying that this tunnel business is dangerous."

"Of course it is! Men were never meant to burrow through the ground like rabbits, any more than they were meant to fly, or breathe underwater. And people tend not to like it when an army appears out of a hole in the ground."

"You could be killed, father-in-law."

I ran my fingertip over another blade and gasped when it cut me. I sucked at the thin trickle of bright red blood. "It's possible."

"Then I'm coming with you."

I shook my head. "No, Davus—"

"It was agreed that I would come along to protect you. You haven't had much need for protection until now."

"No, Davus. I promised your wife that I'd bring you home alive."

"And I promised *your* wife the same thing!"

We stared at each other blankly, then both laughed. "Then I suppose it's a question of which of them we're more afraid of," I said. After a heartbeat, we spoke in unison: "Bethesda!"

I sighed. "Very well, Davus. I think I saw a mail shirt over there that might be big enough to fit you."

Our outfits were convincing enough to fool the grubmaster, at least. Granted, the man hardly looked at us as we passed by, bowls extended for a helping of millet porridge. He did notice our relative sizes; Davus received a portion twice the size of mine.

We ate hastily, then set out. The camp, so quiet and still in the hour before dawn, was now bustling with excitement. Messengers ran to and fro, officers shouted, bright-eyed soldiers whispered to each other as they formed ranks. Everyone seemed to sense that this was a special day.

We descended the hill, keeping the city wall and the contravallation to our right. Ahead and below, hidden from the watchers on the city walls, I spotted a curving fold in the hillside shaded by oak trees, just as Vitruvius had described it. The little hollow was already densely packed with men, their helmets visible through the leaves as we descended.

A well-worn path led down into the hollow. Men stepped aside, jostling each other to make room for us. A glance at their equipment showed that I had not been far off the mark in choosing our own gear. We were inconspicuous, in that regard at least.

The men talked in low voices. Behind me I heard someone say, "How old is that one? You don't see many graybeards on special missions."

Another soldier shushed him. "What are you thinking, courting hubris on this of all days? Or don't you care to live long enough to have your own gray beard?"

"I didn't mean it as an insult," said the first soldier.

"Then keep your mouth shut. If a fellow can live that long fighting in Caesar's army, he must have the gods on his side."

The first soldier grunted. "What about the big one with him? I don't remember ever seeing him at training drills. I thought the call for this mission was strictly for short fellows like us. That big ox is liable to stop up the tunnel like a cork in a bottle!"

"Shut up! Here comes the man himself. This is it!"

Flanked by officers, Trebonius appeared on the hillside above us. He was dressed in full regalia, wearing a crested helmet and a sculpted chest plate that caught flashes of morning sunlight through the shimmering oak canopy. I tugged at Davus's elbow. "Lower your face. And hunker down, as best you can."

Trebonius pitched his orator's voice just loud enough to fill the hollow. "Soldiers! The auspices are favorable. The augurs have declared this a good day for battle—more than good, a propitious day for Caesar and Caesar's men. Today, if the gods see fit, the gates of Massilia will be opened, thanks to your efforts. You will greatly please Caesar, and Caesar will duly reward you. But let me repeat what I have said from the beginning of this siege: When Massilia falls, Caesar, and Caesar only, shall decide her fate. There will be no looting, no rape, no arson. You all understand this, I know. Remember your training. Follow the orders of your mission commander. Now the operation begins. No cheering! Silence! Save your voices for later, when you can let out a victory cry from the walls of Massilia."

Trebonius saluted us. As a body, we saluted back.

"Fall in!" an officer shouted. Around us, everyone began to move, but toward what I couldn't tell. Davus stayed close beside me, hunkering down. We followed the flow like grains of sand in an hourglass. The hollow became noticeably less crowded. Men were disappearing as if the earth itself had swallowed them. There seemed to be no precise order; each man simply moved into the queue as quickly and efficiently as he could. I shuffled forward.

Suddenly, the mouth of the tunnel was before me. Stout timbers outlined a black hole in the hillside. For an instant I froze. What sort of madness had brought me to such a moment? But there was no backing out. Trebonius was watching. Davus jostled me from behind.

"Take it!" said the same voice that had ordered us to fall in. I held out my hand and a lighted taper was pressed into it. "Remember your training," said the officer. "Don't let it go out!"

I moved forward, lowering my head and holding the taper as steadily as I could; my hand shook. I entered the mouth of the tunnel. Behind me I heard a clank and a grunt—the noise of Davus's helmet striking the lintel.

We proceeded at a steady pace. The tunnel was level at first, then began gradually to descend. A framework of timbers supported the walls and the roof. In most places the tunnel was barely wide enough for two men to pass each other. At a few points, where it threaded a course between two rock faces, it constricted even more. The roof was never quite high enough for me to stand fully upright. I had to walk slightly stooped. Poor Davus practically had to bend himself in two.

The tunnel stopped descending and became level again. The pace slackened. Occasionally we came to an abrupt standstill. Men bumped into each other. Tapers were dropped or blown out, then quickly relit from another. Without them the darkness would have been absolute.

We stopped, then shuffled forward; stopped again, then shuffled forward. The atmosphere was humid and stale. Smoke from the tapers burned my eyes. A cold clamminess settled over me. I breathed dank air into my lungs.

The tunnel began almost imperceptibly to ascend. We came to another standstill. Time passed. No one spoke.

At last, in the absence of orders or movement, some of the men began to whisper. The sound was like hissing heard though a trumpet. Occasionally, from the vaguely lit stretches before me or behind, I heard grim laughter. What sort of gruesome banter were the men passing back and forth? Meto's sense of humor had changed much in the years since he became a soldier; it had grown more vulgar and cruel, more mocking of god and man alike. Laughing in the face of Mars, he called it; whistling past Hades. Sometimes, Meto said, with certain death looming ahead—his own death or his enemy's—a man had no choice but to scream or laugh. What would happen if a single man in the tunnel began to scream and panic? I thought about that and was thankful for the release of an occasional burst of harsh laughter.

A chain of whispers came from the head of the line. The young soldier in front of me turned and said, "This is where we wait while the sappers dig out the last bit of earth. Pass it on." I relayed the message to Davus. When I turned back, the young soldier ahead was still looking at me. His voice had been familiar; I suddenly realized that he was the one who had been talking about me behind my back out in the hollow. By the flickering light of his taper, he looked hardly older than a child.

His scrutiny was intense, but not unfriendly. His eyes were unnaturally wide. He looked nervous.

I smiled. "Since you were wondering, I happen to be sixty-one years old."

"What?"

"I overheard you ask your friend before we entered the tunnel. 'How old is that one?' you said."

"Did I?" He looked chagrined. "Well, you *could* be my grandfather. Or even my great—"

"Enough of that, young man!"

He grinned lopsidedly. "Maybe Fortune put me next to you. Marcus said the gods must like you, if you've managed to grow—as old as you have—making your living with a sword. What do you think? Maybe a bit of your good luck will rub off on me today."

I smiled. "I'm not sure I have much luck left to spare right now."

Suddenly a deep, muffled *boom!* ran through the tunnel, as if lightning had struck the earth nearby. I felt it in my ears and toes and teeth. Another *boom!* sounded, and another.

"What—what's that?" The young soldier's voice broke. He rolled his eyes up. "Where's it coming from?"

"It's the battering-ram," I said, trying to keep my voice steady. "We must be directly under the wall."

The soldier jerked his head. "They warned us about that. But I didn't think . . . it would be so . . ."

Boom! A trickle of sand fell from the rafter overhead. The soldier clutched my forearm.

"It's far off," I said. "Hundreds of feet away. The vibration travels through the stones. It seems closer than it is."

"Of course. It's far away." He loosened his grip and released me. He had clutched my forearm hard enough to leave nail marks.

The booming stopped, then resumed; stopped, then resumed again, over and over. The tunnel roof just above my head seemed particularly affected. Trickles, then clods, then lumps of earth fell down on me. Occasionally the young soldier gripped my arm impulsively.

The air became more dank and foul and smoky. Our tapers burned to nothing; fresh ones were passed down to us from the tunnel entrance. Pails of earth and stones were passed back from the sappers at the head of the line. "They said we wouldn't have to get our hands dirty," joked the man behind Davus in mock-complaint. The young soldier giggled nervously. Hours seemed to pass.

Finally the sappers began to pass back shovels and other digging tools. Then the sappers themselves began to depart, heading back up the line toward the entrance. They squeezed past me easily enough, but getting past Davus proved to be a challenge. "What in Hades is that giant doing in here?" muttered one of them.

Davus whispered in my ear. "It'll be soon now, won't it, father-in-law?"

"I imagine so."

I tried to gird myself for what lay ahead. I had never been a soldier, but years ago I had fought beside Meto in his first battle, at Pistoria, where Catilina met his end; and only months ago I had witnessed the final hours of the siege of Brundisium and had very nearly died there. I had some idea of the dangers and the terrors that might lie ahead. But like every soldier, I imagined another scenario. Perhaps all would go smoothly. We would catch the Massilians unaware, their attention diverted by the battering-ram, exactly according to Trebonius's strategy. We would encounter virtually no resistance and open the gates with hardly a struggle. Trebonius would make his triumphant entry without bloodshed. The Massilians would see the hopelessness of resistance; they would lay down their arms. Davus and I would shrug off our armor, slip away, and search the city until we found Meto, alive and well and very surprised to see us. With the city taken, Meto's secret mission would be at an end, and he would surrender himself to Trebonius, present proof of his loyalty to Caesar, and all would be well.

How many others in the tunnel at that moment were comforting themselves with equally optimistic scenarios of the hours to come?

Boom! Boom! Boom! A hard, heavy clump of earth fell on my head, knocking me forward against the young soldier. Davus gripped my shoulder to steady me.

Then, from ahead of us, there came another sound. It was nothing like the thunder of the battering-ram. It was a continuous, unending crescendo. A roar.

My ears tingled. I thought I heard screams, but they were drowned out by the incessant booming and swallowed by the sudden roar.

A burst of cool wind struck my face. The wind blew out the taper in my hand, and every taper ahead of me. We were plunged into darkness. The wind continued to blow, carrying the smell of water.

There was no mistaking the screams now, weirdly distorted by the tunnel so that they combined into a kind of monstrous groan, like the roar of spectators at the circus. I heard the explosive crack and crash of rafters being broken into splinters.

My skin turned hot. My heart pounded. By reflex I steeled myself. A part of me knew it would do no good.

The wall of water struck.

V

In an instant, faster than thought, the young soldier was thrown against me like a stone from a catapult, knocking the breath out of me.

Then all was a roar of chaos and confusion. It seemed to me that I stood on a trapdoor that had suddenly opened, but instead of falling down I fell up. From behind, something circled my chest and lifted me. Somehow I was lodged against the roof of the tunnel, in a cavity of some sort, above the rushing flood, facing down on it. The darkness was not quite absolute; a single flame still flickered from somewhere.

Just beneath me, I gazed into the dark, glittering eyes of the terrified young soldier. He clung to me as the water rushed around him and over him. I tried to grip him in return, but the rush of water and bodies and debris was too great. Something struck his head, so hard that his whole body gave a tremendous jolt. His eyes rolled up. He slipped from my grasp and vanished, lost to the foaming cataract.

Impossibly, I seemed to hover just above the surface of the flood, like a dragonfly. In its depths I saw hands, feet, faces, glinting swords, armor and chain mail, and lumps of broken wood rush by, each glimpsed for an instant and then gone.

The flood went on and on and on. Finally the roar quieted. The rush of water slowed and finally became still. I heard gurgling noises, the lapping of little waves, unaccountable creaks and pops and shudders and groans. Strangely changed from before—duller and deeper—I heard the distant *boom!* of the battering-ram against the walls of Massilia.

And I heard another sound, so close it seemed almost a part of me. It was Davus behind me, above me, breathing into my ear like a runner whose heart might burst.

As these events unfolded, all was chaos, inexplicable—most inexplicable of all, the fact that I was still alive. Gradually I began to realize what had happened.

An instant before the flood reached us, Davus put one arm around me from behind. When the flood struck, our feet were knocked from under us; but Davus gripped the rafter above us, and so we pivoted upward. So much earth had been dislodged by the vibrations from the battering-ram that a cavity had opened in the roof. Davus jammed his feet and elbows against the edges of the cavity, kept hold of me, and somehow maintained his grip on his wildly flickering taper, all at once.

Davus had exhibited great strength and extraordinary reflexes before. Still, to have acted so quickly and surely in the face of such sudden, overwhelming catastrophe seemed more than human. What god had seen fit to save me this time?

When he managed to catch a breath, Davus whispered, "We're alive. I can't believe it."

But for how long? I thought, staring at the dark, turbid water beneath us. "Davus, I think you can let go of me now."

He released his grip. I slid gently into the water. My feet found the bottom. Standing on tiptoes, stretching my neck, I was able to keep my chin just above the waterline. The cavity in the roof offered the only escape from the water. In finding its equilibrium, the flood had left us this isolated pocket of air.

Something solid but yielding bumped against my ankle. I shuddered, knowing it was human flesh.

Davus slowly, carefully extricated himself from the cavity. The trick was to keep his taper lit and above the waterline. His feet dropped with a splash that sent water into my nostrils. I sputtered and blinked. An instant later Davus was standing beside me, holding his taper safely aloft. His helmet grazed the top of the cavity.

As the shock of the catastrophe began to subside, and with it the thrill of having survived, I began to realize what a terrible pass we had come to. We had escaped one death only to face another, even more horrible. The men who were swept away and drowned at least died suddenly and without dread.

I cursed myself. Why had I come? I had known it was madness when I saw the tunnel entrance before me. Why had I allowed Davus to come with me? I had made a widow of my only daughter. Massilia had already claimed Meto. Now it would claim the two of us as well.

"The bottom of this taper is wet," said Davus. "It won't stay lit much longer."

That would be even more dreadful: to be plunged into utter darkness, buried alive like a condemned Vestal with no hope of rescue.

I suddenly realized that the booming of the battering-ram had ceased. Word of the inundation must have reached Trebonius. The invasion by tunnel had failed. The operation had been canceled. The siege tower with the battering-ram had been rolled back from the walls. In the world above us, the battle was over.

"What happened, father-in-law? The flooding, I mean."

"I don't know. The Massilians must have known about the tunnel, or guessed. Perhaps they dug a reservoir inside the wall, an inner moat. They'd have had to pump water from the harbor to fill it, but they have engineers for that, every bit as clever as Vitruvius. When the sappers finally broke though, the water rushed in. It probably killed every man in the tunnel."

"Except you and me."

"Yes," I said grimly.

"What are we going to do, father-in-law?"

Die, I thought. Then I looked in his eyes and felt a jolt. Davus had not asked the question idly. He was looking to me for an answer. He was fearful, but not despairing. He truly expected to live because, as always, his wise old father-in-law would think of something. Davus's strength and reflexes had just saved our lives. Now it was my turn to return the favor.

"How long can you hold your breath?" I said.

"I don't know."

"Long enough to swim from here to the end of the tunnel?"

"We're going to swim out?"

"We can hardly walk."

"Back the way we came?"

I shook my head. "Too far. The opening inside Massilia must be closer."

"But what if it's blocked? I heard timbers breaking. If the earth gave way—"

"If there's an obstruction, we'll simply have to get past it, won't we?"

Davus thought about this and nodded. By the light of the wavering flame, I studied his perfectly chiseled nose, his bright eyes, and strong chin. My daughter had found him handsome despite his simple nature, and without my consent he had became the father of my grandchild. Curious, I thought, that of all the faces in the world, his should be the last I would ever see. Stranger still, that I should find myself faced with drowning in a hole beneath the earth. Drowning was the death I had always most feared, and the one I had least expected to encounter on this day, in this place.

I was a poor swimmer. Davus might have the lungs and the strength to swim to safety, but did I?

"When shall we try it?" he asked.

It would be hard to abandon the safety of the cavity as long as there was light from the taper. But if we waited until the taper burned out and we were plunged into utter darkness, I might lose my nerve, along with all sense of direction. " 'It's like pulling a thorn . . . ,' " I quoted.

" 'Quickly done is best done,' " said Davus, finishing the proverb. "I should go first, in case there's something blocking the way."

"A good idea," I granted. If I went first, and my lungs and strength gave out, I would merely block Davus's way. "We should take off our armor. Too heavy. Here, I'll hold the taper while you take off yours. Turn around. I'll help you with the straps." When he was done, I handed back the taper and set to unbuckling my own armor. Keeping my head above water while reaching down to remove the greaves protecting my shins was hardest. Davus held my shoulder with one strong arm.

"What about our swords?" he said.

I touched the scabbard at my waist. "We might need them. To cut through something," I added. The thought terrified me.

"And our helmets?" he said.

"We should keep them on. Protect our heads. Who knows what we might swim into?"

He nodded. The taper was growing dimmer.

I felt a thickness in my throat. "Davus, we've been through a lot together. At Brundisium, you saved my life—"

"I thought you saved mine!" he said, and grinned. Not for Davus any last-minute, sentimental farewells.

"We'll talk about it later," I said, "after we're out of this mess. Do you think they'll still have wine at the taverns in Massilia, or will they have run out because of the blockade? I'm thirsty."

Davus seemed not to hear. He thrust out his jaw and narrowed his eyes. "Are you ready, father-in-law?"

I tried to draw a deep breath, but my chest was tight, as if circled by an iron band. I swallowed hard. "Ready."

Davus handed me the taper. Our eyes met for an instant, then he turned and disappeared beneath the surface. Before I could reconsider, I sucked in a breath and tossed the taper into the water.

There was a brief hiss, then instant and total darkness. I closed my eyes and ducked beneath the surface. I stroked with my arms, kicked with my feet. Briefly I had a terrifying illusion of propelling myself into an endless black void. Then my outstretched fingers brushed against the sides of the tunnel. I swam blindly forward, using the walls of the tunnel to guide me.

Something cold touched my face, then seemed to slither snakelike against my chest and belly. I grabbed at the thing to thrust it away, but instead became locked in a strange embrace of hard metal and yielding flesh. I was puzzled at first, then horrified. It was the body of a soldier. I recoiled, but his limbs were tangled around me. I thrashed madly until the corpse released me, then swam frantically forward.

The way was clear. My heart boomed in my ears and my lungs felt as if they might burst, but the swimming was effortless. I stroked and kicked, and began to think that escape might be possible after all.

Then my helmet struck something hard. I was dazed. I reached up to feel the jagged stump of a broken rafter above me, sharp as a javelin. What if the way ahead was ringed with broken timbers? I imagined Davus, bigger than I, even more vulnerable, impaled on a spike, thrashing, bleeding, helpless, blocking the way, making it impossible for me to get past him. The image was so real that for an instant I thought of turning back. But that was impossible. I could never hope to find the pocket of air again, not in absolute darkness.

I froze, too frightened to go on, too frightened to turn back. I lost my nerve completely. Spots of light danced before my eyes and became faces in the darkness. They were the anonymous faces of the dead all around me, receding to infinity.

Time stopped. The pressure in my lungs overwhelmed everything else, even panic. I kicked with my feet, stroked with my arms, and swam blindly, as hard as I could, heedless of the danger. I swam so fast I caught up with Davus. His foot kicked my helmet. In desperation I imagined grabbing his leg and pulling myself past him, swimming ahead of him, breaking through to the surface.

On the next stroke, where my fingertips should have touched the guiding walls, there was nothing. The sides of the tunnel were suddenly gone.

I opened my eyes. Up ahead I saw a faint, watery light. Between me and the light, Davus loomed in foreshortened silhouette. I saw him stop and turn about, like wing-footed Mercury suspended in midair. He reached back. I held out my hand. Davus gripped it.

My strength had given out. Somehow Davus knew. With one arm stroking, he pulled me up, up, up toward a growing circle of light. For an instant I saw the world of light and air as a fish might see it, peering up from a pond. Seen through the water, the men who stood at the edge peering down at us were wavering and elongated. Their bright garments flickered like multicolored flames.

An instant later I broke the surface. The light hurt my eyes. I sucked in a long, inverted scream. Ahead of me, Davus collapsed, half in the water and half out, heaving and gasping. I crawled past him, desperate to be clear of the water completely. I rolled onto my back and shut my eyes, feeling warm sunshine on my face.

VI

I must have lost consciousness, but only for a moment. I slowly woke to a confusion of voices surrounding me, speaking Greek—men's voice, old men, speaking on top of each other. The babble narrowed to an argument between two voices.

"But where in Hades did these two come from?"

"I'm telling you, they must have tunneled through. I saw when it happened—big bubbles in the moat, then a weird sucking sound, and then a whirlpool. Look how far the water's dropped!"

"Impossible! If a tunnel broke through, and the reservoir flooded it, how did these two swim against the current? It doesn't make sense. It's uncanny, the way they came flailing out of the water."

"You always look for religious explanations! Next you'll be saying Artemis coughed them up. They dug under the wall, I tell you."

"They don't look like sappers. They don't look much like soldiers, either."

"Oh, no? They're wearing helmets, aren't they? I say, kill them!"

"Shut up, you old coot. We'll hand them over to the soldiers when they get here."

"Why wait? Do you imagine these two would think twice before cutting down a group of old Massilians gabbing in the market square?"

"They look harmless."

"Harmless? Those are swords in their scabbards, you idiot. Here, you fellows, help me take their weapons. Take their helmets, too." I felt myself jostled about on the sand and heard splashes nearby.

"Look, the older one's coming to his senses. He's opening his eyes."

I blinked and looked up to see a circle of old men staring down at me. Some drew back in alarm. Their consternation almost made me laugh. The simple fact of being alive made me feel giddy. "Argue all you want," I said, mustering my Greek. "Just don't throw me back."

My Greek may have been rusty and my accent uncouth, but that hardly justified the onslaught that followed.

The most belligerent of the old men—the one who'd argued to kill us on the spot—began to thrash me with a cane. He was a skinny, bony creature, but he had surprising strength. I covered my head with my arms. He deliberately aimed for my elbows.

"Stop this! Stop at once!" The voice was a new one, a man's. It came from a short distance away. "Slaves, restrain that horrible old man."

My attacker backed away, slashing his cane to fend off two half-naked giants who suddenly loomed over me. The old man was furious. "Damn you to Hades, Scapegoat! If your slaves lay a finger on me, I'll report you to the Timouchoi."

"Oh, really? You forget, old man, *I'm* untouchable." The voice was high-pitched, harsh, and grating.

"For now, maybe. But what about later? Eh, Scapegoat? When the time comes to put an end to you, I swear I'll kick you off the Sacrifice Rock myself."

There were gasps from the circle of old men. "Calamitos, you've gone too far!" said the one who'd been arguing with him. "The goddess—"

"Artemis has abandoned Massilia, in case you haven't noticed—as well she might, given the impiousness of this wretched city. Caesar pinches us in a vise, and what solution do the Timouchoi come up with? A scapegoat to take on the city's sins! So now we starving citizens shrivel to scarecrows while that scarecrow grows fatter every day." The old man threw his cane against the ground so hard it broke in two. He stalked off in a fury.

"Blessed Artemis! The old coot can't help being ugly and bad mannered, but there's no need to be blasphemous as well." I strained my neck and saw that the voice of my rescuer came from a nearby litter attended by a retinue of bearers. "Slaves! Pick up those two fellows and put them here in the litter with me."

The slaves looked down at me dubiously. One of them shrugged. "Master, I'm not sure the bearers can carry all three of you in the litter. The big one looks awfully heavy. I'm not even sure he's alive."

I rolled toward Davus, alarmed. He lay motionless on his back, his eyes shut, his face pale. A moment later, to my relief, he coughed and his eyelids fluttered.

"If the burden's too much, then you'll simply have to run home and fetch more slaves to carry us," said my mysterious protector, his grating voice made more grating by exasperation.

"Wait, Scapegoat!" The cooler-headed of the two old men who had been arguing over me stepped forward. "You can't simply run off with these men. They've come from outside the city. That one spoke Greek with a Roman accent. Despite his blasphemy, Calamitos was right about one thing—they might be dangerous. For all we know, they're assassins, or spies. We must hand them over to the soldiers."

"Nonsense. Am I not the scapegoat, duly chosen by the priests of Artemis and invested by the Timouchoi? For the duration of the crisis, all godsends are mine, to dispose of as I see fit. That includes fish washed up on the shores of Massilia—and I hereby claim these two stranded fish. No doubt they were cast upon this man-made beach by Artemis herself. The big one looks like a beached whale."

"The fellow's mad!" muttered one of the old men.

"But legally he may be right," said another. "Godsends do belong to the scapegoat. . . ."

While the old men argued among themselves, strong arms scooped me up and swung me around. I was in no condition either to resist or assist. They carried me like dead weight. In glimpses I took in my surroundings. We were in a corner of the city. Looming over us were the high walls of Massilia, very different when seen from within, for they were lined with platforms and crisscrossed with stairways, and at their foot was the half-drained reservoir from which we had emerged. A little ways off, twin towers flanked the massive bronze gate that was the main entrance into the city. Past the gate the wall bent sharply back and fronted the harbor, for beyond that stretch of wall I saw the tops of ships' masts.

I was carried toward a litter, which sat alone in the middle of the large square that opened off the main gate. All the buildings facing the square appeared empty. Windows were shuttered; shops were closed. Except for the litter bearers, there was hardly a person in sight.

The green curtains of the litter parted. I was gently placed upon a bed of green cushions. Opposite me, reclining among more cushions, was my rescuer. He was dressed in a green chiton that matched the cushions and the curtains of the litter; so much green was confusing. His gangly limbs seemed too long for the space; he had to bend his knees up sharply to accommodate me. He was thick in the middle, but his face was gaunt. The hair on his head was pale and thin. A narrow strip of wispy beard outlined his sharp chin.

A moment later, the two slaves who had carried me, joined by two others from among the bearers, managed to carry Davus to the litter. I moved over and they deposited him beside me. He looked about, bleary-eyed.

The stranger seemed to find us amusing. His thin lips curved into a smile and there was laughter in his dull gray eyes. "Welcome to Massilia, whoever you are!"

He clapped his hands. The litter was hoisted aloft. I felt nauseous. Our host noticed my distress.

"Go ahead and be sick if you need to," he said. "Try to do it outside the litter; but if you can't manage, don't worry. If you soil a few cushions, I'll simply throw them away."

I swallowed hard. "It will pass."

"Oh, don't hold it in!" he advised. "A man should never restrain his body's natural impulses. If nothing else, I've certainly learned that in the last few months."

Beside me, Davus recovered his wits. He stirred and sat upright. "Father-in-law, where are we?"

Our host answered. "You are in the most wicked city on earth, young man, and you've come at the most wicked time in her history. I should know; I was born here. And here I'll die. In between I've known wealth and poverty, joy and bitterness. Mostly poverty and mostly bitterness, to be honest. But now, in her final hour, my city forgives me and I forgive her. We exchange the only things we have to give, her final bounty for my final days."

"Are you a philosopher?" asked Davus, frowning.

The man laughed. It was like the sound of a scythe cutting thick grass. "My name is Hieronymus," he said, as if to change the subject. "And yours?"

"Gordianus," I said.

"Ah, a Roman, as the old men suspected."

"And this is Davus."

"A slave's name?"

"A freedman; my son-in-law. Where are you taking us?"

"To my tomb."

"Your tomb?" I asked, thinking I had misunderstood his Greek.

"Did I say that? I meant to say my home, of course. Now lie quietly and rest. You're safe with me."

From time to time I stole a glance between the curtains that sealed the box. At first we kept to a wide, main road. Not a shop was open and the street was empty, allowing the bearers to make good time. Then we turned off the main way into a maze of lesser roads, each more narrow than the last. We began to ascend, gradually at first, then more sharply. The bearers did a good job of keeping the box level, but nothing could disguise the sharp turns as they went around switchbacks, taking us higher and higher.

Finally the litter lurched to a halt. "Home!" declared Hieronymus. He folded his limbs and exited the box with the slow grace of an overfed stick insect. "Do you need assistance?" he called to me over his shoulder.

"No," I said, stepping out of the box onto wobbly legs. Davus stepped out after me and laid a hand on my shoulder to steady us both.

"However you came to be inside the city, it was clearly an ordeal for you both," said Hieronymus, looking us up and down.

"What would comfort you? Food? Wine? Ah, from the look on your faces, I see it's the latter. Come, we shall drink together. And none of the local swill. We'll drink what they drink in Rome. I think I still have some of the good Falernian left."

The house had been built along Roman lines, with a small foyer and an atrium that opened onto the rest of the dwelling. It was a rich man's house, with sumptuously painted walls and a fine mosaic of Neptune (or, since we were in a Greek city, Poseidon) in the atrium pool. Beyond a formal dining room, at the heart of the house, I glimpsed a garden surrounded by a peristyle of red and blue columns.

"Shall we take our wine in the garden?" said Hieronymus. "No, on the rooftop, I think. I love to show off the view."

We followed him up a flight of stairs to a rooftop terrace. Tall trees on either side of the house provided shade and seclusion, but the view toward the sea was clear. The house had been built on the crest of the ridge that ran through the city. Below us the ridge dropped off sharply, so that we looked down on rooftops that descended in steps toward the city walls. Beyond the walls, the sea extended to a horizon of scudding blue clouds. Off to the left, I could see a bit of the harbor and the rugged coastline beyond. Opposite the mouth of the harbor were the islands behind which Caesar's warships lay moored. Shielding my eyes against the lowering sun, I could see one of the ships peeking around the bend of the farthest island. The ship was tiny at such a distance, but the air was so clear I could make out long-shadowed sailors moving about the deck.

Hieronymus followed my gaze. "Yes, there it is, Caesar's navy. They think they're hiding around the bend, but we can see them, can't we? Peek-a-boo!" He fluttered his fingers in a simpering wave and laughed at his own absurdity, as if aware that such childishness was at odds with the lines of ancient suffering that creased his face.

"Were you hereabouts to witness the little naval battle we had a while back? No? It was something to see, I'll tell you. People

lined the walls down there to watch, but I had the perfect vantage point right here. Catapults hurling missiles! Fire sweeping
the decks! Blood on the water! Nine of our ships lost. Nine out
of seventeen—a catastrophe! Some sunk, some captured by Caesar. What a humiliating day for Massilia that was. I can't tell
you how much I enjoyed it." He stared grimly at the now placid
spot where the battle had taken place, then turned to me and
brightened. "But I promised you wine! Here, sit. These chairs
are made of imported terebinth. I'm told they shouldn't be left
out of doors, but what do I care?"

We sat in the full sunshine. A slave brought wine. I praised
the vintage, which was unmistakably Falernian. Hieronymus insisted I drink more. Against my better judgment I did. After
his second cup, Davus fell asleep in his chair.

"The poor fellow must be exhausted," said Hieronymus.

"We very nearly died today."

"A good thing you didn't, or else I'd be drinking alone."

I looked at him keenly, or as keenly as I could after a third
cup of Falernian. So far he had asked not a single question about
us—who we were, how we had entered the city, what we had
come for. His lack of curiosity was puzzling. Perhaps, I thought,
he was merely being patient, biding his time, allowing me to
recover my wits.

"Why did you come to our rescue?" I asked.

"Mainly to spite those old men who hang about the market
square, the ones who were kicking you and discussing you like
a fish that needed gutting."

"Do you know them?"

He smiled ruefully. "Oh, yes, I've known them all my life.
When I was a boy, they were men in their prime, very sure of
themselves, full of their own importance. Now I'm a man and
they're old, with nothing better to do than hang about the
square all day, spreading slanders and commenting on everyone's
business. The square is shut down now—there's nothing left to
buy in the shops—but there they still go, day after day, haunt-

ing the place." He smiled. "I like to drop by in the litter every now and then just to taunt them."

"Taunt them?"

"They used to treat me rather badly, you see. The market square was where I used to spend my days, too . . . when I didn't have a roof over my head. That old coot Calamitos was the worst. He's gotten even crankier since the food shortages began. What a joy to see him so flustered he broke his cane! When I think of the times he struck me with it. . . ."

"I don't understand. Who are you? I heard them call you 'Scapegoat.' And the old man said he'd report you to the Ti-mouchoi. Who are they?"

He stared grimly at the sea for a long moment, then clapped his hands. "Slave! If I'm to tell the story, and if my new friend Gordianus is to hear it, we shall both require more wine."

VII

"What do you know about Massilia?" asked Hieronymus.

"It's far, far from Rome," I said, feeling a stab of homesickness, thinking of Bethesda and Diana and my house on the Palatine Hill.

"Not far enough!" said Hieronymus. "Caesar and Pompey have a brawl, and Massilia is close enough to take a blow. No, what I mean is, what do you know about the city itself—how it's organized, who runs it?"

"Nothing, really. It's an old Greek colony, isn't it? A city-state. Here since the days of Hannibal."

"Since long before that! Massilia was a bustling seaport when Romulus was living in a hut on the Tiber."

"Ancient history." I shrugged. "I do know that Massilia sided with Rome against Carthage, and the two cities have been allies ever since." I frowned. "I know you don't have a king. I suppose the city's run by some sort of elected body. You Greeks invented democracy, didn't you?"

"Invented it, yes, and quickly discarded it, for the most part. Massilia is run by a timocracy. Do you know what that means?"

"Government by the wealthy." My Greek was coming back to me.

"By, for, and of the wealthy. An aristocracy of money, not birth. Just what you might expect from a city founded by merchants."

"Not a good place to be a poor man," I said.

"No," said Hieronymus darkly. He stared intently into his wine cup. "Massilia is run by the Timouchoi, a body of six hundred members who hold office for life. Openings occur as members die; the Timouchoi themselves nominate and vote on replacement candidates."

"Self-perpetuating." I nodded. "Very insular."

"Oh, yes, within the Timouchoi the attitude is very much 'us' and 'them,' those on the inside and those on the outside. You see, a man must be wealthy to join the Timouchoi, but it takes more than just money. His family must have held Massilian citizenship for three generations, and he himself must have fathered children. Roots in the past, a stake in the future, and here in the present, a great deal of money."

"Very conservative," I said. "No wonder the Massilian system is so famously admired by Cicero. But is there no people's assembly, as in Rome, where the commoners can make themselves heard? No way for ordinary folk to at least vent their frustrations?"

Hieronymus shook his head. "Massilia is ruled by the Timouchoi alone. Of the six hundred, a rotating Council of Fifteen deal with general administration. Of those fifteen, three are responsible for the day-to-day running of the city. Of those three, one is selected First Timouchos, the closest thing we have to what you Romans call a 'consul,' chief executive in times of peace and supreme military commander in times of war. The Timouchoi make the laws, keep order, organize the markets, regulate the banks, run the courts, hire mercenaries, equip the navy. Their grip on the city is absolute." As if to demonstrate, he tightened his fingers around the cup in his hand until his knuckles turned white. The look in his eyes made me shift uneasily.

"And what is your place in this scheme of things?" I asked quietly.

"A man like me has no place at all," he said dully. "Oh, *now* I do. I'm the scapegoat." He smiled, but his voice was bitter.

Hieronymus called for more wine. More Falernian was brought. Such largesse in a city under siege seemed nothing less than profligate.

"Let me explain," he said. "My father was one of the Timouchoi—the first of my family to rise so high. He was made a member just after my birth. A few years later, he was elevated to the Council of Fifteen, one of the youngest men ever elected to that body. He must have been a man of great ambition to rise so high, so fast, leapfrogging past men from richer, older families than ours. As you might imagine, there were those among the Timouchoi who were jealous of him, who believed that he had stolen honors properly due to them.

"I was his only child. He raised me in a house not unlike this one, up here on the crest of the ridge where the old money lives. The view from our rooftop was even more spectacular than this; or perhaps my nostalgia embellishes it. We could see all Massilia below, the harbor filled with ships, the blue sea stretching on and on to the horizon. 'All this will be yours,' he told me once. I must have been quite small because I remember that he picked me up, put me on his shoulders, and turned slowly about. 'All this will be yours. . . .' "

"Where did his money come from?" I asked.

"From the trade."

"The trade?"

"All wealth in Massilia comes from the slave and wine trade. The Gauls ship slaves down the Rhodanus River for sale to Italy; the Italians ship wine from Ostia and Neapolis to sell to the Gauls. Slaves for wine, wine for slaves, with Massilia in the middle, providing ships and taking her cut. That's the foundation of all wealth in Massilia. My great-grandfather began our fortune. My grandfather increased it. My father increased it more. He owned many ships.

"Then the bad times came. I was still quite young—too young to know the details of my father's business. He told my mother that he had been betrayed by others, cheated by men among the Timouchoi whom he had considered his friends. He had to sell his ships, one by one, to pay his creditors. It wasn't enough. Then our warehouse near the harbor burned to the ground. My father's enemies accused him of setting the fire himself to destroy records and avoid debts. My father denied it." Hieronymus paused for a long moment. "If only I had been older, able to understand all that was happening. I'll never know the truth— whether my father was responsible for his own ruin, or whether others destroyed him. It's a painful thing, never to know the whole truth."

"What became of him?"

"He was suspended from the Council of Fifteen. The Timouchoi began proceedings to expel him."

"Were there criminal charges?"

"No! It was worse than that. He had lost all his money, don't you see? In Massilia there's no greater scandal. What matters to a Roman most?"

"His dignity, I suppose."

"Then imagine a Roman stripped completely of his dignity, and you may understand. Without wealth, a man in Massilia is *nothing*. To have possessed wealth and to have lost it—such a thing could happen only to the worst of men, men so vile they've offended the gods. A man like that must be shunned, despised, spat upon."

"What became of him?"

"We have a law in Massilia. I imagine it was devised for just such men as my father. Suicide is forbidden, with penalties exacted upon the suicide's family—unless a man applies to the Timouchoi for permission."

"Permission to take one's own life?"

"Yes. My father applied. The Timouchoi took up the matter as they might have taken up a trade bill. It saved them the embarrassment of expelling him, you see. The vote was unanimous. They were even so kind as to supply him with a dose of hemlock. But he didn't take it."

"No?"

"He chose the harder way. Down there, where the land meets the sea, do you see that finger of rock that juts up through the city wall, so massive they had to build the wall around it?"

"Yes." The rock was naked of vegetation, its summit stark white against the blue sea.

"Its official name is the Sacrifice Rock. Sometimes people call it Suicide Rock, or Scapegoat Rock. If you're agile enough, you can climb onto it from the battlements of the city wall. If you're fit enough, you can climb from the base to the top without using the walls at all. It's not as steep as it looks, and there are plenty of footholds. But once you reach the top, it's a frightening place. The view over the edge is dizzying—a long, sheer drop to the sea. When the wind is high at your back, it's all a man can do to keep from being blown off."

"Your father jumped?"

"I remember that morning vividly. It was the day after the Timouchoi approved his request. He dressed in black and left the house without a word. My mother wept and tore her hair, but she didn't try to follow him. I knew where he was headed. I went up on the roof and watched. I saw when he reached the foot of the rock. A crowd had gathered to watch him climb. He looked so small from our roof—a tiny black figure scaling a white finger of rock. When he reached the top, he didn't hesitate, not even for an instant. He stepped over the edge and vanished. One moment there, the next—gone. My mother was watching from a window below me. She let out a scream the moment he vanished."

"How terrible," I said. From old habit, I sifted the unresolved details of his story. "What became of the hemlock?" As soon as I asked, I knew the answer.

"Creditors came to drive us out of the house the next day. My mother could never have borne that. They found her in her bed, as peaceful as if she slept. She broke the law by drinking the hemlock provided for my father; broke the law as well by mixing it with wine, because wine is strictly forbidden to women in Massilia. But no one sought to prosecute her. There was nothing left to confiscate, and no one left to punish but me. I suppose they thought I had already been punished enough for the sins of my parents." He took a deep breath. "I resent her, sometimes, for not staying with me. I resent him, as well. But I can't blame them. Their lives were over."

"What became of you?"

"For a while I was grudgingly passed from one relative to another. But they all considered me to be cursed. They didn't want me in their homes for fear that the curse would rub off. At the first sign of trouble—a fire in the kitchen, a sick child, a slump in the family business—I was tossed out. At last I ran out of relatives. I looked for work. My father had given me good tutors. I knew philosophy, mathematics, Latin. I probably knew more about the trade than I realized, having picked it up from my father. But no one among the Timouchoi would hire me. You might think one of these exiled Romans who keep popping up in Massilia would have found me useful, but not one of them would touch me for fear of offending the Timouchoi.

"Now and again I found work as a common laborer. It's not easy for a free man to make a living by manual labor—too many slaves about who can do the same work for no wages. I can't say that I ever succeeded at anything except staying alive. Some years I barely managed that. I've worn other men's cast-off rags, eaten other men's garbage. I've swallowed my shame and begged for alms. For long periods I've had no roof over my head. Sun and wind turned my skin to leather. Just as well; a hard hide served me well when fellows like that old coot Calamitos took a cane to me, calling me a vagrant, a good-for-nothing, a parasite, the son of a cursed father and an impious mother."

"Calamitos—is he one of the Timouchoi?"

"Artemis, no! None of that gang of old fools is rich. They're contemporaries of my father who never amounted to much. When I was a boy they were all afire with ambition and wracked by their jealousy, Calamitos especially, of my father and his success. After my father died, it gave them great pleasure to gloat over my squalor and to vent their cruelty on me. Nothing comforts the wretched like having someone even more wretched to despise."

The sun was lowering and the wind was beginning to rise. The tall trees on either side of us shivered and pitched, and their shadows grew longer.

"A terrible story," I said quietly.

"Merely a true one."

"The way you described the Sacrifice Rock—you must have climbed it yourself."

"A few times. The first time was out of curiosity, to see what my father had seen, to know the place where he ended."

"And after that?"

"To follow him, if the moment seemed right. But I never heard the call."

"The call?"

"I don't know how else to explain it. Each time I climbed up, I fully intended to jump. What was there to keep me in this accursed world? But once I reached the top, it never felt right. I suppose I expected to hear my father and mother calling to me, and they never did. But soon now . . . very soon. . . ."

"What did Calamitos mean when he called you 'Scapegoat'?"

He smiled bitterly. "That's another of our charming ancient traditions. In times of great crisis—plague, famine, military siege, naval blockade—the priests of Artemis choose a scapegoat, subject to approval by the Timouchoi, of course. Ideally it's the most wretched creature they can find, some pathetic nonentity whom no one will miss. Who better than a child of suicides, the lowest of the low, that irritating beggar who haunts the market square, whom everyone will be glad to be rid of? There's a bit of a ceremony—*xoanon* Artemis presiding over clouds of incense, chanting priests, that sort of thing. The scapegoat is dressed in green, with a green veil; the goddess has no desire to see his face. Then the priests parade the scapegoat through the city, with all the onlookers dressed in black as if for a funeral, the women ululating laments. But at the end of the procession, the scapegoat arrives, not at a tomb, but at a very fine house especially prepared for his arrival. Slaves bathe him and anoint him with oil, then dress him in fine clothes—all in this partic- ular shade of green, which is the scapegoat's color. More slaves pour costly wine down his throat and stuff him with delicacies. He's free to move about the city, and a fine litter—green, of course—is provided for his use. The only problem is, he might as well be in a tomb. No one will talk to him. They won't even look at him. Even his slaves avert their eyes and say no more than they have to. All this luxury and privilege—it's only a pretense, a sham. The scapegoat lives a sort of death-in-life. Even as he indulges in every physical pleasure, he begins to feel . . . utterly alone. Slightly . . . unreal. Invisible, almost. Perhaps that's only to be expected. All this time, if you believe the priests of Artemis, by some mystical means his person is collecting the sins of the entire city. Well, that might make *anyone* feel a bit out of sorts."

"What is the end of all this?"

"Ah, you're eager to jump ahead. Better to shun the future and live in the moment! But since you ask: when the moment is right—I'm not sure how the priests determine this, but I suspect the Council of Fifteen has a say—at the right moment, when all the sins of the city have attached themselves to the pampered, bloated, satiated person of the scapegoat, then it will be time for another ceremony. More incense and chanting, more onlookers dressed in black, more ululating mourners. But this time, the procession will end—down there." He pointed toward the finger of rock. "Suicide Rock, Sacrifice Rock, Scapegoat Rock. I don't suppose the name matters. My misery began there. There my misery will end."

He expelled a long sigh, then smiled wanly. "Surely, my friend, you've been wondering why I've asked you no questions about yourself, why I seem so curiously incurious about two Romans who bubbled up out of that inner moat? Here's your answer. I don't care who you are or where you came from. I don't care if you're here to murder the First Timouchos, or to sell Caesar's secrets to that motley colony of Roman exiles who've washed up in Massilia. I'm simply glad for the company! You can't imagine what it means to me, Gordianus, to sit here on this rooftop as the day wanes, sharing this splendid view and this splendid wine with another man, enjoying a civilized conversation. I feel . . . not so alone, not so invisible. As if all this were real, not merely a pretense."

I was weary from the day's ordeal and disquieted by the scapegoat's story. I looked sidelong at Davus, who was gently snoring, and felt envious.

While we had talked, the sun had slipped beyond the watery horizon. It was the darkling hour. The line between sea and sky blurred and dissolved. Ethereal patches of silver light hovered here and there on the face of the water. Nearer at hand, shadows deepened. Warmth still rose from the paving stones beneath our feet, but puffs of cooler air eddied from the tall trees on either side, shrouded deeply now in their own shadows.

"What's that?" whispered Hieronymus, leaning forward, his voice urgent. "Down there . . . on the rock!"

Out of nowhere, two figures had appeared about halfway up

the face of the Sacrifice Rock. Both were climbing upward; one was substantially ahead of the other, but the lower figure was gaining.

"Is that . . . a woman, do you think?" whispered Hieronymus. He meant the upper figure, who wore a dark, voluminous, hooded cloak that flapped in the wind to reveal what had to be a woman's gown beneath. Her movements were halting and uncertain, as if she were weak or confused. Her hesitation allowed the lower figure to continue closing the gap between them. Her pursuer was certainly a man, for he was dressed in armor, though without a helmet. His dark hair was cut short and his limbs looked dark against the white stone and the pale blue of his billowing cape.

Beside me, Davus stirred and opened his eyes. "What . . . ?"

"He's chasing her," I whispered.

"No, he's trying to stop her," Hieronymus said.

The twilight played tricks on my eyes. The harder I stared at the distant drama on the rock, the more difficult it was to discern the crabbed movements of the two figures. It was almost easier to watch their progress from the corner of my eye.

Davus leaned forward, suddenly alert. "That looks dangerous," he offered.

The woman paused and turned her head to look behind her. The man was very close, almost near enough to grasp her foot.

"Did you hear that?" whispered Hieronymus.

"Hear what?" I said.

"She shrieked," agreed Davus.

"That might have been a seagull," I objected.

The woman put on a burst of speed. She gained the summit of the rock. Her cloak blew wildly about her. The man lost his footing and scrambled on the rock face, then recovered and scurried up after her. For an instant they merged into a single figure; then the woman vanished, and only the man remained, his figure outlined against the leaden sea beyond.

Davus gasped. "Did you see that? He pushed her!"

"No!" said Hieronymus. "He was trying to stop her. She jumped!"

The distant figure knelt and looked over the precipice for a long moment, his pale blue cape thrashing in the wind. Then he turned about and climbed down the rock face, not straight down the way he had come but angling toward the nearest connecting section of the city wall. As soon as he was close enough he leaped from the rock onto the battlement platform. He stumbled when he landed and apparently hurt himself. He broke into a run, limping slightly and favoring his left leg. There was no one else on the platform, the Massilians having earlier moved all their men to the other side of the city to deal with the assault from Trebonius's battering-ram.

The limping runner reached the nearest bastion tower and disappeared into the stairwell. The base of the tower was hidden from view. There was nothing more to see.

"Great Artemis! What do you make of that?" asked Hieronymus.

"He pushed her," Davus insisted. "I saw him do it. Father-in-law, you know how keen my eyes are. She tried to cling to him. He pushed her away, over the edge."

"You don't know what you're talking about," said Hieronymus. "You were asleep when I explained to Gordianus. That's the Sacrifice Rock, also called the Suicide Rock. He didn't chase her up the face of it. She went there to kill herself, and he tried to stop her. And he very nearly did—but not quite!" The hard lines around his mouth suddenly loosened. He covered his face. "Father!" he moaned. "Mother!"

Davus looked at me with a puzzled frown. How could I explain the scapegoat's misery?

I was saved from the attempt by the arrival of a breathless slave, a young Gaul with a red face and unruly straw-colored hair. "Master!" he cried to Hieronymus. "Men downstairs! The

First Timouchos himself, and the Roman proconsul! They demand to see . . . your visitors." The slave cast a wary glance at
Davus and me.

That was all the warning we had. The next moment, with a
great tramping of feet, soldiers emerged from the stairway onto
the rooftop terrace, their drawn swords gleaming dully in the
gloaming.

VIII

Davus reacted at once. He jumped up from his chair, pulled me to my feet, pushed me to the far side of the terrace, then took a stance before me. He had no weapon, so he raised his fists. Back in his slave days, he had been trained to be a bodyguard. His trainers had done a good job.

"Look behind you, father-in-law," he whispered. "Is there any way to jump from the roof?"

I looked over the short railing of the terrace. In the courtyard below I saw more soldiers with drawn swords.

"Not an option," I said. I laid a hand on his shoulder. "Step back, Davus. And drop that boxer's stance. You'll only antagonize them. We're the intruders here. We must trust to their mercy."

I took a deep breath. Hieronymus had given me plenty to drink, but nothing to eat. I was light-headed.

The soldiers made no move to attack us. They fell into a line, swords drawn but lowered, and simply stared at us. Hieronymus flew into a frenzy.

"What are you doing here? This is the sacred residence of the scapegoat! You can't bring arms here. You can't enter at all without permission from the priests of Artemis!"

"How dare you invoke the goddess, you impious dog!" The booming voice came from the man who had evidently dispatched the soldiers up the stairs and who now followed behind them. His armor was magnificent, as bright as a newly minted coin. A pale blue cape trailed behind. The horsehair crest on the helmet carried under his arm was likewise died pale blue. The color matched his eyes. They seemed too small, as did his thin nose and narrow mouth, for such a broad forehead and an even broader jaw. His long, silver hair was swept back like a mane.

"Apollonides!" said Hieronymus, uttering the name like a curse. Through gritted teeth, to me, he added, "The First Timouchos."

Another man followed Apollonides, wearing the armor of a Roman commander. A copper disk on his breastplate was embossed with a lion's head. I recognized him at once; but then, I knew he was in Massilia and was not surprised to see him. Would he recognize me? We had met only briefly, and months ago.

"By all the gods!" Lucius Domitius Ahenobarbus put his hands on his hips and stared at me. "I don't believe it. Gordianus the Finder! And who is this big fellow?"

"My son-in-law, Davus."

Domitius nodded, pulling thoughtfully at the red beard across his chin. "When did I last see you? Don't tell me—at Cicero's house in Formiae. The month was Martius. You were on your way to Brundisium. I was on my way here. Ha! When the old men who hang about the market square told Apollonides that two Romans had dragged themselves out of the inner moat, he wanted to be sure they weren't a couple of my men gone astray before he cut off their heads. A good thing I came along to identify you! Who'd have thought . . . ?"

His brow darkened. I could read the change as clearly as if

he'd spoken his thoughts aloud. He had finally remembered not just my name and my association with Cicero; he now recalled that I was Meto's father. If Meto had come to Massilia, secretly loyal to Caesar but seeking a position with Caesar's enemies, it was to Domitius that he would have offered his services. Had they met? What had passed between them? What did Domitius know of Meto's whereabouts? Why was his expression suddenly so dark?

"Who is this fellow?" demanded Apollonides impatiently. Clearly, from the way they conversed, he and Domitius considered each other to be of equal rank—one, supreme commander of the Massilian forces; the other, commander of the Roman troops in Massilia loyal to Pompey and the Roman Senate.

"His name is Gordianus, called the Finder. A Roman citizen. We've met before, once, briefly." Domitius squinted and studied me as he might a map turned upside-down.

"Loyal to Caesar or to Pompey?" Apollonides looked at me more as if I were a strange animal; tame or feral?

"That's a very good question," said Domitius.

"And how did he come to be in the city?"

"Another good question."

Together they stared at me.

I crossed my hands before me and took a deep breath. "I hate to change the subject," I said slowly, "but we've just witnessed something very alarming. Over . . . there." I pointed toward the Sacrifice Rock.

"What are you talking about?" Apollonides glared at me. "Answer my question! How did you get into the city?"

"A woman and a man—a soldier, to judge by his clothing—just climbed that finger of rock. The three of us sat here and watched them. One of them went over the edge. The other ran off."

Now I had his attention. "What? Someone jumped from the Sacrifice Rock?"

"The woman."

"No one is allowed to climb the Sacrifice Rock. And suicide without approval is strictly forbidden in Massilia!" barked Apollonides.

"So is murder, I should think."

"What?"

"The man pushed her!" Davus explained.

I cleared my throat. "Actually, there's some disagreement about that."

Apollonides stared at us through narrowed eyes, then waved to one of the soldiers. "You there, take some men and go to the Sacrifice Rock. Don't set foot on it, but examine the area all around. Look for signs that anyone ventured onto the rock. Ask questions. Find out if anyone saw a man and a woman climbing it."

"The woman wore a dark cloak," I offered. "The man was in armor, without a helmet. He had a pale blue cape . . . rather like yours, Timouchos."

Apollonides was taken aback. "One of my officers? I don't believe it. You've fabricated the whole episode to avoid answering my questions!"

"No, Timouchos."

"First Timouchos!" he insisted. His red face contrasted strongly with his pale blue cape. I saw a frazzled man at the end of a trying day, without an atom of patience left.

"Of course, First Timouchos. You ask how we came to be here. The fact is, Trebonius's men dug a tunnel under the city walls. It was to come out near the main gate—"

"I knew it!" Apollonides pounded a fist into his open palm. "I told you, Domitius, the battering-ram assault this morning was only a diversion. Trebonius knows better than to think he can bring down the walls of Massilia with such a toy. While we were distracted, he meant to send a smaller force through a tunnel and take the main gate. Is that what you're saying, Finder?"

"Exactly, First Timouchos."

"The whirlpool that was seen, and the drop in the water level in the inner moat—you said it must be due to a leak, a fault in our own earthworks, Domitius!"

Now Domitius's face flushed red, clashing with his copper-colored beard. "I'm not an engineer. I only suggested the idea off the top of my head."

"Instead, it was just as *I* thought—Trebonius has been planning all along to tunnel his way in. I knew it! That's why I dug that trench and pumped it full of water, to thwart just such an attempt. And it worked! Tell me I'm right, Finder." He beamed at me. Now I was his friend, the bearer of good news.

I swallowed a lump in my throat. "The tunnel was full of soldiers, waiting to emerge the moment the sappers broke through. We waited for hours. We could hear the boom of the battering-ram farther down the walls . . ." I lowered my eyes. "Suddenly, the tunnel was flooded. A rush of water came though, carrying everything before it."

"Perfect!" exclaimed Apollonides. "All those soldiers flushed through the tunnel like rats through a Roman sewer!" Domitius scowled at this, but said nothing. "But you, Finder—how did you survive?"

"My son-in-law pulled me into a cavity in the ceiling of the tunnel. We waited until the flooding settled, then swam out. As far as I know, we were the only survivors."

"I think the gods must like you, Finder." Apollonides looked sidelong at Hieronymus. "No wonder the wretched scapegoat scooped you up and fetched you home with him. He thinks you'll bring him good luck."

"You have no right to be here!" Hieronymus suddenly shrieked. "The scapegoat's house is sacred. Your presence here is sacrilege, Apollonides."

"Fool! You don't know what you're talking about. I have the right to enter any house that may be harboring enemies of Massilia." Apollonides returned his gaze to me. "Is that the case here, Finder? What were you doing in that tunnel with Trebonius's men, if not taking part in an armed invasion of the city?"

"First Timouchos, look at me. I'm an old man. I'm not a soldier! I'm not a partisan for either side, and neither is Davus. We've traveled overland from Rome. We spent one night in Trebonius's camp. I wanted to enter the city, and I saw a way to do it. Davus and I disguised ourselves and slipped into the ranks. Trebonius didn't know. He'd have been furious if he found out. My business here in Massilia is neither military nor political. It's personal."

"And what exactly is this 'personal' business?"

"My son, Meto, was last seen in Massilia." I looked sidelong at Domitius, whose expression remained enigmatic. "I've come to look for him."

"A missing child?" The idea appeared to strike a sympathetic chord in Apollonides, who nodded slowly. "What do you think, Domitius? You know this fellow."

"Not that well." Domitius crossed his arms.

"Proconsul," I said, addressing Domitius with the formal title to which he aspired, knowing he fancied himself, and not Caesar, to be the Roman Senate's legally appointed governor of Gaul. "If Cicero were here, he'd vouch for me. You and I ate together at his table in Formiae; we both slept under his roof. Did you know that he once called me 'the most honest man in Rome'?" The quotation was accurate. I saw no need to add that Cicero had not necessarily intended it as a compliment.

Domitius tilted his head back and breathed in sharply through his nostrils. "I'll take responsibility for these two, Apollonides."

"Are you sure?"

Domitius hesitated for a heartbeat. "Yes."

"Good. That's settled, then." Apollonides yawned, showing molars to rival those of a Nile river-horse. "By Hypnos, I'm tired. And hungry! Will this wretched day never end? I'd hoped for a moment's peace, but now I suppose I must go and check the condition of the inner moat to make sure it's still holding water."

He turned to leave. Some of his soldiers broke from their ranks to precede him down the stairs. At the second step he stopped and looked back. "Oh, Finder—if the story you tell is true, I suppose you had the last laugh on Trebonius today, infiltrating his ranks and getting through that tunnel alive. We had a good laugh at him, too. That battering-ram he sent against the city wall? We finally got the better of it. Some of my soldiers managed to lower a rope noose, capture the head of the ram, and haul it up. A good thing; all that booming was giving me a headache. You should have seen the reaction on that hillside where Trebonius and his engineers gather. They were furious! That battering-ram shall make a fine trophy. Perhaps, after we've broken the siege and sent Trebonius packing, I'll display it on a pedestal in the market square."

He turned and took a few more steps.

"First Timouchos!" I called. "The . . . incident . . . on the Sacrifice Rock. The soldier and the woman—"

"The murder!" insisted Davus.

"You heard me dispatch my men," snapped Apollonides, stopping again. "I shall look into the matter. It's no longer your concern."

"But I heard you order them not to set foot on the rock. If you won't even allow them to examine the place where—"

"No one may set foot on the Sacrifice Rock! That includes you, Finder." He gave me a penetrating look. "The priests of Artemis sanctified it during the same ritual that invested the scapegoat. From the time that a scapegoat is invested until the day he fulfills his destiny, the Sacrifice Rock is sacred ground, forbidden to all. The next person to set foot on it, and not until the priests of Artemis say so, will be your friend Hieronymus here. That will also be the *last* time he sets foot on it." He shot a sardonic glance at our host, then turned, quickly descended the steps, and disappeared, his soldiers following.

"Not a bad fellow, for a Greek," said Domitius under his breath.

"Where are *your* soldiers, Proconsul?" asked Hieronymus suspiciously.

"My bodyguards are outside the house," said Domitius. "Apollonides wouldn't let me bring them in. He's that pious, at least—no foreigners bearing arms in the scapegoat's house. Don't worry. They'll stay where they are until I tell them otherwise. By Hercules, I'm hungry! I don't suppose, to show a bit of hospitality. . . ."

Hieronymus stared back at him glumly for a long moment, then clapped his hands and instructed a slave to bring food. Hieronymus then withdrew, sulking, into the house.

"I'll eat far better here than I would at Apollonides's house," Domitius confided. "This fellow gets all the best cuts. There's a priest of Artemis who sees to it. The city's facing serious shortages, but you'd never know it from the way they stuff this goose."

Lamps were brought onto the terrace, then trays of food, along with little tripod tables. Seeing the feast made me dizzy from hunger. There were steaming slices of pork glazed with honey and aniseed, a pâté of sweetbreads and soft cheese, a gingery fava bean puree, a barley soup flavored with dill and whole onions, and little must cakes speckled with raisins.

Domitius ate like a starving man, popping fingers into his mouth and sucking them clean. Davus, seeing such manners, made no pretense to refinement and did likewise. I was tormented by hunger but hardly able to eat, my stomach seized by sudden anxiety about Meto. What did Domitius know? I tried a few times to raise the subject, but Domitius refused to respond until he had eaten his fill. What was he playing at?

At last he sat back, took a long swallow of wine, and let out a burp. "The best meal I've had in months!" he declared. "Almost worth the trip to this godforsaken city, don't you think?"

"I came here—"

"Yes, I know. Not for the food! You came to look for your son."

"Do you know Meto?" I asked quietly.

"Oh, yes." Domitius stroked his red beard and was silent for a long time, content to observe my discomfort. Why did he look so smug? "Why have you come here looking for him, Gordianus?"

"I received a message in Rome, sent anonymously, claiming to come from Massilia." I touched the pouch that hung from my belt, felt the small wooden cylinder inside, and wondered if the parchment it contained had survived the flood. "The message said that Meto . . . was dead. That he'd died in Massilia."

"An anonymous message? Curious."

"Please, Proconsul. What do you know about my son?"

He sipped his wine. "Meto arrived here several days before Caesar's army did. He said he'd had enough of Caesar; said he wanted to join our side. I was skeptical, of course, but I took him in. I confined him to quarters and gave him light duties— nothing sensitive or secretive, mind you. I kept an eye on him. Then a ship from Pompey arrived, the very last ship in before Caesar launched his little navy to blockade the harbor. Pompey sent word on various subjects—his hairbreadth escape from Caesar at Brundisium, his position in Dyrrhachium, the morale of the senators in exile from Rome. And he specifically mentioned your son. Pompey said that 'incontrovertible evidence'—his phrase—had come into his hands that Meto was indeed a traitor to Caesar and should be trusted.* That seemed to settle the matter; the last time I ignored Pompey's advice I had cause to regret it—though there was plenty of blame to go around." He referred to his humiliation by Caesar in Italy when Pompey had urged Domitius to withdraw before Caesar's advance and join forces, but Domitius had insisted instead on making a stand at Corfinium; Domitius had been captured, attempted suicide (and failed), then was pardoned by Caesar and released, whereupon he fled to Massilia with a ragtag band of gladiators and a fortune of six million sesterces.

"But despite Pompey's message," he went on, "I still had my

---

* See *Rubicon* (St. Martin's Press, 1999).

suspicions about your oh-so-clever son. Milo warned me. You must remember Titus Annius Milo, exiled a few years back for murdering Clodius on the Appian Way?"

"Of course. I investigated the matter for Pompey."

"So you did! I'd forgotten that. Did you somehow . . . offend . . . Milo?"

"Not to my knowledge."

"No? Well, for whatever reason, I'm afraid Milo wasn't fond of your son. Suspected him right off. 'The boy's no good,' he told me. I might have paid Milo no mind—when was Milo ever known for sound judgment?—but he echoed my own instincts. I continued to watch your son very closely. Even so, I could never quite catch him at anything. Until. . . ."

Domitius turned his head and gazed at the view, sipping his wine in silence for so long that he seemed to have forgotten his thought.

"Until what?" I finally said, trying to keep my voice steady.

"Do you know—I think Milo himself should tell you. Yes, I believe that would be best. We'll go and see him right now. We can gloat about what a fine meal we've just had, while Milo dines on stale bread and the last of the fish-pickle sauce he brought from Rome."

When I first met him at Cicero's house months ago, I had decided that Domitius was a pompous, vain creature. Now I saw that he was also petty and spiteful. He seemed to relish my distress.

We bade the scapegoat farewell. Hieronymus invited Davus and *I* to return later to sleep under his roof that night. Even as I promised that we would, I wondered if I lied. Just because I had escaped death twice already that day, there was no reason to think it might not come for me yet.

Had death come already for Meto? Domitius had so far refused to tell me, but I kept thinking of his words: *Milo wasn't fond of your son.* Why he had spoken in the past tense?

IX

The way to Milo's house took us through a district of large, fine houses. More than a few, I was surprised to see, had thatched roofs—a reminder that we were not in Rome, where even the poor sleep with clay tiles over their heads.

The moon was so bright that we made our way without torches. The only sound was the tramping of Domitius's body-guards on the paving stones. The narrow streets of Massilia, almost empty by daylight, were even more deserted after dark. "Martial law," Domitius explained. "A strict curfew. Only those on state business can be abroad after nightfall. Anyone else is presumed to be up to no good."

"Spies?" I said.

He snorted. "Thieves and black marketeers, more likely. Apollonides's greatest fear now isn't Trebonius with his tunnels and battering-rams; it's famine and disease. We're already feeling the shortages. As long as the blockade holds, the situation can only get worse. If the people become hungry enough, they're likely to break into the public granaries. Then they'll discover just how bad the situation really is. The Timouchoi fear an uprising."

"The authorities didn't stockpile enough grain for a siege?"

"Oh, quantity isn't the problem. There's a full store of grain—but half of it is ruined with mold. Emergency stores have to be replaced every so often; once every three years is the rule in most cities. Apollonides can't even tell me when the stores were last replenished. The Council of Fifteen thought it was a wasteful expense. Now their niggardliness has gotten the better of them, and my men are reduced to half rations."

Domitius had left Italy with six million sesterces, I recalled; money enough to sail to Massilia and hire an army of Gaulish mercenaries once he arrived, with plenty left over. But no amount of riches could feed an army if there was no food to be purchased.

"Don't misunderstand me," he continued. "Apollonides is a good man, and he's not a bad general. He knows everything there is to know about ships and war machines. But like all Massilians, he's a merchant at heart, forever calculating and looking for a profit. These Greeks are clever, but they have a narrow view of things. They're not like us Romans. There's a fire they lack, a bigger way of looking at the world. They'll never be more than minor players in the great game."

"Does Apollonides have children?" I asked. I was remembering the way he had abruptly softened when I explained that I had come to Massilia seeking my son.

"Of course. No man can join the Timouchoi unless he has offspring."

"Ah, yes. The scapegoat explained that to me."

"But in Apollonides's case, it's a bit of a delicate subject. You'll see. Or *not* see, rather." He smiled at a secret joke.

"I don't understand."

"Apollonides has only one child, a daughter named Cydimache. Her ugliness is legendary. Well, she's more than ugly; a monster, really. Hideous. Born with a harelip and her face all misshapen, like a lump of melted wax. Blind in one eye and has a hump on her back."

"Babies like that are usually exposed at birth," I said. "Discreetly gotten rid of."

"Indeed. But Apollonides's wife had already miscarried twice, and he was desperate to become a Timouchos, and for that he needed offspring. So he kept Cydimache and got himself elected to the next opening among the Timouchoi."

"He had no more children?"

"No. Some say his wife's labor with Cydimache left her barren. Others say that Apollonides himself was too afraid of fathering another monster. At any rate, his wife died a few years ago, and Apollonides never remarried. Despite her deformities, they say that Apollonides genuinely loves his daughter, as much as any father could."

"You've seen her?"

"Apollonides doesn't hide her away. She rarely goes out, but she dines with his guests. She hides her face with veils and rarely speaks. When she does, her voice is slurred, on account of her harelip I suppose. I did get a glimpse of her face once. I was crossing the garden of Apollonides's house. Cydimache had paused at a rose bush. She'd pulled aside her veils to smell a bloom, and I surprised her. Her face was a sight to stop a man's heart."

"Or break it, I should think."

"No, Finder. Beauty breaks a man's heart, not ugliness!" Domitius laughed. "I'll tell you this: The face of Cydimache is not a sight I ever care to see again. I don't know which of us was more unnerved. The girl fled, and so did I." He shook his head. "Who'd have thought such a creature would ever find a husband?"

"She's married?"

"The wedding took place just before I arrived in Massilia. The young man's name is Zeno. Quite a contrast to his wife; damned good-looking, in fact. Not that my taste runs to boys—although faced with a choice of Zeno or Cydimache . . . !" He laughed. "Some people claim it was a love match, but I think that's just these Massilians' sense of humor. Zeno comes from a modest but respectable family; he married her for money and position, of course. This is his means to become a Timouchos—if he can manage to get Cydimache with child."

"Apollonides was satisfied with the match?"

"I don't suppose many young men with prospects were lining up to woo the monster, not even to become the son-in-law of the First Timouchos." Domitius shrugged. "The match seems to have worked. Zeno and Cydimache sit at Apollonides's right hand every night at dinner. The young man treats her with great deference. Sometimes they talk in low voices and laugh quietly among themselves. If you didn't know what was under the veils"—he made a face and shuddered—"you might think they were as lovestruck as any other pair of newlyweds."

A Gaulish slave girl with braided blond hair answered the door at Milo's house. She was scantily clad even for such a warm night. Her Greek was poor and atrociously accented, but it was obvious she had not been purchased for her language skills. She giggled incessantly as she invited Domitius, Davus, and myself into the foyer. The only light was the lamp she held in her hand; outside the scapegoat's house, fuel, like food, was severely rationed in Massilia. The oil was of low quality. The rancid-smelling smoke at least helped to cover the odor of unwashed humanity that permeated the house. Instead of running to fetch her master, the girl simply turned and yelled for him.

"I'd have expected a bodyguard to answer the door," I muttered to Domitius under my breath. "I seem to recall that Milo took a large party of gladiators with him when he went into exile."

Domitius nodded. "He's hired his gladiators out to the Massilians as mercenaries. Most of them, anyway; I suppose he kept one or two for bodyguards. They must be somewhere about, probably as drunk as their master. I'm afraid dear Milo has rather let himself go. It might have been different if Fausta had accompanied him into exile." He referred to Milo's wife, the daughter of the long-deceased dictator Sulla. "She would have insisted on keeping up social appearances at least. But Milo, on his own—"

Domitius was interrupted by the appearance of the man himself, who shuffled into the foyer carrying a lamp in one hand and clutching a silver wine cup in the other, barefoot and wearing nothing but a loincloth.

It had been three years since I had last seen Titus Annius Milo, during his trial in Rome for the murder of the rival gang-leader Clodius. Against Cicero's advice, Milo had refused to observe the time-honored tradition that an accused man should appear unkempt and in rags before the court. His pride mattered more to Milo than pandering for sympathy. Defiant to the end, infuriating his enemies, he had appeared at his own trial meticulously groomed.

His appearance had changed considerably since then. His hair and beard were grayer than I remembered and badly needed trimming. His eyes were bloodshot and his face bloated. He was even more scantily clad than the slave girl—his haphazardly arranged loincloth looked as if it might come undone at any moment—but not nearly as pretty to look at. His burly wrestler's physique had lost its shape, like a clay sculpture gone soft from the heat. He needed a bath.

"Lucius Domitius—dear old Redbeard himself! What an honor." The wine on Milo's breath overpowered even the rank smell of his body. He handed his lamp to the slave girl and slapped her on the rump. She giggled. "Hope you haven't come around sniffing for supper. We finished our day's rations before noon. We're having to drink our supper, aren't we, my dove?"

The girl giggled madly. "But who are these fellows you've brought with you, Redbeard? I'm sure I don't know the big one; handsome brute. But this graybeard—great Jupiter!" His eyes sparkled, and I saw a hint of the old, wily Milo. "It's that hound who used to hunt for Cicero—when he wasn't snapping at Cicero's fingers. Gordianus the Finder! What in Hades are you doing in this godforsaken place?"

"Gordianus has come in search of his son," Domitius explained, his voice flat. "I told him that you were the man to talk to."

"His son? Oh, yes, you mean"—Milo hiccupped violently—"Meto."

"Yes. It appears that Gordianus received an anonymous communication, claiming to come from Massilia, informing him of Meto's demise. He's come all this way, even managed to get inside the city walls at great peril, because he wants to know the truth of the matter."

"The truth," Milo said blearily. "The truth never did me a bit of good."

"About my son," I asked impatiently, "what can you tell me?"

"Meto. Yes, well . . ." Milo refused to meet my gaze. "A sad story. Very sad."

I was utterly exhausted, confused and disoriented, far from home. I had come to Massilia for one reason only, to discover Meto's fate. Domitius had teased me, coyly indicating that Milo knew the answer; now Milo seemed unable to complete a sentence. "Proconsul," I said to Domitius through gritted teeth, "why can't you tell me yourself what's become of Meto?"

Domitius shrugged. "I thought Milo would want the privilege of telling you himself. He's usually such a braggart—"

"Damn you!" Milo threw his cup against the wall. Davus dodged the splashes. The slave girl emitted a noise between a shriek and a giggle. "This is indecent, Redbeard. Indecent! To bring the man's father into my house, to taunt us both like this!"

Domitius was unperturbed. "Tell him, Milo. Or else I will."

Milo blanched. His face turned pale. A sheen of sweat covered his naked flesh. His shoulders heaved. He clutched his throat. "Little dove! Bring me my ewer. Quickly!"

Maniacally giggling, the blond slave girl put down the lamps, skittered across the room, disappeared for a moment, and then hurried back bearing a tall clay vessel with a wide mouth. Milo dropped to his knees, seized the arms of the ewer, and loudly vomited into it.

"For pity's sake, Milo!" Domitius wrinkled his nose in disgust. Davus seemed hardly to notice; his attention was riveted instead on the slave girl, who, leaning over to assist her master, was inadvertently revealing heretofore unseen portions of her lower anatomy. Plautus himself never staged a more absurd tableau, I thought. I wanted to scream from frustration.

Gradually, with the slave girl wiping his chin, Milo staggered back to his feet. He seemed considerably less drunk, if not exactly sober. He looked utterly wretched.

I couldn't resist. "A pity the judges at your trial never saw you in such a state. You might never have had to leave Rome."

"What?" Milo blinked and looked about, dazed.

"Meto," I said wearily. "Tell me about Meto."

His shoulders slumped. "Very well. Come, we'll sit in the study. Little dove, hand me one of those lamps."

The house was a cluttered mess. Clothes were strewn about the floor and festooned over statues, dirty bowls and cups and platters were stacked everywhere, unfurled scrolls overflowed from tables onto the floor. In the corner of one room a recumbent figure, presumably a bodyguard, lay noisily snoring.

Milo's study was the most cluttered room of all. There were chairs for all four of us, but first Milo had to clear away scraps of parchment, piles of clothing (including an expensive-looking but badly wine-stained toga), and a yowling cat. He dumped them all on the floor. Hissing, the cat fled the room.

"Sit," Milo offered. He pulled a wrinkled tunic over his head, sparing us the sight of his sweaty, corpulent chest. "So you want to know what's become of your son." Milo sighed and averted his eyes. "I suppose there's no reason why I shouldn't tell you the whole wretched story. . . ."

X

"Tell me, Gordianus, do you have any idea what your son was *really* up to these past few months?" Milo used his tunic to wipe a speck of vomit from his chin.

"I'm not sure what you mean."

"Were you in on his little game or not? This mime show he attempted, passing himself off as a traitor to Caesar."

I looked him squarely in the eye. Outright lying has never come easily to me, but there are subtler ways of skirting the truth. "I know that Meto and Caesar parted ways when both of them were last in Rome. That was in the month of Aprilis, after Caesar ran Pompey out of Italy and Domitius was on his way here to Massilia. There was talk of a plot against Caesar, devised by some of his closest officers. Meto was said to be part of that plot. Supposedly the scheme was discovered and Meto had no choice but to flee."

Milo nodded. "That's what your son wanted us all to believe. Perhaps he even made *you* believe it." He raised a shrewd eyebrow. As his intoxication receded, a more familiar Milo came to the fore—the rabble-rousing gang-leader, the politician unafraid of violence, the blustering, unapologetic victim of a legal system as ruthless as himself. Despite his squalid circumstances and his physical decline, Milo was still a very dangerous man. He no longer averted his eyes. "Did *you* believe your son was a traitor, Gordianus?"

I spoke carefully, feeling Domitius's gaze on me. "At first it seemed impossible that Meto could turn against Caesar. There had always been a bond between them, a closeness—"

"We've all heard *those* rumors, as well!" Milo interjected. A barely stifled belch reminded me that he was still more drunk than sober.

I ignored his insinuation and pressed on. "But don't you see, that very closeness was what swayed me to accept that Meto had betrayed Caesar. Closeness can breed contempt. Familiarity can turn love to hate. Who might be more likely to be repelled by Caesar's ruthless ambition, his carelessness in destroying the Republic, than a man who shared the same tent with Caesar day after day, who helped him write his memoirs, who came to see exactly how his mind worked?" Indeed, such had been my reasoning when, for a while, I myself believed that Meto had turned traitor.

Milo shook his head. "If you don't know the truth, then truly I feel sorry for you. Redbeard here was taken in as well," he said, shrugging at Domitius. "So was Pompey, apparently. But not me. Not for a moment!"

"At last the braggart overtakes the drunkard," said Domitius dryly. They exchanged a chilly glance.

Milo went on. "All that talk of Meto changing sides was nonsense. I'm a shrewd judge of character. Don't forget, for years I ran the streets in Rome. It was my gang that did Pompey's dirty work so that he could keep his own hands clean. A friendly candidate needed a good turnout for a speech? My gang was there in full force. Clodius's rabble was hectoring a senator in the Forum? My gang could be there in minutes to clear the place out. An election needed to be postponed? My gang was ready to crack a few heads down at the voting stalls. All at the snap of my fingers." He tried to demonstrate, but his fingers fumbled and made no noise.

"The coins from your purse spoke louder," quipped Domitius.

Milo frowned. "The point is, you don't become a leader of men without learning to judge a man's character, figuring out how best to persuade him, knowing his limits, what he will or won't do—getting under his skin. And I knew from the moment I laid eyes on him here in Massilia that Meto was no traitor. He wasn't dodgy enough. Didn't have the smell of a man who's out just for himself. And what reason did he have to turn on Caesar? All your high-flown talk about love turning to hate is just so much cow dung, Gordianus."

"Some men love the Republic more than they love their imperator," I said quietly.

"Show me one! Show me just one!" he barked, then fell to coughing. His forehead erupted in sweat. "I need a drink," he muttered.

So did I. My throat was so dry I could hardly swallow. "Go on," I said hoarsely.

Milo leaned back in his chair, lost his balance, and came close to falling. Domitius sniggered. Davus rolled his eyes.

Milo recovered himself and went on, unflustered. "Consider my position. Everything went wrong for me in Rome. My trial was a farce. Clodius's mob burned down the Senate House! They didn't even let Cicero finish his speech for me. They drowned him out, screaming for my head. The verdict was a foregone conclusion. Only one man could have saved me—but my dear friend, Gnaeus Pompey, the Great One himself, *turned his back on me!* After all I'd done for him. . . ."

He picked up a discarded loincloth from the floor and mopped his forehead. "Even Fausta refused to come with me into exile. The bitch! Married me because she thought I was a rising star, then jumped off quicker than a flea from a drowning dog when things went sour. So here I landed in Massilia, a man without a country, without a family, without friends. Abandoned. Forgotten. 'Don't fret, Titus,' Cicero told me. 'Massilia is a civilized place full of culture and learning . . . admirable government . . . delightful climate . . . delicious food.' Easy for Cicero to say; he's never even set foot in this Hades-on-earth! He can admire Massilia from a distance, relaxing in his house on the Palatine or at one of his summer places in the countryside. I used to have summer houses. . . ."

He shut his eyes for a moment and sighed, then went on. "Now the whole world's been turned upside-down. Caesar and his outlaw armies are in control of Rome. Pompey and the Senate have fled across the water. Even Rome's oldest allies, these wretched Massilians, aren't safe. And where does that leave me? Milo, who was always loyal, even when it harmed his own prospects. Milo, who was abandoned by his friends, even the Great One, just because of a stupid, stupid, stupid incident on the Appian Way.

"With everything in such a muddle, you might think that Pompey would be ready to take me back, eager to make amends. But, no! A message comes from Pompey." He launched into an uncanny impersonation of the Great One at his most pompous: " 'Stay in Massilia, good Milo. Stay right where you are! The verdict against you stands, and the law must be respected. Your choice remains the same: exile or death. It's Caesar and his ilk who advocate allowing political exiles to return to Rome; I cannot possibly do the same, even for a friend such as you—*especially* for a friend such as you. In spite of the current crisis—indeed, *because* of the crisis—there can be absolutely no exceptions to the severe majesty of Roman law.' In other words: 'Stay put in Massilia, Milo, and rot!' "

By the dim lamplight, I saw the sparkle of tears in his eyes. Please, gods, I prayed, spare me the spectacle of Milo weeping.

He drew a deep breath and went on. "What I needed, you see, was some way to get back into Pompey's good graces, to impress him—to put him in my debt if I could. But how, stuck here in Massilia with only a handful of gladiators, and those already hired to the Massilians as mercenaries? Then it occurred to me: What if I were to expose a dangerous spy? And not just any spy, but a spy planted in our ranks by Caesar's own hand, a spy Pompey himself had instructed us to trust? That would be no small thing. Step one in the rehabilitation of Milo!

"First, I had to get Meto to trust me. That was the easy part. Look at me! I'm not blind to my own condition. I know how far I've fallen. I go naked all day. I live in a house that stinks of urine. I'm a Roman exiled from Rome, a man without prospects, without even dignity—bitter, desperate, the ideal candidate for recruitment in a dangerous game. Oh, yes, Meto came to me; he searched me out at once. He thought he was being subtle, I'm sure, but I could read his thoughts as if he spoke them aloud. Poor old Milo, abandoned by all; he should be easy to lure over to Caesar's cause, ripe and ready to stab his old friend Pompey in the back. I simply went along; I let Meto seduce me. Slowly, surely, he wormed his way into my confidence. I made a great deal of it, the day I was finally ready to show him that message from Pompey telling me to stay put. I wept real tears when I read it to him; that wasn't acting.

"After that it was only a matter of time. I could sense the day approaching. Even before it happened, I knew the very hour Meto would make his move, the way a farmer can smell rain on the wind. It happened in this room. I was ready for him. The trap was laid. Do you see that wooden screen in the corner? Redbeard here was concealed behind that screen. Come on, Redbeard, why don't you show our visitors how you hid and listened? We can reenact the moment."

"Get on with it!" snapped Domitius.

"It's a beautiful screen, isn't it? Carved from terebinth in Libya, I think. That's gold leaf along the border. Fausta's father owned it; imagine the uses wily old Sulla must have found for such a screen to hide behind! I brought it with me when I left

Rome. Fausta wanted to keep it, but I smuggled it out from under her nose. I wonder if she ever missed it?"

"Tell the story, Milo!" I whispered hoarsely.

He lowered his eyes. "You won't like the ending."

"Tell me!"

"Very well. You have to realize, Redbeard here thought I was deluded. Said my mind was addled from too much bad Massilian wine. 'You're wrong about Meto,' he told me. 'The man can be trusted; Pompey himself says so. What Meto knows about Caesar and the way his mind works could fill a book. His value to us is immeasurable.' Ha! Don't glare at me like that, Redbeard. You're the one who insisted on bringing Gordianus into my house. If I needle you a bit, you'll just have to bear it.

"So there was Redbeard listening behind the screen, and in that storage room beyond he managed to stuff ten or so hand-picked soldiers—probably the same bodyguards escorting him tonight. Meto didn't suspect a thing. At some point Redbeard made a shuffling noise. Meto glanced at the screen. I told him it was a rat. And so it was!" Milo laughed. Domitius stared at him coldly.

"Meto and I talked around and around each other. The little dove fetched wine, and I pretended to be drunk—well, perhaps I wasn't entirely pretending. Drunk or not, I turned in a performance worthy of Roscius the actor. My part was the diver who's stepped to the precipice and needs just a puff of air at his back to take the plunge; the coward who's mustered his last scrap of courage and needs only one more turn of the screw to reach the sticking point; the lover bursting with emotion who can't quite bring himself to be the first to say, 'I love you.' Around and around we talked, your son and I, with Redbeard fidgeting behind that screen, about to sneeze at any moment, for all I knew. The suspense was terrible. I imagine it made my performance all the more convincing.

"Finally, Meto made his play. 'Milo,' he said, 'you're trapped in Massilia. Domitius treats you like a slave. You have no hope of reconciliation with Pompey. Desperate times demand desperate actions. Perhaps you should consider a radical move.'

" 'But where else is there for me to go?' I asked. 'After Massilia, the next port of call is Hades.'

"Meto shook his head. 'There's another choice.'

" 'Caesar, you mean? But Caesar would never have me. He relies too much on the good will of the Clodians. That rabble would turn on him in an instant if he took me in.'

" 'Caesar is beyond needing the Clodians,' said Meto. 'He's bigger than the Clodians now. Bigger than Rome. He can ally himself with whomever he chooses.'

" 'But you've turned your back on Caesar,' I said.

"Meto looked at me squarely. 'Perhaps not,' he said.

"I told him, 'I can't deny that I've thought about it. It seems to me that it's the only choice I have left. But I'd need a go-between, someone to help me cross to the other side. Tell me, Meto, are you that man?'

"Meto nodded. Why, at that precise moment, Redbeard felt it was necessary to make such a show of knocking the screen down, I don't know. My heart almost flew out of my mouth. Meto was on his feet with his dagger drawn in an instant. He saw Redbeard, saw the look on my face, saw the first of the soldiers burst out of the storage room. It should have all been over in an instant. Instead. . . ." Milo stopped and took another drink.

"Tell me!"

"No need to shout, Gordianus. Let Redbeard tell you. It's his story from here on."

Domitius looked at me coldly. "I'd given my men instructions to capture Meto, not to kill him if they could help it. They were too cautious."

"Too clumsy!" interjected Milo.

"It happened very quickly," Domitius went on. "Meto was out of the room before my men could catch him. I had more men posted at the front door, but Meto surprised us by running into the garden and climbing onto the roof. He jumped down into a side alley and ran to the back of the house. I had more men posted there, but he got past them. They chased after him. He was a fast runner. He might have eluded them entirely, but one of my men threw a spear and managed to graze his hip. That slowed him down. Still, he managed to reach the city wall, down where it runs along the sea. He climbed the stairs up to the battlements, not far from the Sacrifice Rock—"

"The Sacrifice Rock!" I whispered, remembering vividly what I had seen there at twilight.

"He wasn't mad enough to leap from the rock," said Domitius. "The surf and the rocks below would kill any man. Instead, he ran farther on, to a bend where the sheer wall drops to deep water. Perhaps that was his goal all along; he may have scouted out the place in advance, planning for just such an emergency. I suppose it's barely possible that a man could dive from the wall and swim all the way out to the islands where Caesar's ships are moored. Meto might have made a clean escape. . . ."

My heart pounded in my chest. "But?"

"But that's not what happened. My men stayed close on his heels. They were almost on him when he jumped. One of them swears he pierced Meto with an arrow on his way down, but that may be idle boasting. The fall alone might have killed him. He disappeared beneath the water. When my men saw his body break the surface, they showered him with arrows. The sun was in their eyes, casting a glaring light on the waves, which made it hard to see, but some of the men swear they saw blood on the water. They all saw his body being swept out to sea by the current. They say he didn't kick or flail his arms, as any conscious man would; he simply floated like a cork for a while, then disappeared below the surface."

Domitius sat back and crossed his arms, looking pleased with himself. "Well, then, Gordianus, is that what you wanted to know? Is that what you came all this way to find out? Your son died an outlaw, pursued by soldiers of the legal proconsul of Gaul. I suppose you can take some comfort in the fact that he died loyal to his imperator, if not to Rome."

The whole world seemed to have contracted to that squalid, dimly lit room. Milo's face was in shadow, impossible to read. Domitius wore an expression of smug satisfaction. I had never shared my son's love for Caesar, but how small these men seemed in comparison!

I felt a gentle hand on my shoulder. "Father-in-law, you're exhausted. The scapegoat promised us a bed for the night. We should go now."

I rose without a word and left Milo's study. Milo, almost tripping, hurried after us. "The little dove will show you out," he said. "And I'll send one of my gladiators along to show you the way. There's a curfew, but no one's likely to question you in this neighborhood. If they do, just mention Redbeard." He lowered his voice and laid a hand on my arm. "Gordianus, it gave me no pleasure, exposing your son for what he truly was. Meto was no more honest with me than I was with him. Caesar would never have taken me in. Never! Meto tried to deceive me, just as I deceived him." I tried to draw my arm away, but Milo clutched it and lowered his voice to a whisper. "I'm not proud of myself, Gordianus. What I've done, I had to do!"

My eyes were hot with tears. I pulled my arm free. As I hurried on, behind me I heard Domitius address the empty room: "But who sent the anonymous message that brought Gordianus to Massilia? *That's* what *I'd* like to know. . . ."

XI

I scarcely remember our moonlit journey through the streets of Massilia and our return to the scapegoat's house. Hieronymus took one look at my face and nodded gravely. "Ah, bad news," he said quietly. Without another word he showed Davus and me to a room with two beds. My mind was in such turmoil that I couldn't imagine sleeping. Sleep came nonetheless, as quickly and deeply as if I had been drugged.

I dreamed. Missiles flew from catapults. Flaming bodies plummeted from siege towers. At my side the engineer, Vitruvius, blithely chattered on about machines of death. He was interrupted by a hooded soothsayer who tugged at his elbow and loudly whispered in his ear, "Tell the Roman he has no business here." A soldier in a fluttering blue cape hurried past, limping slightly, and disappeared in a hole in the ground. I took Davus's hand and told him we had to follow. The hole led straight to Hades. I saw a disembodied head levitating amid vents of steam and jets of flames, ringed by blood at the severed neck. "Catilina!" I cried. The head flashed a sardonic grin and vanished. A cloaked figure stepped out of the mist. She pulled away her veils and I confronted the grossly misshapen *xoanon* Artemis come to life. "Marry me," the thing said, and I started back in horror. Suddenly all Hades was flooded. Bodies floated past. Flames hissed and died out. All was darkness. The water kept rising. I sucked in a breath and felt the burn of saltwater in my throat and nostrils. I felt a strange mixture of relief and dread, and a sadness that crushed me like a stone. Was it my own watery death I dreamed of, or Meto's?

I woke, thinking: Even in my dreams, my son refuses to appear. Then I realized that Davus was standing over me, his hand on my shoulder, his face drawn with concern.

"Where are we?" I asked. The words came out in a gasp. I had been sobbing in my sleep.

"The scapegoat's house. In Massilia."

I blinked and nodded. "What time is it?"

"After dark."

"But it was after dark when we went to bed. Surely. . . ."

"It's nighttime again. You slept all day. You needed it."

I sat up and groaned. My joints were stiff. Every muscle ached. The journey, the ordeal in the flooded tunnel, the revelations of the previous night had drained all my resources. I felt as hollow as a reed.

"You must be hungry," said Davus.

"No."

"Then sleep some more." He gently pushed me back.

"Impossible," I said, remembering my nightmares with a shudder. And that was all I remembered until I woke again the next morning.

Had I not known for a fact that we were in the middle of a city under siege, blockaded by land and sea, threatened by famine and disease, I would never have guessed it from our breakfast at the scapegoat's house. We were given farina sweetened with pomegranates and honey, dates stuffed with almond paste, and all the fresh figs we could eat.

Rested and fed, I sat alone on the scapegoat's rooftop terrace and began to realize the predicament into which I had put Davus and myself. From the moment I had received the message about Meto, I had thought only of coming to Massilia to discover the truth, and had never thought beyond that. I had always assumed that I would find Meto alive, or at worst discover that he had vanished. Instead, the anonymous message had been borne out. My son was dead and his body lost. There was nothing more for me to do in Massilia, but thanks to my own perseverance and ingenuity, I was trapped there.

Was it for this that the gods had saved me when the tunnel was flooded? I had thanked them at the time, forgetting that they always have the last laugh.

At least in Rome I could have shared my grief with Bethesda and Diana and my other son, Eco, and the daily rhythms of the city would have afforded some distraction. In Massilia, there would be nothing for me to do but brood.

I had no friends in Massilia. Milo had as good as murdered my son. Domitius despised me, and I despised him. Apollonides had dismissed me as beneath his interest. Hieronymus alone had been hospitable to me, but over his head hung a cloud of ruin and death that only depressed me further. I felt what many a Roman exile must have felt in Massilia: helpless and hopeless, cut off from all that makes life worth living. Even if Hieronymus continued to grant me food and shelter, how could I continue to exist in such a state, hour after hour, day after day?

My emotions ran through a gamut of recriminations. I

blamed myself for coming to Massilia. I blamed Milo for having laid the bait that ruined Meto. I blamed Meto for having accepted such a dangerous mission. I blamed Caesar for a multitude of sins—for having seduced my son (in every sense, if the rumors that reached my ears were true), for having sent him on a fool's errand to certain death, for having crossed the Rubicon in the first place. The vanity of the man, to believe that his destiny should eclipse all else, that the whole world was made to quiver in his shadow! How much suffering had he caused already? How many more sons would die before he was done? Meto had loved the man, had given his life for him. For that, I hated Caesar.

If I closed my eyes, I could see Meto clearly. Not one Meto, but many: as a small boy in the house of Crassus at Baiae, where he had been born a slave and where I first met him; walking proudly if a little uncertainly through the Forum at the age of sixteen on the day he first put on his manly toga; dressed as a soldier—the first time, with a shock, I ever saw him in armor—in Catilina's tent just before the battle of Pistoria. He had been a bright, beautiful child, full of laughter. He had grown into a sturdy, handsome young man, proud of his battle scars. Each time he came home after campaigning in Gaul with Caesar, I greeted him with a mixture of elation and dread, happy that he was alive, fearful that I would find him maimed or disfigured or crippled. But the gods had seen fit to keep him alive and whole through all his battles. Until now.

A small voice in my head whispered: *But Meto's body was never found. He might still be alive . . . somehow . . . somewhere.* I refused to listen. Such delusions were merely weakness. They could lead only to disappointment and even greater misery.

And so I went round and round, from grief to anger, from bittersweet memories to doubt, from delusions of hope to hard, cold reason, and back to grief, resolving nothing. I sat on the terrace of the scapegoat's rooftop, staring for hours at the Sacrifice Rock in the distance and the uncaring sea beyond.

So a day or two passed, or perhaps three or four, perhaps more. My memory of that time is unclear. Both Davus and Hieronymus left me mostly to myself. Food was served to me occasionally, and I suppose I ate it. My bed was made for me each night, and I suppose I slept. I felt dull and remote, as disembodied as the levitating head of Catilina in my nightmares.

Then, one morning, Hieronymus announced that a visitor had come to see me and was waiting in the atrium.

"A visitor?" I asked.

"A Gaulish merchant. Says his name is Arausio."

"A Gaul?"

"There are a lot of them in Massilia."

"What does he want?"

"He wouldn't say."

"Are you sure it's me he wants?"

"He asked for you by name. Surely there can't be more than one Gordianus the Finder in Massilia."

"But what can he possibly want?"

"There's only one way to find out." The scapegoat raised an eyebrow and gave me a hopeful look, such as a careworn mother might give to a child recuperating from a fever.

"I suppose I should see him, then," I said dully.

"That's the spirit!" Hieronymus clapped his hands and sent a slave to fetch the visitor.

Arausio was a man of middle age with thinning brown hair, a ruddy complexion, and a drooping mustache. He wore a plain white tunic; but to judge by the well-made shoes on his feet, he was a man of means; and to judge by his gold necklace and gold bracelets, not averse to advertising it. His manner was skittish and he kept his distance from Hieronymus, who remained nearby on the terrace. He had a superstitious fear of the scapegoat, I realized, a dread of contagion. What, then, had induced him to enter the scapegoat's house?

He took stock of his surroundings. Did I imagine that he gave a start when he saw the view of the Sacrifice Rock in the distance? "My name is Arausio," he said. "Are you Gordianus, the one they call 'the Finder'? "

"I am. I didn't realize that anyone in Massilia had heard of me."

He flashed an unpleasant smile. "Oh, we're not all quite as ignorant in this backwater town as you might think. Massilia may not be Athens or Alexandria, but we do try to keep abreast of what's happening in the great world beyond."

"I'm sorry. I never meant to suggest—"

"Oh, that's quite all right. We're used to Romans turning up their noses when they come here. What are we, after all, but an outpost of second-rate Greeks and barely civilized Gauls just off the road to nowhere?"

"But I never said—"

"Then say no more." The man held up his hand. "I'll state my business, which you may or may not deign to find of interest. My name, as I said, is Arausio, and I'm a merchant."

"In slaves or wine?" I asked. Arausio raised an eyebrow. "I'm told it's one or the other here in Massilia."

Arausio shrugged. "I handle a little traffic in both directions. My grandfather used to say, 'Romans get lazy; Gauls get thirsty. Send slaves in one direction and wine in the other.' We've done well enough. Not quite as well as *this.*" He gestured to the house around us. His eyes swept the view. Again I saw him focus sharply on the Sacrifice Rock, then tear his eyes away.

He suddenly dropped his abrasive manner like a shield he no longer had strength to carry. "They say . . . you saw it happen," he whispered. "Both of you." He ventured a glance at Hieronymus.

"Saw what?" I asked. But of course he could mean only one thing.

"The girl . . . who fell from the rock." His voice was strained.

Hieronymus crossed his arms. "She didn't fall. She jumped."

"She was pushed!" Davus, who had been standing discreetly out of sight inside the doorway, felt obliged to step forward.

I gazed at the Sacrifice Rock. "Girl, you say. But why 'girl,' and not 'woman'? The three of us saw a figure in a woman's gown and a hooded cloak. We couldn't see her face or even the color of her hair. She was fit enough to climb the rock, but she did so haltingly. Perhaps she was young, or perhaps not." I looked at Arausio. "Unless you know more than we do."

He thrust out his jaw to stop it from quivering. "I think . . . I may know who she was."

Hieronymus and Davus both stepped closer.

"I think . . . the girl who fell . . . was my daughter."

I raised an eyebrow.

Arausio's voice was suddenly choked and bitter. "He led her on, you see. Right up until the moment he married that monster, he led Rindel to think he might choose her instead."

"Rindel?" I said.

"My daughter. That's her name. *Was* her name."

"Who led her on?"

"Zeno! The son of a whore said he loved her. But like every other lying Greek, all he cared for in the end was bettering himself."

Zeno. Where had I heard the name recently? From Domitius, I recalled, when he told me the tale of Apollonides and his hideously deformed daughter, Cydimache. The young man who had recently married Cydimache was named Zeno.

"Do you mean the son-in-law of the First Timouchos?"

"That's the one. *We* weren't good enough for him. Never mind that I could buy and sell Zeno's father if I wanted. Never mind that Rindel was one of the most beautiful girls in Massilia. We're Gauls, you see, not Greeks; and no one in our family has ever been elected to the Timouchoi. In this town, that puts us just one step above the barbarians in the forest. Even so, Zeno could have married Rindel. Greeks and Gauls do marry. But Zeno was too good for that. Curse his ambition! He saw his chance to leap to the top, and he took it, over the head of my poor Rindel."

A part of me, frozen with grief for Meto, simply wanted the man to go away. But another part of me grudgingly stirred. I was curious. Looking at Arausio, his face now nakedly showing his misery, I felt a pang of sympathy as well. Were we not both fathers grieving for lost children? If I understood correctly, his daughter and my son had ended their lives within a few hundred feet of each other, beneath the same wall, claimed by a plunge into the same unforgiving sea.

"She was desperately in love with him," Arausio went on. "Why not? Zeno's handsome and charming. He dazzled her. The young can't see beneath the surface of things. When he told her he loved her in return, she thought that was the end of it. She'd found her bliss and nothing could spoil it. I can't say I wasn't pleased myself; he'd have made a good match. Then Zeno stopped calling on her. And the next thing we knew, he'd married Cydimache. It broke Rindel's heart. She wept and tore her hair. She shut herself away; wouldn't eat or talk to anyone, not even to her mother. Then she took to slipping out of the house, disappearing for hours at a time. I was furious, but it did no good. She said it helped her to take long walks alone. Imagine that, a young girl walking the streets in broad daylight by herself, unescorted! 'People will think you've gone mad,' I told her. Perhaps she *was* going mad. I should have kept a closer eye on her, but with everything in such chaos, . . ." He shook his head.

"What makes you think it was Rindel we saw on the Sacrifice Rock?" I asked. "And how did you hear about it? How did you know that we saw it happen?"

"Massilia is a small town, Gordianus. Everyone's talking about it. 'The scapegoat has two Romans staying at his house, and you won't believe what the three of them saw—a man chased a woman up the Sacrifice Rock, and over she went. And one of these Romans is a character named Gordianus, called the Finder; investigates for people like Cicero and Pompey, digs up scandal and snoops under people's sheets.' "

That was not exactly how I would have described my livelihood, but I felt curiously flattered to discover that my name was sufficiently well-known to provide fodder for gossip in a city where I had never previously set foot. Of course, anything to do with the scapegoat would be of interest to the locals, and any death at the Sacrifice Rock would excite speculation.

"As for why I think it must have been Rindel. . . ." There was a catch in Arausio's voice. He cleared his throat and pressed on. "That morning she went missing again. Out for another of her long walks, I thought. But I had other things to worry about. That was the day the Romans brought up the battering-ram. For all we knew, the walls of the city might come down at any moment. As it turned out, the walls held; our soldiers even captured the battering-ram for a trophy. But Rindel. . . ." He cleared his throat. "Rindel never came home. Night fell, and the curfew, and still no sign of her. I was angry, then worried, then frantic. I sent slaves to search for her. One of them came back with the rumor about a girl who had been seen on the Sacrifice Rock pursued by a soldier—an officer in a blue cape." His eyes bored into mine. "Is it true? Is that what you saw?"

"The man wore a pale blue cape," I acknowledged. I remembered it fluttering in the wind.

"Zeno! It must have been him. I knew it! Rindel must have found him and confronted him. He'd led her on, betrayed her, broken her heart—married that monster instead. Who knows what Rindel said to him, or what he said to her? And it ended with him driving her up the rock, and then—"

"No one drove anyone," objected Hieronymus. "The woman we saw led, and the man chased after her. He was clearly trying to stop her. The tragedy is that he failed. The woman *jumped*."

"No, Arausio is right," insisted Davus. "The woman was trying to get away from the man. Then he caught up with her. He *pushed* her over."

Arausio looked at me. "What do you say, Gordianus?"

Both Hieronymus and Davus looked to me for vindication. I turned my gaze to the Sacrifice Rock. "I'm not sure. But both versions can't be true."

"It matters, don't you see?" Arausio leaned forward. "If Zeno pushed Rindel, then it was murder. The heartless beast!"

"*If* the woman was Rindel; *if* the man was Zeno."

"But it must have been them! Rindel never came home. She couldn't simply disappear, not in a city as small as Massilia, with every exit blocked. It was her on that rock. I know it was! And the man was Zeno, wearing his blue officer's cape; you saw that for yourself."

"And if it *was* your daughter and Zeno, and if the only witnesses to the event were the three of us on this terrace, then there are at least two different opinions of what may have occurred—and no way to reconcile them."

"But there is a way. There's someone who knows the truth," insisted Arausio. "Zeno!"

I nodded slowly. "Yes, if it was Zeno we saw in the blue cape, then he alone can tell you exactly what happened, and why."

"But he never will! He lied to my daughter about loving her. He'll lie about this as well."

"Unless he could be compelled to tell the truth."

"By whom? His father-in-law, the First Timouchos? Apollonides controls the city police and the courts. He'll stop at nothing to protect his son-in-law and avoid a scandal." Arausio lowered his eyes. "But there *will* be a scandal. Word is already out. Everyone knows there was a death at the Sacrifice Rock. No one knows yet who it was, but word will spread soon enough. 'I heard it was the daughter of that Gaulish merchant Arausio,' they'll say. 'Rindel was her name. She went crazy after Zeno spurned her. Her father should have seen it coming.' And I should have. I should have locked her in her room! How could she bring such shame on her family? Unless I can show that Zeno pushed her, everyone will assume that she killed herself. An illegal suicide, unsanctioned by the Timouchoi—an offense to the gods at the very moment they sit in judgment on the city, deciding whether Massilia lives or dies! How can I bear it? This will be the ruin of me!"

I felt a sudden chill toward the man. He had come to us grief-stricken at the disappearance of his daughter. Now he seemed more concerned about damage to his own reputation. But the scapegoat had a different reaction. Hieronymus knew what it meant to suffer the onus of public humiliation and ruin in Massilia, to be outcast for the sins of others. He looked at Arausio with tears in his eyes.

"That's why I've come to you, Finder," said Arausio. "Not just because you witnessed the thing, but also because of what they say about you. You find the truth. The gods guide you to it. I know the truth—my daughter didn't jump; she must have been pushed—but I can't prove it. Apollonides could squeeze the truth out of Zeno, but he'll never do it. But maybe there's some other way to bring out the truth, and if there is, you're the man to find it. Name your fee. I can afford it." As proof, he slipped one of the thick bracelets from his wrist and pressed it into my hand.

The yellow gold was worked with images of a hunt. Archers and hounds pursued an antelope, and overseeing all was Artemis, not in her guise as the strange *xoanon* of the Massilians, but in the traditional image of a robust young woman with long, graceful limbs, armed with a bow and arrow. The workmanship was exquisite.

"What did your daughter look like?" I asked quietly.

Arausio smiled weakly. "Rindel's hair was blond. She wore it in braids, like her mother. Sometimes her braids hung free. Sometimes she wound them about her head. They shimmered like ropes of gold, like that bracelet in your hand. Her skin was white, as soft as rose petals. Her eyes were blue, like the sea at midmorning. When she smiled. . . ." He drew a shuddering breath. "When Rindel smiled, I felt like a man lying in a field of flowers on a warm spring day."

I nodded. "I, too, have lost a child, Arausio."

"A daughter?" He looked at me with tears in his eyes.

"A son. Meto was born a slave and not of my flesh, but I adopted him and he became a Roman. When he was a boy, he was full of mischief and laughter, bright as a newly minted coin. He grew quieter as he grew older, more thoughtful and withdrawn, at least in my presence. I sometimes thought he was more reserved and somber than a young man his age ought to be. But every now and then he still laughed, exactly the way he'd laughed when he was a boy. What I would give to hear Meto laugh again! The sea below the walls of Massilia claimed him, as you say it claimed your daughter. I came all the way from Rome to find him, but he was gone before I arrived. Now there's nothing more I can do to help my son. . . ."

"Then help my daughter!" begged Arausio. "Save her good name. Help me to prove that she never jumped from the Sacrifice Rock. Prove that Zeno murdered her!"

Davus cleared his throat. "As long as we're stuck here in Massilia, father-in-law, we could use the money. . . ."

"And surely," added Hieronymus, "you need something to occupy you, Gordianus. You can't go on as you have been, sitting and brooding on this terrace from sunrise to sunset."

Their advice had no influence on me. I had already made up my mind.

"Ever since we saw the incident on the Sacrifice Rock, there's something I've been wondering about." I spoke slowly, trying to choose my words carefully, although there was no delicate way to speak of the matter. "Others have fallen from the Sacrifice

Rock before—scapegoats . . . suicides. Were their remains never found? I should think they might eventually have . . . washed up on shore." I was thinking of the woman we had seen. I was also thinking of Meto.

Hieronymus lowered his eyes. "My parents were never found," he whispered.

Arausio cleared his throat. "The current can be very strong, depending on the season and the time of day. Yes, sometimes bodies have washed up on shore, but they never enter the harbor; the current won't allow that. Bodies have been found miles from Massilia—or never found at all, because so much of the coastline consists of steep, jagged rocks. A body washed onto the shore is likely to be torn to pieces among sharp rocks, or hidden in some inaccessible grotto, or sucked into a seacave where even the eyes of the gods can't see."

"After the naval battle with Caesar, there must have been scores of bodies in the waters offshore," I said.

Arausio nodded. "Yes, but not one of them was recovered. If they were cast onto the shore, and if they could be seen and reached, it was the Romans who claimed them, not us. The Romans control the shoreline."

"So, even if the woman we saw was washed back to the shore—"

"If anyone found her, it would have been the Romans. Here in Massilia, we would never hear of it."

"I see. Then we should give up any hope that we might yet identify the woman by her . . . remains." My thoughts turned again to Meto. What had become of his body? Surely, if it had been found and identified by Caesar's men, Trebonius would have known, and would have told me. It seemed most likely that Meto, like Rindel—if indeed the woman was Rindel—had been swept out to sea beyond recovery, swallowed forever by Neptune.

I sighed. "Then we must determine the woman's identity by some other means. We can begin with practical considerations. For example, what was the woman on the Sacrifice Rock wearing when we saw her that morning? And was it the same as what your daughter was wearing the last time she left your house?"

It was Hieronymus's recollection that the woman on the rock had worn a dark gray cloak. Davus thought it was more blue than gray. I remembered it as more green than blue. As far as Arausio could recall, none of his daughter's garments fit any of those descriptions, for she preferred bright colors, but he couldn't be certain. His wife and household slaves knew Rindel's wardrobe better than he did; perhaps one of them could either remember or, by elimination, deduce exactly what Rindel had been wearing on the day she left home for the last time.

We talked a bit more, but Arausio was wrung out and unable to think clearly. I told him to go home and see what else he could learn from his wife and slaves.

After he left, I sat on the terrace, idly fingering the gold bracelet and studying the changing light on the Sacrifice Rock and the sea beyond. Suddenly I noticed that Davus was looking at me sidelong, a smile of relief on his lips.

XII

Apparently it was my day for receiving visitors. No sooner had
Arausio left, than a slave came running to tell Hieronymus that
two more callers had arrived, again asking for Gordianus the
Finder.

"Greeks or Gauls?" asked Hieronymus.

"Neither, Master. Romans. They call themselves Publicius and
Minucius."

The scapegoat raised an eyebrow. "I thought you had no
friends in Massilia, Gordianus."

"I've no idea who they are. Perhaps it's another inquiry about
what we saw on the Sacrifice Rock."

"Perhaps. Will you see them?"

"Why not?"

A few moments later two men slightly younger than myself
were shown onto the terrace. The taller, balding one was Publicius; the shorter, curly-headed one Minucius. Even without
their names I would have known them for Romans by their

dress. In Massilia, the Greeks wore the knee-length chiton or the draped chlamys, while the Gauls wore tunics and sometimes trousers; but these men were dressed in togas, as if outfitted for some formal event in the Roman Forum. But what sort of man, even a Roman, dons a toga on a warm day in a foreign city under siege?

Their togas looked freshly washed and had been impeccably draped across their shoulders and folded over their arms. I wondered if they had helped each other to arrange their garments; could one find a slave this far from Rome who knew the proper way to drape a toga? Despite their gravity, there was something comical about them; they might have been a pair of wide-eyed farmers come to the city to petition a magistrate in the Forum. It seemed absurd, especially given the state of affairs in Massilia, that they should have dressed so formally merely to call on Gordianus the Finder.

Their manner was stiff. When Hieronymus introduced me, they stuck out their jaws and gave me a military salute in unison, striking their fists against their breasts.

They appeared to have mistaken me for someone else. I was about to say as much when Publicius spoke up. The emotion in his voice overwhelmed his dignified bearing and caused him to stammer. "Are you—I mean, are you really—are you *the* Gordianus?"

"I suppose. The name is fairly uncommon," I allowed.

His shorter companion elbowed him. "Of course it's him! There can be only one Gordianus the Finder."

"Perhaps not," I said. "Some philosophers teach that each man is unique, but others believe that we each have a double."

Publicius laughed out loud. "And a wit! Of course, you would be. So famously clever and all that." He shook his head, beaming at me. "I can hardly believe it. I'm actually seeing you in the flesh!" His eyes sparkled, as if he were Jason and I the fleece. I found his scrutiny disconcerting.

Minucius saw my discomfort. "You're wary, Finder—and

rightly so, in this godforsaken city." He lowered his voice. "Spies everywhere. And pretenders."

"Pretenders?"

"Frauds. Impostors. Liars and rogues. Misleaders of the credulous."

"You make Massilia sound like Rome."

I was serious, but they again took my words for wit and cackled. Whom on earth had they mistaken me for? A popular comedian from the stage? Some wandering philosopher with a cultish following?

"I think, citizens, that you may have confused me with another Gordianus."

"Surely not," said Publicius. "Are you not the father of Meto, Caesar's close companion?"

I drew a sharp breath. "I am."

"The same Gordianus who fought alongside his son Meto, then barely old enough to don a manly toga, under the banner of the great Lucius Sergius Catilina—"

"Catilina the Deliverer!" intoned Minucius in a sudden rapture, with folded hands and upturned eyes.

"—at the battle of Pistoria?"

"Yes," I said quietly. "I was at Pistoria . . . with Meto. And Catilina. That was years ago."

"Thirteen years ago, last Januarius," noted Minucius. "Thirteen is a mystical number!"

"You and your son were the only followers of Catilina to survive that battle," continued Publicius. "All the others perished alongside the great Deliverer. Nothing in this universe occurs without a reason. We are all part of a divine plan. The gods chose you, Gordianus, and your son, to carry the memory of Catilina's last moments."

"Did they? All I remember is a great deal of noise and confusion, and screaming, and blood everywhere." And fear, I thought. I had never known such fear as when the Roman troops assembled against Catilina began to converge upon us there on that battlefield in northern Italy. I was there, suited in mismatched armor with a sword in my hand, for only one reason: because my son, with the hot-headed enthusiasm of a sixteen-year-old, had decided to cast his lot with the doomed leader of a doomed revolution, and if I could not persuade him to abandon Catilina, I had determined to die fighting at his side. But in the end it was Meto who saved me, who abandoned the battlefield to drag me, unconscious, to a safe refuge where we two alone, of all those who fought alongside Catilina, survived. The next day, in the victors' camp, I saw the head of Catilina mounted on a stake. He had been a man of immense charm and wit, radiating an infectious sensuality; nothing could have brought home more vividly the totality of his destruction than the sight of that lifeless head with its gaping mouth and empty eyes. It haunted my nightmares still. So much for the revolution Catilina had promised his followers; so much for the leader these men still, inexplicably, insisted on calling "the Deliverer."

"Pistoria!" said Publicius, who intoned the name of the battleground as if it were a holy shrine. "You were actually there, beside the Deliverer himself! Did you hear his last words?"

"I heard the speech he delivered to his troops." Wry and ironical it had been, fearless and without illusion. Catilina had faced destruction with his eyes wide open, perversely defiant to the end.

"And you saw his final moments?"

I sighed. "Meto and I were near Catilina when the fighting began. He planted his eagle standard in the ground. That was the spot where he made his last stand. I saw the standard fall. . . ."

"The eagle standard!" gasped Publicius. "The eagle standard of Marius himself, which Catilina held in trust for the next deliverer to come."

Publicius and Minucius raised their hands and chanted together: "The eagle standard! The eagle standard!"

"Yes, well. . . ." I felt increasingly uncomfortable in the presence of these two fawning acolytes of a dead deliverer. "If you were such staunch supporters of Catilina, why were you not there at Pistoria as well?"

As they had chanted, so they blushed in unison. Publicius cleared his throat. "We and a few others came here to Massilia in advance of Catilina, to clear the way for his arrival. Up until very near the end, it was in his mind to escape to Massilia, here to plan his triumphant return to Rome. But in the end, alas, he could not abandon the country and the people he sought to deliver from the Senate's tyranny. Catilina chose martyrdom over exile. He made his stand at Pistoria and fell there. It was left to us, the handful of his followers who had fled to Massilia, to keep his memory alive."

"To keep his dream alive!" added Minucius.

"And now the gods have led you here, Gordianus the Finder. Have led both you and your son to Massilia! It can only be a sign that the faith we have kept alive all these years has been justified, that the gods have looked down upon us and given us their blessing."

"My son—how did you know he was here?"

"Because he came to us, of course. He sought us out in secret. When he revealed to us who he was—"

"No one less than Meto, who fought with Catilina at Pistoria, who crossed the Rubicon with Caesar—"

"We could hardly believe it. It was a sign, of course. A sign of the gods' favor—"

"*Favor?*" I snapped. "You fools! My son is dead."

There was an awkward silence. My two visitors gazed sidelong at each other, keeping their mouths shut but working their eyebrows and lips, as if debating some point purely by an exchange of facial expressions. Finally Publicius stepped forward. He took my hand, which hung limply at my side.

"Come with us, Gordianus. We have something to show you. And something to tell you."

"Tell me now, then."

He shook his head gravely. "No, not here." He looked askance at Hieronymus and lowered his voice. "This place is . . . not suitable." *Impure,* he meant. Unclean, on account of the scapegoat. "Come, Gordianus. You must see what we have to show you. You must hear what we have to say."

I swallowed hard. The visit from the Gaulish merchant had distracted me, had lured me with a puzzle to take me out of myself and away from my misery. The visit from these latter-day Catilinarians had plunged me back into an unhappy past and an even more miserable present. What of any consequence could they show me? What could they tell me that I didn't already know? I looked to Davus, who saw my indecision and gave an eloquent shrug, as if to say, *Why not? What have we to lose, father-in-law, stuck here on the edge of nowhere?*

"Very well," I said. "Davus and I will go with you."

"And where are you taking my guests?" inquired Hieronymus, who clearly thought as little of the two Romans as I did.

"That, Scapegoat, must be a secret," said Publicius, with his nose in the air.

"But I'm this man's host, and as such I'm obliged to look after his safety. Before he leaves my home, you'll have to tell me where you're taking him."

Publicius and Minucius conferred in whispers. At last Publicius looked up. "I don't suppose there's any harm in telling *you,*" he said, with the unsubtle implication that the scapegoat's days were numbered. "We're taking Gordianus to the house of Gaius Verres."

Verres! The name was synonymous with corruption, extortion, limitless greed, and the very worst sort of misgovernment. As my two visitors conducted Davus and me through the streets of Massilia, I wondered what possible link could connect these last pitiful sheep from Catilina's flock to the most notorious of all Roman exiles.

It was Cicero who had prosecuted Gaius Verres a little over twenty years ago. The case had been a major scandal and established Cicero as the preeminent advocate in Rome, even as it destroyed Verres, who fled for Massilia before the court could deliver its damning verdict. The charge against Verres was extortion and criminal oppression of the people of Sicily during his three years as provincial governor of the island. Roman governors have always been notorious for exploiting their provinces and lining their own purses at the expense of the governed, while the Senate, whose members all hope for the opportunity to do the same themselves someday, turns a blind eye. It was indicative of the egregiousness of Verres's conduct that he was actually brought to trial for his offenses.

According to Cicero, who had also served as an administrator in Sicily, Verres had not only extorted the populace and plundered their civic treasuries, but had virtually stripped the island bare of every beautiful man-made object. Verres's appetite for fine works of art amounted to a mania. He especially loved paintings of the sort done in encaustic wax on wood, not least because they could easily be carried off, and he assiduously built himself a collection of the best pictures to be gleaned from every public space and private gallery in Sicily. But his greatest passion was for statues. Before Verres, every town square in Sicily, even the humblest, was decorated with the statue of a local hero or some particularly venerated deity; after Verres, the pedestals stood empty—except in those instances where the scoundrel, to squeeze even more money from the locals, had forced them to erect statues of himself, charging them outrageous sums for the privilege. Anyone who dared to oppose him, whether Sicilian or Roman, was ruthlessly disposed of. His behavior while he controlled the island was more that of a pirate than a provincial governor.

As soon as Verres's tenure was up and he returned to Rome, the Sicilians sought restitution from the Roman Senate and looked for a way to prosecute the man who had robbed them. Cicero took up their cause and, despite all Verres's legal finagling and the Senate's reluctance to prosecute one of its own, Cicero and the Sicilians eventually prevailed. The evidence assembled against Verres was so damning that even the Senate had to act; and as the trial progressed, Verres chose to flee Rome rather than face the verdict. The connoisseur of fine art set another fashion in his choice of destination; Verres fled for Massilia, and in the twenty years of political chaos that ensued, wave upon wave of Roman political exiles would follow him.

I knew who Gaius Verres was, of course—what Roman didn't?—but I had I never laid eyes on him. I knew that he was here in Massilia, but I had never expected our paths to cross. But then, nothing predictable or expected had occurred since the moment we emerged from the flooded tunnel into the city. More and more it seemed to me that Massilia was an unfamiliar world with its own peculiar rules of logic to which I must bend, willingly or not.

Verres's house was not far from the scapegoat's, somewhere along the way to Milo's house. Within her encircling walls, Massilia was a small city, and her fashionable district was very compact.

The house itself surprised me by its opulence. One thinks of exiles living in ruin and misery, or at least in reduced circumstances. But the house of Verres was even more ostentatious than that of the scapegoat, with a brightly colored facade in shades of pink and yellow, and elaborate columns flanking the entrance. A slave admitted us at once; the Catilinarians were obviously familiar visitors. The foyer was floored with yellow marble with swirling red veins, and, like a Roman house, had niches on either side housing the busts of Verres's ancestors. Or so I thought upon first glance. When my eyes adjusted to the dimness, I saw that the busts were not of ancestors after all, unless Verres claimed descent from the likes of Pericles, Aeschylus, and Homer. He had used the niches reserved for sacred display to show off specimens from his sculpture collection!

A slave led us deeper into the house. Statues and paintings were everywhere. Many of the paintings were installed on the walls, jammed close together, but others were stacked in narrow spaces between pedestals and walls, and some were even piled atop each other in corners. But the paintings, as vivid as many of them were—portraits, pastoral scenes, episodes from *The Iliad* and *The Odyssey,* erotic tableaux—faded into the background. It was the statues that dominated the house, and not just in the niches and the usual spots in front of columns or under archways. There were scores of statues, perhaps hundreds, so crowded together in some rooms that only a narrow pathway had been left clear. Their arrangement made no sense; Diana with her bow and arrow thrust her elbow into the nose of some obscure Sicilian statesman and appeared to take aim directly at the head of a seated Jupiter only a few feet way, whose stern gaze was directed at a pair of rearing life-size stags done in marble and flawlessly painted, even to the white spots on their flanks. The house was large and the rooms spacious, but it was not a palace, and a palace would have been required to properly contain so much art. As it was, I had the peculiar feeling of having stumbled into a very crowded but ominously silent house party, where the strange mix of guests were all made of bronze and marble—gods and animals, dying Gauls and cavorting satyrs, nude athletes and long-dead playwrights.

It was a kind of blasphemy to treat works of art, especially images of the gods, in such a fashion, with no respect for their unique power and singularity. I shuddered.

"Why in Hades have you brought me here?" I asked Publicius.

"You'll see," he said in hushed voice. "You'll see!"

We were led at last to the garden at the house's center, where an immensely fat man in a red tunic rose from a bench to greet us. A fringe of white hair circled his perfectly round head. A strand of tiny pearls and lapis beads peeked out from between the folds of fat that circled his neck. Rings of silver and gold glittered on his fingers. Among them I saw what looked like an iron citizen's ring. Verres had no right to wear it. The court's verdict had stripped him of his citizenship.

"Publicius! Minucius! How good to see you again. Welcome to my house."

"I swear to Artemis, he gets bigger each time we see him," said Publicius under his breath in a tone more full of wonder than disdain, and then, louder, "Gaius Verres! How kind of you to welcome us. We bring two guests, newly arrived from Rome."

"Ah! Rome. . . ." Verres's beady eyes glimmered. "So near, yet still so far away. Some day. . . ."

"Yes, some day," Publicius agreed wistfully. "And perhaps not so long from now, from the look of things. The world has turned upside-down."

"And shaken out these two," said Verres, regarding Davus and myself.

"Ah, yes, let me introduce you. Gaius Verres, this is Gordianus, called the Finder. The father of Meto," he added in a hushed voice.

If Publicius expected our host to be impressed, the fat man disappointed him. Verres looked me up and down as if appraising an object newly offered for acquisition. His rudeness was almost refreshing after the obsequious fawning of the Catilinarians. "When I was last in Rome, you were known as Cicero's hunting dog," he said gruffly. He spat the name Cicero as if it were an epithet.

"Perhaps," I said, staring at him coldly. "But you haven't been in Rome for a very long time, Gaius Verres." The Catilinarians winced. "At any rate, I had nothing to do with your trial."

Verres grunted. He turned his attention to Davus and raised an eyebrow. "And this big fellow?"

"Davus is my son-in-law."

Verres crossed his arms and pulled at his several chins. "A model worthy of the great Myron himself. I should like to see him naked. But with what sort of props? He's too grown-up for Mercury. His features are not intelligent enough to pass for Apollo. Not coarse enough for Vulcan, or old and worn enough to be Hercules, though perhaps some day. . . . No, I have it! Give him a helmet and a sword and he could be Mars. Yes, especially scowling like that. . . ."

Misreading Davus's frown of consternation as anger, Publicius hurriedly spoke up. "Gordianus and Davus arrived in the city only a few days ago. It was the day of the battering-ram—"

"Yes, yes, I know," said Verres. "Everyone in Massilia has heard the story by now. Two Romans swam in through a flooded rat hole and were scooped up by the scapegoat, who's now fattening them up—though why, no one can imagine, since it's the scapegoat who'll wind up as the main course one of these days."

This casual impiety induced an uncomfortable silence in the two Catilinarians. Publicius bit his lip. Minucius lowered his eyes. Clearly, of the three, Verres had by far the strongest personality. A tyrant he had been, and a tyrant he remained, even if his shrunken kingdom extended only as far as the walls of his own house.

"Well, then," Verres went on, "I suppose I can guess why you've come. Not to see my ivory Jupiter from Cyzicus, or the Apollo I brought back from Syracuse; nor to savor the beauty of my Ephesian Alexander, or experience the very rare sight of my miniature Medusa, which was executed by a student of Praxiteles. Did you know that the snakes on her head were carved from solid carnelian? Incredibly delicate! The largest is no thicker than my little finger. The Syracusans said the snakes were sure to break if I dared to move her, but not one of them suffered even a chip when I shipped her to Rome . . . and then here to Massilia."

"Fascinating, Gaius Verres," said Publicius, in a tone that indicated he had heard the tale more than once. "But what we actually came to see—that is, what we came here to show Gordianus, so that he might behold it once again with his own eyes—"

"Yes, yes, I know why you've come. It's why you always come."

Verres called for a slave, spoke to him in a whisper, and sent him from the room. The slave returned with a bronze key, a big, bulky thing with numerous notches, and a flickering lamp. Why a lamp, when the sun was still up? Verres took the key and the lamp and dismissed the slave. "Follow me," he said.

We left the garden. A long hallway led to the back of the house, where a flight of stairs descended steeply to a subterranean level.

The underground passage was so narrow that we had to proceed in single file. Verres and the Catilinarians went ahead of me, with Davus in the rear. The floor was treacherous and uneven. The wavering flame from Verres's lamp was too weak to light our feet, but it did illuminate the masses of spiderwebs above our heads. In places the ceiling sagged; Publicius and Davus, the tallest among us, had to stoop.

At last the winding subterranean passage terminated in a bronze door. There was a scraping noise as Verres pushed the key into a keyhole and worked it back and forth. The walk had required no special exertion, yet Publicius and Minucius both took labored breaths. By the flickering lamplight I saw that they trembled.

Davus took my arm and whispered in my ear. "Father-in-law, I don't like this. Who knows what's in that room? It might be a prison. Or a torture chamber. Or . . ."

Or a hiding place, I thought. The Catilinarians had spoken of Meto. He had come to them, they said, sought them out. They told me they had something to show me, something I could see only at the house of Verres. I felt a sudden rush of irrational excitement and found myself breathing as heavily as the others.

The door swung inward on creaking hinges. Verres stepped inside, leaving the rest of us in darkness. "Well, then, come on," he said. Publicius and Minucius stepped forward, visibly shaking. Davus insisted on stepping in front of me so as to enter ahead of me. I was the last to step inside the long, narrow room.

XIII

It was neither a prison nor a torture chamber, but the most obvious and logical thing to be found behind a bronze door beneath a rich man's house: a treasure room. The chamber was crowded with ornately decorated jewelry boxes and urns heaped with coins, small silver statuettes and talismans carved from precious stones. On the walls were mounted antique weapons and military regalia of the sort collectors fancy. Amid this clutter, my eyes were drawn to something at the far end of the room. It stood apart, with space cleared around it so that it could be seen clearly.

I recognized it at once and felt a sudden, painful stab of nostalgia. I had first seen it in a setting in some ways similar to this, illuminated by lamplight in a place of darkness. It had been in a mine north of Rome where Catilina and his inner circle were hiding. The thing was made of silver, perched atop a tall pole festooned with a red and gold pennant. Through the gloom, I peered up at the eagle with its beak held high and its wings spread. But for the glimmer of silver it might have been a real bird, frozen in glory.

"The eagle standard of Catilina," I whispered.

"You remember!" said Publicius.

Of course I did. How could I forget? I had last seen it tumbling to earth at Pistoria, lost in the chaos of the battle, marking the spot where Catilina fell.

Publicius touched my arm and whispered in my ear, "This was what your son came here to find. That was his true mission to Massilia!"

I gazed up at the eagle, fascinated by the play of light and shadow across its spread wings. "What are you saying? I don't understand."

"Before Catilina, it was Marius who carried the eagle standard—Marius the mentor and hero of Caesar—in his campaign against the Teutones and the Cimbri, here in Gaul."

"That was a long time ago," I said.

"Yes, even before Caesar was born. Marius defeated the Teutones and the Cimbri. He returned to Rome in triumph with the eagle standard. Years later he prepared to carry it into war once again, against Mithridates in the East. But then Sulla, who had been his lieutenant, turned against him and waged civil war. Sulla marched on Rome itself! In the end, Marius was killed, and the eagle standard fell into Sulla's bloodstained hands. He made himself dictator—but only for a while, because Sulla soon died, consumed by worms that grew out of his own flesh. A horrible death, but no more than he deserved; the gods dealt with him justly. And then—no one quite knows how—the eagle standard came into the possession of Catilina."

"The Deliverer!" cried Minucius, clutching his breast.

"For many years Catilina hoarded it in secret, biding his time," Publicius continued.

I nodded. "Cicero claimed that Catilina kept the eagle of Marius in a hidden room and bowed down to worship it before plotting his crimes."

"The criminal was Cicero!" said Publicius vehemently. "Such a man could never understand the true power of the eagle standard. Catilina kept it safely hidden until the time came to carry it into battle again, against the same forces that Marius had fought, the oppressors of the weak, the defilers of the pure, the false pretenders who fill the Senate and mock the virtues that once made Rome great."

Minucius, in a breathless, impatient voice, took up the story. "But the time was not yet right—Catilina was premature; his cause was doomed. Only we few who fled to Massilia were left to preserve his memory, and for a while longer the gods allowed the serpents who ruled the Senate to hold sway. The murderers of Catilina cut off the Deliverer's head and showed it off as a trophy . . . but they never found the eagle standard! If they had, they would have destroyed it, melted it down, reduced it to a shapeless lump, and cast it into the sea. But the eagle eluded them."

"For years we searched for it," said Publicius, pressing his colleague aside, clutching at me and pushing his face close to mine. "We hired agents, offered rewards, followed false leads—"

"Those who tried to dupe us and cheat us lived to regret it!" cried Minucius.

"But the eagle had vanished. We despaired—"

"Some of us lost hope—"

"We feared that our enemies had found it after all, and destroyed it." Publicius sucked in a breath and turned his head to gaze up at the silver eagle. "Yet all along, here it was! Here in Massilia, safe and sound in this vault! Hidden underground, in darkness, behind a bronze door. As if the eagle had known where to rendezvous with its next owner."

I looked up at the eagle, then past Publicius and Minucius to Verres, who pursed his lips but said nothing.

"Then Gaius Verres is now your leader?" I asked.

"Not at all!" said Publicius. "Verres is merely the keeper of the standard, holding it in trust for its next, true owner. What better place for it to reside, temporarily at least, than here, forgotten by the world at large and safe from its enemies?"

I nodded. "And who is this next, true owner?"

"But surely that's obvious! Caesar, of course. Caesar will complete what Marius and Catilina began. Caesar will abolish the Senate; he's already driven them into exile. Caesar will remake the Roman state—"

"Remake the world!" cried Minucius.

"That is his destiny. And he'll do it under this standard. When the walls of Massilia fall and the city opens her gates to Caesar, and the imperator himself strides in, resplendent in glory, the eagle shall be here, waiting for him. Do you think it was merely coincidence that Massilia was Caesar's first destination after taking Rome? Oh, no! Rumors had already reached him that the eagle standard of Marius was here in Massilia. He came here to find it. But the Timouchoi sided with Pompey and closed their gates to Caesar. The fools! To obtain what is rightfully his, Caesar was forced to lay siege. But a man like Caesar has recourse to more subtle tools than catapults and siege towers. He also sent your son here—Meto, who once fought beside Catilina—to confound Caesar's enemies and search for the missing eagle standard."

"And now *you've* come," whispered Minucius. "The father of Meto! You, too, fought beside the Deliverer. When Caesar returns to claim Massilia, *you* shall be here to witness the moment he takes possession of the eagle standard. Do you see how the gods bring all things to a head? The strands they weave out of our mortal lives are like a pattern visible only from the heavens; we here on earth can only guess at their designs." He shook his head and smiled, bemused by the wonder of it all.

The narrow vault suddenly seemed airless and cramped, and the treasures strewn about the room as tawdry as the masses of crowded statues in the rooms above our heads. The eagle standard itself, briefly invested with magic by the sheer enthusiasm of the acolytes, was merely another object after all, beautiful and precious but made by human hands for an all-too-human purpose, now reduced to one of a thousand items in the inventory of a shamelessly greedy miser.

I shook my head. "What does any of this matter to me? My son is dead."

Publicius and Minucius exchanged a significant glance. Publicius cleared his throat. "But you see, Gordianus, that's where you're wrong. Your son is *not* dead."

I looked at him dumbly. From the corner of my eye, a flicker of light created the illusion that the silver eagle stirred. "What did you say?"

"Meto is not dead. Oh, yes, everyone *thinks* he is; everyone but us. We alone know better. Because we've seen him."

"Seen him? Alive? Where? When?"

Minucius shrugged. "More than once, since he supposedly drowned. He appears when we least expect it. Part of his mission is to prepare the way for Caesar, and for that, of course, the silver eagle must be ready—"

"To Hades with the silver eagle!" I shouted. Davus gripped my arm to restrain me. "To Hades with Caesar, where he can join Catilina for all I care! Where is Meto? When can I see him?"

They recoiled as if struck, gazed up at the eagle, and then averted their eyes, as if ashamed to have brought a blasphemer into its presence. "You've suffered much, Gordianus," said Publicius through gritted teeth. "We acknowledge your sacrifice. Still, there can be no excuse for such impiety."

"Impiety? You bring me into this . . . into such a"—I could not think of a word to describe the house of Gaius Verres—"and you accuse me of impiety! I want to see my son. Where is he?"

"We don't know," said Minucius meekly. "He comes to us at the time and place of his own choosing. Just as Catilina does—"

"What?"

"Oh, yes, we see Catilina quite often here in the streets of Massilia." Minucius shook his head. "You say he's in Hades, but you're wrong. His lemur has never rested, never left the earth since the battle of Pistoria. As he planned to come here in life, so his lemur journeyed here in death. He sometimes affects the guise of a soothsayer, hiding himself in a cloak and cowl so that no one can see his face or the scar of the wound that separated his head from his shoulders. . . ."

I remembered the soothsayer who appeared out of nowhere at the temple of the *xoanon* Artemis and rode with us as far as the ruined forest outside Massilia, the one whom the Roman soldiers jokingly called Rabidus. The cowled figure had said to me: *Nothing in this place is what it appears to be. Nothing!* And later, to the soldiers: *I know why the Roman has come here. He's come to look for his son. Tell the Roman to go home. He has no business here. There's nothing he can do to help his son. . . .*

The vault was suddenly as cold as a tomb. I shuddered and clenched my teeth to stop them from chattering.

"Meto comes to you, then—" There was a thickness in my throat that made it hard to speak. "Meto comes to you as a lemur. Like Catilina?"

Publicius shrugged. His voice was quiet now, no longer angry. "Who can say? What does it matter? Meto played his role in the story of the eagle standard, as did Catilina before him; as yet may you, Gordianus. Why else did the gods send you here to Massilia?"

"Why, indeed?" I muttered. I felt hollow, as I had felt in my lowest hours at the scapegoat's house, drained of anger, of hope, even of the disdain I felt for these simpering disciples and their strange cult. I looked past them to Verres, who gazed back at me with a sardonic expression, barely able to contain his amusement. I could not even muster the energy to feel disgust for him. I felt nothing.

"Take me away from here, Davus," I whispered. "I need air."

We stepped out of the room, but Verres held the lamp, and without it the passage was pitch-black. I was reminded of the flooded tunnel and felt dizzy. We waited while Verres locked the bronze door, then pressed ourselves against the wall while he awkwardly squeezed ahead of us to lead the way out. The forced contact with his corpulent body repulsed me. The smell of his perfume, mixed with his sweat and the smoke from the lamp, was nauseating.

We ascended the stairs, emerged into the house, and proceeded to the garden, then to the foyer, without a word. At the door, the Catilinarians hesitated. If they had more to say, I was in no mood to hear it.

"You needn't escort me back to Hieronymus's house," I said. "Davus and I can find the way."

"Then we shall leave you now," said Minucius.

They each clasped one of my hands and looked into my eyes. "Have strength, Gordianus," said Publicius. "The moment of our deliverance is coming very soon. All questions will be answered." Then the two of them departed.

I swayed, feeling a bit dizzy. Davus held my arm.

Behind me, Verres laughed. "They're both completely mad, of course," he said. "And they're not the only two. There are quite a few of those fanatics here in Massilia, clinging to Catilina and his so-called dream. Can you believe it? Completely mad, every one of them."

I turned to face him. "And you, Gaius Verres? What word would you use to describe yourself?"

He shrugged. "Acquisitive, I suppose. And shrewd—I hope. Ten years ago, when one of my contacts in Italy offered to sell me that eagle standard, I thought it might be a good investment—a unique acquisition, certainly—but I had no idea it might someday purchase my return to Rome."

"What are you talking about?"

"Mad our two friends may be, but they're right about one thing: Caesar *does* want the eagle standard. Oh, not for some mystical purpose. And not for political reasons, either; all the old Marian supporters have already rallied to his side. No, he wants it for sentimental reasons. Marius was his mentor, after all, and a kinsman; and Catilina was his friend. I've always suspected that Caesar would have openly supported Catilina, if the moment had been right."

"Those two think that Caesar headed straight for Massilia to claim the thing."

Verres laughed. "Anyone who can read a map knows why Caesar made a detour to this spot: Massilia happens to be on the way to Spain, where Caesar must first dispose of Pompey's troops before he can make any further moves. Nonetheless, he wants the eagle standard—and I happen to own it. Surely such a prize will be worth the redemption of a single harmless exile such as myself."

"You expect Caesar to restore your citizenship in return for the eagle?"

"A fair bargain, I should think."

"You're merely using the Catilinarians, then?"

"As they hope to use me. They disgust me. I suppose I disgust them. But we have one thing in common: We're all homesick. We want to go back to Rome. We want to go home."

"So do I, Gaius Verres," I whispered. "So do I."

Davus and I headed back toward the scapegoat's house. My mind was in a tumult. The Catilinarians, casually claiming to have seen Meto since his fall into the sea, had cruelly raised my hopes, then dashed them. They were mad, as Verres had said. And yet . . . a part of me clutched at even this tattered shred of hope that Meto might somehow be alive. Was it because I hadn't seen his dead body with my own eyes that I couldn't accept the hard fact of his death? Uncertainty allowed for doubt, and doubt allowed for hope; but false hope was surely crueler than the grief of certain knowledge.

What was I to make of the two acolytes' reference to visitations from a hooded figure they claimed to be the restless lemur of Catilina, whose appearance sounded strangely similar to the hooded soothsayer the Roman guards had called Rabidus? Could it truly have been the spirit of Catilina I met in the wilderness outside Massilia? Had Catilina himself tried to warn me away from the city, knowing that my son was already dead?

Over and over I imagined the sight of Meto plummeting from the high wall into the sea. The image became confused with my memory of the woman we had watched as she scrambled up the rock face and then vanished, either because she was pushed, or jumped, or fell. . . .

I walked through the streets of Massilia in a daze, hardly aware of my surroundings, letting Davus lead the way. When he touched my arm and whispered in my ear, I gave a start.

"I'm not sure, father-in-law, but I think we're being followed."

I blinked and looked around, for the first time taking notice of others in the street. There were more people about than I had realized. Life in Massilia went on despite the siege. "Followed? Why do say that?"

"There are two fellows who seem always to be about a hundred paces behind us. We've just completed a circuit of the block around Verres's house, and they're still there."

I turned and saw that we stood once again before the door to Verres's house. My wits were so dulled, I hadn't even noticed that Davus had just led me in a circle.

"Are they closing on us?"

"No, they seem to be keeping their distance. And I think . . ."

"Yes?"

"I think they may have followed us earlier, when we left the scapegoat's house. I wasn't sure, then. But it must be the same two."

"Probably agents of the Timouchoi, keeping an eye on the scapegoat's Roman guests," I said. "If the authorities are having us watched, there's not much we can do about it. Do you recognize these two? Might you have seen them before, perhaps among Apollonides's soldiers?"

Davus shook his head. "They stay too far back for me to get a good look at their faces." He frowned. "What if they're not from the Timouchoi? What if someone else is having us followed?"

"That seems unlikely." Or did it? If I had learned anything since my arrival in Massilia, it was to expect the unexpected.

I glanced behind us, attempting to do so casually. "Which ones are they?"

Davus shook his head. "You can't see them now. They've stepped out of sight. But father-in-law . . . haven't we seen *him* before?"

I turned my head and followed Davus's gaze down a narrow side street, where a group of twenty or so women, all clutching empty baskets, had gathered before a closed storefront, whispering and wearing furtive expressions, drawn, it was painfully obvious, by some black marketeer's promise of contraband rations on offer in a certain place at a certain hour. What would the Timouchoi think of that?

"I see a lot of women, Davus, but no men."

"There, a little beyond the women, wearing a hood. It's the soothsayer we met outside Massilia!"

I drew a sharp breath. The figure could be seen only in glimpses, yet somehow, like Davus, I perceived it at once to be the soothsayer. But that was impossible; how could he have gotten inside the city walls? Our minds were playing tricks on us; the Catilinarians had mentioned a hooded visitor, and that had brought the soothsayer to the forefront of our thoughts. The figure was probably not a man at all, but simply another of the women standing a little beyond the crowd. And yet . . .

I stepped into the side street and walked toward the crowd of women. Davus followed. Did I only imagine that the hooded figure beyond the crowd gave a sudden start?

Davus gripped my arm. I tried to shake him off, but he tightened his grip. "Father-in-law, there they are again—the two who've been following us. Beyond the soothsayer, at the far end of the street. They must have circled around."

I saw the two men Davus was talking about. They were too distant for me to see their faces, dressed in plain brown chitons with nothing to set them apart. The hooded figure, turning his head, seemed to see them as well, and gave another start. I tried to move toward him, through the crowd of women. The look on my face must have alarmed them; I heard exclamations in Greek too fast for me to follow, and then they began to scatter like startled birds. They thought that Davus and I were agents of the Timouchoi come to break up their black market.

For a moment all was confusion, then the narrow little side street was suddenly empty. The women had vanished. So had the two men at the far end of the street. So had the hooded figure—if indeed he had ever been there.

XIV

I dreamed that night of Meto's toga day, when he turned sixteen and for the first time put on his manly toga for a promenade through the Forum in Rome. The night before he had panicked and been paralyzed with doubt; how could a boy born a slave ever truly become a Roman? But I had comforted him, and on the appointed morning my heart soared with pride to see him stride through the Forum, a citizen among citizens.

In my dream, all was exactly as it had been on that day, except that I never saw Meto's face; in a strange way I didn't see him at all, for where he should have been there was a kind of gap in my vision, a nothingness, an empty blur. Yet the dream-Forum through which our little retinue progressed was somehow even more vivid than life, super-real, teeming with color and noise. We passed by the great temples and across the public spaces. We mounted the long flight of steps that led to the summit of the Capitoline Hill, and on the way up, who should pass us coming down but a group of senators, including none other than

Caesar. Ever the politician, always eager to ingratiate himself with potential supporters, Caesar congratulated Meto on his toga day, even though he scarcely looked at him. Was that the first time Meto and Caesar met face to face? It must have been. Who could have imagined then how closely their destinies would intertwine?

In my dream, Caesar was especially vivid. His face was almost a caricature of itself, the high cheekbones and lofty forehead slightly exaggerated, the bright eyes sparkling feverishly, the thin lips drawn into a characteristic smile, as if at some secret joke shared only by Caesar and the gods.

The senators moved on. Our retinue proceeded upward. Atop the Capitoline my old friend Rufus observed the auspices, searching the sky for birds in order to read the will of the gods. We waited a long time for any bird at all to appear. Finally a great winged shape darted like lightning across the sky and landed at our feet. The eagle stared at us and we stared back. I had never seen one so close. I could have reached out and touched it, had I dared. Suddenly, with a great beating of wings, it departed. What did it mean? The eagle was Jupiter's favorite, the most divine of birds. According to Rufus, to have seen one on Meto's toga day, especially so close, was the best of all possible omens. But even then I felt vaguely apprehensive; and later, when Meto first saw the eagle standard of Catilina, it had seemed to him a further sign of the gods' will, a marker for his destiny, and I think it must have been in that very instant that he truly became a man, which is to say that he moved irrevocably beyond my control and into dangers from which I could no longer protect him.

I was suddenly transported, as happens in dreams, to a place completely different. I was in the treasure chamber beneath the house of Gaius Verres, amid the clutter of shimmering coins and jewel-encrusted artifacts. It seemed to me that Meto was in the room as well, but invisible. The eagle standard loomed over us, uncannily lifelike—and then, suddenly, the eagle was alive! It let out a shriek and flapped its wings, trying to take flight in the confined space, thrashing madly, rending the air with its beak and its dagger-sharp talons. I covered my eyes. The dream became a nightmare of screams, blood, confusion.

And then I awoke.

Davus was gently shaking me. "Father-in-law, wake up! Something important is happening."

"What?" I shook my head, confused and uncertain where I was.

"A ship arrived during the night—"

"A ship?"

"It slipped past the Roman blockade. An advance messenger. Reinforcements are coming—ships full of soldiers—sent by Pompey!"

The nightmare clung to me like cobwebs. I sat up, reached blindly for the ewer beside the bed, and splashed water onto my face. The room was shadowy but not completely dark, illuminated by the faint glow that precedes the dawn. For a fleeting instant it seemed to me, beyond any doubt, that Meto was in the room. I looked about and, not seeing him, felt certain nonetheless that he must be there, present but somehow invisible. Davus saw me staring into space and wrinkled his brow.

"Father-in-law, are you ill?"

I took a long time to answer. "No, Davus. Not ill. Just sick at heart. . . ."

This seemed to reassure him. "Then you'd better get up. The whole town is awake, even though it's not yet daylight. People are out in the streets, on rooftops, hanging out windows, calling back and forth to each other. I can't follow the Greek, but Hieronymus says—"

"Hieronymus says, let their timbers rot and Poseidon take them!" Our host stood in the doorway, a dour look on his face.

I cleared my throat. "Is it true, what Davus says? A ship arrived in the night?"

"A fast-sailing messenger ship. Apparently it slipped past the blockade and into the harbor without being seen by the Romans. Amazing how quickly the news spread across the city, like wildfire jumping from rooftop to rooftop."

"And more ships are on the way?"

"So goes the rumor. One of Pompey's admirals has reached a Massilian garrison called Taurois just a few miles up the coast. They say he has eighteen galleys—an even match for Caesar's fleet." He sighed glumly. "Come, Gordianus. Get dressed and take breakfast with me."

I rubbed my eyes and wondered which was more precarious, the dream world I had just left or the one I had awakened to. Would there ever again come a time when I could wake in the morning and know, with blessed, boring predictability, exactly what each hour of the day would bring?

We breakfasted on the rooftop terrace. The privileged venue, with its lofty seclusion looking out on distant views, gave a sense of removal, but the palpable excitement in the city penetrated even there. From the street below came snatches of conversation as passersby speculated on the size and quality of the expected reinforcements, predicted the annihilation of the blockading navy, gloated over the terrible revenge to be exacted against Caesar's forces. A trumpeter blew his horn in the street; a crier announced that all slaves were confined to their households and that all able-bodied citizens were to report at once to the dockyards, by order of the Timouchoi. From nearby temples came chants of praise to the strange *xoanon* Artemis of the Massilians and her brother Ares. Out at the wall along the sea, a steady stream of women, children, and old men funneled into the bastion towers, wound their way up the stairwells, and poured out along the battlements.

"Was this how it was on the day the Massilian navy sailed out to take on Caesar's ships?" I asked Hieronymus.

He followed my gaze to the wall. "Exactly. All the noncombatants gathered on the wall to watch. Standing like statues and peering at the sea, or huddled in little groups, or pacing nervously about. All torn between hope and the terrible fear that everything might go wrong—as it did, last time." A faint, sardonic smile bent his lips. "Do you see how some have brought blankets and parasols and even small folding chairs? They've come prepared to stay all day. Last time those same spectators brought baskets of food as well. Watching men kill each other is hungry work. But I don't see anyone carrying a basket today. Not enough rations, I suppose. Would you care for another piece of bread, Gordianus? Perhaps a stuffed date?"

The slanting light of the rising sun glinted across the face of the Sacrifice Rock. Although it looked as if its summit would afford the best possible view of the harbor and the waters beyond, the spectators shunned it and kept to the man-made battlements.

"Do you know, Davus," I said, "I have a sudden impulse to see the Sacrifice Rock."

"We can see it from here."

"Yes, we can. But I want to have a closer look."

Davus frowned. "Apollonides told us that the rock is off-limits. It's sacred ground, forbidden, for as long as the scapegoat is still—" He realized what he had said and averted his eyes from Hieronymus.

I nodded. "And we have obediently kept our distance. Until now. On any other day, snooping around the wall and the Sacrifice Rock, we'd have instantly drawn attention to ourselves. We'd have been ordered to keep away, maybe even arrested. But today, with the authorities distracted and so many people out, perhaps we can take advantage of the crowd and its confusion." I put another stuffed date in my mouth and savored it. "Eat your fill, Davus. We may not be able to eat again for a while; it would hardly be seemly to carry food into a hungry crowd forced to do without."

Out in the streets, no one seemed to take any notice of me, but Davus attracted curious looks. Slaves had been confined to quarters and every able-bodied citizen had been summoned to the dockyards. Other than a handful of soldiers stationed here and there to keep order, there was not a young man to be seen among the women, children, and graybeards heading for the battlements. With his broad shoulders and tall frame, Davus stood out.

But no one prevented us from merging with the others who were filing into the nearest bastion tower to mount the stairwell that led up to the battlements. This was the tower into which the soldier in the light blue cape had vanished after the woman plunged from the precipice. These were the steps by which he had fled from his crime, if indeed there had been a crime for him to flee. We were retracing his route in reverse. Every step took us closer to the Sacrifice Rock.

Halfway up, I paused to catch my breath. Davus waited beside me while others passed by. "Any sign of those shadows that followed us yesterday?" I asked, peering down the hollow center of the stairwell.

"Not that I've seen," said Davus. "The two men I saw yesterday would stand out in this crowd almost as much as I do."

We pressed on and soon emerged from the bastion onto the platform that ran along the battlements. To our right, toward the sea, the crowd was pressed thickly all along the outer wall, where people jostled one another to get the best view. I turned and looked in the opposite direction, toward the spine of hills and jumbled rooftops of the city. I searched for the scapegoat's house in vain until Davus pointed it out to me; then I clearly saw the green-clad figure of Hieronymus sitting on his rooftop terrace with tall trees on either side. If he saw us, he gave no sign. Beyond the skyline of the city, I could see the summit of the high hill upon which Trebonius had established his camp and from which the commander was no doubt at that very moment keeping watch on the city and the sea beyond.

Turning back toward the sea, I could see only glimpses of blue through the crowd. Davus, able to peer over the throng, told me he could see from the harbor mouth to the islands offshore and beyond. Away from the wall, the crowd was thin enough for us to thread our way toward the Sacrifice Rock, which loomed up as we approached. The weathered finger of limestone was white with patches of gray and streaks of black running down its smooth hollows and sinuous contours. It rose higher than the wall and extended farther outward, overhanging the sea far below like the jutting prow of a ship. As we approached the rock, the crowd grew thinner, and the section of the wall nearest the rock was completely empty. No doubt the Massilians hung back out of superstitious awe and respect for the rock's sanctity, but there was also a more practical reason; beyond a certain point, the jutting rock obscured the view of the islands outside the harbor and completely blocked the view of the harbor mouth.

Where the wall abutted the rock, the building stones had been expertly cut to fit without a gap, and the looming rock bulged out over the battlements, forming a sort of shallow cave. We had seen the man in the blue cape jump from the rock onto the wall. I found the approximate spot where he must have landed and looked up at the overhanging lip of rock. From rock to wall was a jump of at least ten feet, perhaps more. The man had stumbled when he landed, I recalled, and had limped as he ran toward the bastion tower, favoring his left leg.

It appeared, at first, that we had reached a dead end; short of scaling the overhang, there was no way to get onto the rock and over it and then to the next stretch of wall. But this was not quite the case. At the left-hand corner where the wall abutted the rock on the city side, the overhang slanted sharply down and receded considerably. Shallow steps, some scarcely more than toeholds, had been crudely chiseled out of the stone. It would require a considerable step, angling out over a sheer drop, to reach the first toehold, and the ones that followed were erratically spaced and appeared to follow a circuitous path, having been cut more in accordance with the peculiar contours of the rock than to match the measure of a man's footsteps. To climb onto or off of the rock using these toeholds would require a considerable amount of agility and strength, not to mention nerve and patience, which was probably why the man in the blue cape had bypassed them to take the shortcut of simply jumping down onto the wall.

Davus looked at me and raised an eyebrow. "Shall I go first, father-in-law? I'll have an easier time stepping up to that first notch. Then I can reach back to give you a hand if you need help."

"*If* I need help? You're very tactful, Davus. Even at your age, I'd have hesitated to take that first step. Hurry, then, while no one's watching."

I glanced at the crowd over my shoulder, then watched with bated breath while Davus reached up to grasp the stone face with both hands, raised his left foot to gain the toehold, and swung his body up and briefly out over a corner of empty space between the rock and the wall. He paused, testing his balance and calculating his next move, then swung up and back, again over empty space, and raised his right foot to the next toehold. The maneuver brought his center of gravity squarely back over the rock, and I heard him release a sigh of relief an instant before I did.

"Now you," he said. He extended his hand. Had his arm been any shorter, I couldn't have reached it.

His grip was strong. With my other hand I clutched at the rock face and raised my left foot as high as I could. The toehold was just out of reach—until Davus gave me a steady pull and lifted me high enough for my toes to slip over the notch. I propelled myself upward and swung out over empty space, feeling suddenly queasy and out of control.

"Steady," Davus whispered. "Keep your eyes on the rock and don't look down. Do you see the next step?"

"Yes."

"It's not as far as it looks."

"Somehow, I don't find that particularly reassuring."

Davus's grip remained firm. I raised my right foot, searched clumsily for the toehold, then found it. I took another swing over empty space, and for a vertiginous instant I knew beyond any doubt that if Davus were not gripping my hand I would have lost my balance and fallen. I glanced down. It was a sheer drop for most of the way. Eventually a falling body would hit either the wall or the rock and then bounce back and forth between them. I shut my eyes and swallowed hard.

A moment later, I was securely on the Sacrifice Rock, my balance regained. Another easy step upward and I was on the overhanging lip of the rock, on a relatively level surface. Davus released my hand and proceeded on all fours ahead of me. I scrambled after him.

The view from the Sacrifice Rock was uninterrupted in all directions, but the summit was slightly depressed at the middle, like a furrowed tongue, so that if we crouched, we couldn't be seen by the spectators lining the battlements on either side. We remained visible to anyone who might be gazing out from one of the houses behind us. When I turned to have a look at the scapegoat's rooftop, I saw that Hieronymus had risen to his feet and stood at the edge of his terrace, leaning forward with his hands on the balustrade, watching intently.

Peering over the farther edge of the rock, I looked down upon the section of wall that lay beyond. The crowd was even thicker along this stretch of the battlements; but as on the opposite side, even though here the rock presented no visual barrier, people kept their distance from it. I looked for a way to get down to the wall, but if anything, this side offered even less access than the way we had come; there did not seem to be even crude toeholds for gaining access.

Staying low, I turned toward the sea and crept forward to have a look over the precipice. The rock formed a shelf extending well beyond the line of the wall and then abruptly ended. I lay flat on the rock and poked my head over the edge. Far below, I saw shallow, jagged rocks washed by churning waves that glinted blue-green and gold in the soft morning light.

Davus crept up alongside me and peered over the edge.

"What do you think, Davus? Could anyone survive a drop like that?"

"Impossible! Of course, if it weren't for the rocks . . ."

I looked past him, toward the stretch of wall from which Meto had jumped. There the wall dropped sheer to the sea, with no rocks at the base. *If it weren't for the rocks* . . . what then? A man might strike the water and survive? There was no point in pursuing such thoughts, yet I found myself staring at the blue-green depths as if they held a secret that might be yielded up if only I stared long and hard enough.

Davus suddenly nudged me and pointed. "Father-in-law, look!"

A Massilian galley appeared at the harbor mouth, rowing out toward the open sea. Its deck was crowded with archers and ballistic artillery. Another ship followed it, and another, all with oars flashing in the sunlight. From the top of each mast, a pale blue pennant snapped in the breeze.

As each ship came into view, cheers erupted from the spectators, beginning at the section of the wall nearest the harbor mouth and then spreading toward us, so that successive waves of cheering poured over us. Spectators waved blankets, twirled parasols, or produced bits of cloth and waved them in the air. From the decks of the outbound ships, the walls of Massilia must have presented a lively spectacle of color and motion.

"I thought the Massilian navy had been destroyed," said Davus.

"Not destroyed, only crippled. Rendered too weak to present a challenge to Caesar's ships lying offshore. No doubt the shipbuilders have been hard at work repairing the galleys that survived the battle and refitting old ships—look, there's a vessel hardly bigger than a fishing boat, but they've installed screens to protect the rowers and mounted a catapult on it."

More ships appeared, all flying pale blue pennants. The first to exit the harbor drew up its oars and set sail, swinging round to port to catch a rising wind that propelled it into the channel between the mainland and the islands offshore. The other ships followed the same course, steering adroitly along the coastline and disappearing from sight behind the low hills on the far side of the harbor.

"Where are they off to?" asked Davus.

"Hieronymus said the relief force is anchored a few miles up the coast, at a place called Taurois. The Massilian ships must mean to join them so that they can take on Caesar's fleet together."

"Speaking of which . . ." Davus pointed toward the islands offshore. Sailing out from the hidden harbor on the far side, a galley appeared, followed by others. Caesar's fleet was setting sail in pursuit of the Massilians. Why had they waited so long? According to Hieronymus, Pompey's messenger ship had arrived without alerting the blockade. It seemed that the sudden reappearance of a revamped Massilian navy had taken Caesar's fleet by surprise. Now they were scrambling to react.

The last of the Massilian ships cleared the harbor and headed up the coast before the first of Caesar's galleys managed to maneuver past the islands and set sail after them. It was obvious that the Massilian galleys were faster and more skillfully manned. "If it were nothing more than a race, the Massilians would win without a contest," Davus observed.

"They may have better ships and better sailors," I granted, "but what will happen when they turn about and fight?"

A third voice answered: "If only we Massilians had a Cassandra, like the Trojans, to answer such questions!"

Davus and I both gave a start and looked up. Looming over us, his hands on his hips, his face starkly lit by the morning sun, stood Hieronymus.

XV

"What are you doing here?" I asked.

Hieronymus smiled. "I should think I have more of a right to be here than you do, Gordianus."

"But how—?"

"The easy way, up the face of the rock starting at the ground, the same way the soldier and the woman climbed up. I saw you earlier, swinging onto the rock from the wall. You're both lucky you didn't fall and break your necks."

I heard little shouts of surprise and alarm and lifted my head just enough to look over the edges of the rock at the spectators on either side. "People have seen you, Hieronymus. I think they must recognize you by your green clothes. They're staring . . . pointing . . . whispering."

"So? Let them. They probably think I've come to throw myself off. They'd like that, I imagine; good luck for the fleet. But I've no intention of jumping. That would be premature. It's up to the priests of Artemis to choose the moment." He strode to the precipice and peered over. Davus and I stayed low but moved aside to make room. "It's been a long time since I was up here," he said. "It does give one a strange feeling."

A sudden, powerful gust of wind buffeted the rock. Hieronymus staggered. Davus and I both let out a gasp and reached to grip his ankles. He swayed but managed to brace himself. The flash of panic in his eyes was followed by a brittle laugh. "Our famous wind! It's starting early today. I wonder how it will affect the battle?"

"Hieronymus, sit down! It's not safe to stand."

"Yes, I think I *will* sit. But I won't lie flat, as you're doing. I've no reason to hide. Neither do you. You're with me now. You're with the scapegoat, and if the scapegoat chooses to sit cross-legged on his rock to watch the sea with his friends while we wait for news of the battle, who forbids it?"

"Unless my memory fails me, the First Timouchos forbids it, and quite explicitly."

"Apollonides!" Hieronymus snorted and waved his hand in the air, as if the dictates of the First Timouchos signified no more to him than the buzzing of a fly.

The scapegoat's presence on the rock continued to cause a commotion among the spectators along the battlements, but only for a short while. Eventually people grew tired of pointing and whispering. They knew that the Sacrifice Rock was sacred ground and they knew it was off-limits; but I suspect, like most people, they left the finer points of sacred law to the authorities in charge of such things. If the scapegoat himself should appear on the rock, for all they knew he was supposed to be there. They accepted his presence as part of the day's spectacle, as another of the rituals of battle—like the chanting that echoed from the temples—and they turned to watch the sea.

There was, however, nothing to watch. The last of the Massilian ships had vanished, sailing eastward up the coast. So had the last of the Roman fleet, sailing in pursuit. The battle, if there was to be one, would take place elsewhere, presumably off

Taurois, where the Pompeian relief fleet lay anchored. The spectators had nothing to look at but the empty sea, yet no one seemed inclined to abandon a hard-won spot along the wall. Sooner or later, a ship would appear. Would it be Massilian or Roman? The eyes of Massilia watched, dazzled by morning sunlight glinting off the waves, and waited.

From behind us, never ceasing, came the sound of chanting from the temples. It swelled or receded according to the whims of the wind that carried it to our ears. For long spells I took no notice and forgot about the chanting; then I would suddenly hear it again and realize it had never gone away. Chants to Artemis, chants to Ares, chants to a host of other gods competed for the ears of Olympus. Different chants echoed simultaneously through the city. Sometimes they clashed in dissonance. Sometimes, in rare, evanescent moments, they combined in accidental harmonies of unearthly beauty.

Like everyone else on the wall, we fell to discussing what was happening and what might happen next.

"It's what Apollonides and the Timouchoi have been waiting for, praying for—the arrival of these ships from Pompey," said Hieronymus. "Unless the blockade can be broken, it's only a matter of time until the city falls. Even if Trebonius can't break through the walls, starvation will do his work for him. The famine has started. Do you know, there's even talk of cutting my rations. *My* rations, the scapegoat's portion! That shows you just how badly things are going." On the wall not far away a child was crying persistently, probably from hunger. Hieronymus sighed. "You saw the fleets sail out, Gordianus. How many Massilian galleys did you count?"

"Eighteen, plus a number of smaller craft."

"And Caesar's galleys, how many of those did you count?"

"Eighteen as well."

"And word has it that the fleet from Pompey numbers eighteen vessels as well. No doubt the priests will find some mystical significance in these multiples of eighteen! But what it means in practical terms is that the combined Massilian and Pompeian ships outnumber those of Caesar two to one. A clear advantage that any gambler would appreciate! Except, of course, that we've already seen what happens when Massilian galleys run up against those of Caesar, even when Caesar's ships were built in a rush and manned by infantry—disaster for Massilia! Granted, Pompey's reinforcements should provide at least an even match . . . but why did their commander anchor at Taurois? Why didn't he sail straight to Massilia if his intention is to break the blockade? There's something not quite right about this so-called 're-lief' force. Do you know what I think? I think they're headed for Spain to join with the Pompeian navy there, and this stop in the vicinity of Massilia is no more than a courtesy call, to sniff the wind and see which way it's blowing. Oh, they'll render assistance to Massilia—as long as it's not too much bother. But what sort of fight are they going to put up when they see the kind of warriors they're up against and their own blood begins to color the sea red? Say, what's this?" From his pouch he produced another stuffed date, peered at it distastefully, then flung it into the sea. I heard a little moan from Davus, followed by the sound of his stomach growling.

"You may be right, Hieronymus," I granted. "But you may be wrong. I can imagine another scenario. The fleets do battle and Caesar's ships are destroyed. Why not? Pompey has officers every bit as clever as Caesar's, and fighting men who are just as brave. The blockade is broken. The Timouchoi regain control of the sea and the coastline. Trading vessels can come and go. The city's food stores are replenished; the famine is lifted. As long as the walls hold firm, Massilia can hold off Trebonius indefinitely. Or perhaps do better than that: If these eighteen ships from Pompey arrive in Massilia filled with soldiers, Domitius and Apollonides might even dare to mount a counterattack against Trebonius. Trebonius could be forced to retreat, might even be destroyed. If Massilia can be made into a secure stronghold for Pompey, then Caesar's route back to Italy would be blocked. He could be trapped in Spain. Meanwhile, Pompey could muster his forces in Greece and Asia, sail back to Italy to take on Marc Antony—"

" 'Might' . . . 'Could' . . . 'What if?' " Hieronymus shook his head. "In a universe ruled by capricious gods, anything is possible. But close your eyes. What do you hear? A child crying because it's hungry. Apollonides and the Timouchoi are responsible for that. When Caesar came knocking at our gates, they made a choice—and they chose wrongly. That was the moment to seek the gods' wisdom. Now it's too late. . . ."

So we spent the long day, talking politics and warfare. When those subjects paled, we moved on to others—our favorite Greek dramas and Roman comedies, the relative merits of various philosophers, the prose of Caesar compared to that of Cicero. Hieronymus delighted in being argumentative. Whatever side I took, he took the other, and usually got the better of me. To his advantage, he seemed freshly versed on every subject, like a schoolboy immersed in learning. In his role as scapegoat, his every pleasure had been catered to; books, denied him in his years as a beggar, were among those pleasures. Massilia was famous for its academies and had no shortage of books. They had been delivered to the scapegoat's house by the wheelbarrow-full. He had stuffed himself with scrolls just as he had stuffed himself with food.

Hours passed. The chanting from the temples never ceased.

Davus contributed little to the conversation, except for an occasional grumble from his stomach. I grew hungry too, if the stirring of appetite experienced by a well-fed man when he goes without food for a few hours is worthy of being called hunger. How did it compare to what the spectators along the battlements were experiencing? In a city under siege, noncombatants always receive smaller rations than their defenders. Women, children, and the old are the first victims of famine, and the least able to withstand it. To what level of daily, hourly craving had the spectators around us already descended? How much thinner would they be stretched, and how much longer would they have to endure it? Truly starving people will eat anything to fill their bellies—wood shavings, the stuffing from pillows, even dirt. Hunger robs its victims of every shred of dignity before it snuffs out their lives. And for those who survive starvation, pestilence inevitably follows. Then surrender to the besieger; then rape, plunder, slavery. . . .

Like the spectators along the battlements, I anxiously watched the sea.

"Do you know the Fallacy of *Enkekalymmenos?*" Hieronymus suddenly asked.

Davus furrowed his brow at the long Greek word.

"The Fallacy of the Veiled One," I translated.

"Yes. It goes something like this: *'Can you recognize your mother?' 'Of course.' 'Do you recognize this veiled one?' 'No.' 'Yet this veiled one is your mother. Hence you can recognize your mother . . . and not recognize her.'* "

I frowned. "Whatever made you think of that?"

"I'm not sure. Something I read recently. Aristotle, was it? Or Plato . . . ?"

Davus looked thoughtful. "I don't see the point. You could put a veil over any woman and trick her child into not recognizing her. But—it wouldn't necessarily work." He raised an eyebrow and looked uncommonly shrewd. "What if the child recognized her perfume?"

"I suspect the veil is metaphorical, Davus."

"The fallacy is an epistemological allegory," Hieronymus interjected, but this, too, was Greek to Davus.

I cleared my throat, willing to debate the fallacy out of simple boredom. "How do we know what we know? How can we be sure of what we know? And what do we mean by 'knowing,' anyway? Very often we say we 'know' a person or a thing, when all we really mean is that we know what they look like. To truly know a thing, to know its essence, is knowledge of a different order."

Hieronymus shook his head. "But that's not the point of the fallacy. The point is that you can both *know* and *not know* at the same time. You can be in a state of knowledge and in a state of ignorance about the same subject *simultaneously*."

I shrugged. "That merely describes most people, about most subjects, most of the time. It seems to me—"

"Look!" said Davus. "Look there!"

A ship had appeared, sailing around the headland from the direction of Taurois. By the pale blue pennant atop its mast, we knew at once that it was a Massilian vessel.

A great cheer erupted from the spectators. Old men stamped their feet. Children let out shrill screams. Women who had stood for hours beneath the hot sun swooned and fainted. Although the ship was still too far off to appreciate the sight, many of the spectators waved their bits of cloth in the air.

The cheering grew louder as the vessel approached the harbor entrance. But no other vessel was seen to be following, and the cheering began to fade. Of course, the fact that the ship was arriving alone did not necessarily forebode something sinister; perhaps it was a messenger ship sent ahead of the rest to carry news of victory. Still, there was something disturbing in the way the ship approached, not on a steady course but veering back and forth erratically, as if the crew were shorthanded or completely exhausted. As the vessel drew nearer, it became evident that it had suffered considerable damage. The ramming beak at the prow was in splinters. Many of the oars had been lost or broken, so that the long row along the waterline had as many gaps as a beggar's grin. The remaining oars moved out of time with each other, as if the rowers had no drummer to keep them to a rhythm. The deck was a shambles, with overturned catapults and broken planking, scattered with prostrate bodies that did not move. The crewmen who manned the sail did not wave as they approached the harbor entrance but kept their eyes downcast and their faces averted. One figure in particular I noticed, an officer wearing a light blue cape. He stood alone at the prow of the ship, but instead of facing forward he kept his back to the city, as if unable to bear the sight of Massilia.

The cheering dwindled until it died altogether. A cold silence descended upon the spectators.

All eyes turned toward the headland, watching for the next ship to appear. But when ships were sighted—many ships, a whole fleet sailing in formation—they were not where anyone expected to see them. They were well out to sea, far beyond the offshore islands, barely within sight. They were sailing with all speed in a westerly direction, away from the scene of the battle and away from Massilia.

"Davus, you brag about your keen eyesight. What do you see out there?" I asked, though I already knew what the answer must be.

He shaded his brow and squinted. "Not Massilian ships; no pale blue pennants. And not those rough-hewn galleys of Caesar's, either. But they *are* Roman warships."

"How many?"

He shrugged. "Quite a few."

"Count them!"

I watched his lips move. "Eighteen," he finally announced. "Eighteen Roman galleys."

"The so-called relief ships from Pompey! All together. All intact. Sailing off toward Spain. They didn't take part in the battle at all! They must have hung back, watching and waiting. If the Massilian fleet had looked a fair match for Caesar's, surely they would have joined the fight. This can only mean—"

I was interrupted by a sound so strange, so full of hopeless despair, it froze my blood. The damaged, returning vessel must have reached the harbor and been boarded by those anxiously awaiting it. The crew had delivered their news. The sound I heard must have originated there, with the first men to hear that news. They moaned. Those who stood behind them heard the noise they made and repeated it. That wailing moan was a message without words, more devastating than any words could be.

It spread through the city like flames through a forest, growing louder and louder. It reached the pious in their temples, whose chanting abruptly turned to shouts and screams. It reached the spectators on the wall and moved toward us so rapidly and so palpably that I cringed as it approached and broke over us like a wave of pure despair.

The whole city joined in a great collective moan. I had never heard anything like it. If the gods have ears, they surely heard it, too, yet the heavens gave no response; the sky remained a blank. Even a hard-hearted man can be stirred to pity by a bleating lamb or a whimpering dog. Are the gods so much higher than mortals that they can hear the despair of a whole city and feel nothing?

A kind of madness gripped the spectators along the wall. Women dropped to their knees and tore their hair. An old man climbed atop the wall and jumped into the sea. People turned toward the Sacrifice Rock, pointed at the scapegoat and screamed curses in Greek too fast and too crude for me to follow.

"I think perhaps it's time for me to go home," said Hieronymus. His voice was steady but his face was pale. He had slipped off his shoes while sitting cross-legged on the rock. He stood and bent over to slip them on again, then gave a little cry and reached down. He had stepped on something.

"Pretty," was all he said as he held it up and peered at it. It glinted in the sunlight: a ring made of silver, quite small, as if for a woman's finger, and set with a single stone. The stone was dark and shiny. He slipped it into the pouch that had contained the stuffed dates. I wanted to have a closer look, but Hieronymus was in a rush. More curses were shouted at him. The crowd on either side was gradually converging toward the Sacrifice Rock.

The way down the slanting rock face was simple compared to the method by which Davus and I had climbed onto the summit from the wall. We descended more swiftly than I would have preferred, but I never felt the sort of danger I had felt swinging over empty space with Davus's hand clutching mine. Above and all around us the moaning continued. As we descended, the noise, echoing off the city walls, grew even louder and more unearthly.

Near the base the way grew steeper, so that we had to climb down backwards, facing the rock. As we neared the bottom I looked over my shoulder and was relieved to see that the area looked deserted; I had feared that an angry crowd might await the scapegoat. But where was the green litter that had brought him? It appeared that his litter bearers had panicked and taken flight.

Then I glimpsed a figure in the shadows of a nearby building and almost lost my footing. Davus was beside me. I gripped his arm.

"Look there!" I whispered. "Do you see?"

"Where? What?"

It was the same cowled figure we had first seen outside the city, then again on the way back from Verres's house. "*Enkeka-lymmenos*," I whispered.

"What?"

"The veiled one."

The figure haltingly stepped from the shadows and moved toward the base of the rock as if to meet us. He raised his hands. For a moment it seemed that he intended to push back the cowl and show his face.

Suddenly he stiffened and looked over his shoulder toward the shadows from which he had come. He bolted in the opposite direction, his cloak billowing after him, and vanished.

A moment later I saw what had caused him to flee. A troop of soldiers appeared from the shadows and marched straight to the foot of the Sacrifice Rock.

Their commander signaled for his men to halt, then crossed his arms and glowered up at us. "Scapegoat! Reports reached the First Timouchos that you were seen on the Sacrifice Rock, trespassing on sanctified ground. By order of the First Timouchos,

I command you to vacate the site immediately. The same goes for your two companions."

"Well, really!" said Hieronymus, sounding petulant and a little out of breath. The rock flattened considerably at the base, so that he was able to turn about and take the last few steps facing the officer head-on. Davus followed him, hanging back a bit to make sure that I stepped off the rock safely.

"There, we're off the rock. Now that you've done your job, you can run along," Hieronymus snapped at the officer. "Unless you're here to escort me safely home. My litter seems to have vanished, and there's an ugly mob forming along the battlements—"

"I'm here to escort you, but not to your house," said the officer, sneering.

Hieronymus's sarcasm suddenly deserted him. From behind I saw his fingers tremble. He clenched his hands to stop the shaking. He swayed as if he were dizzy.

If the soldiers did not mean to escort him home, then where?

Massilia had lost its navy. Massilia had been betrayed by Pompey. Her people already faced starvation and pestilence; now they could look forward to capitulation and total catastrophe. Their city was older than Rome, her ancient ally; older even than their mutual enemy, Carthage. But Carthage had been destroyed, obliterated so completely that no trace of that once-great city, or its proud people, remained. Massilia could be destroyed just as completely. Until now, hope had staved off that cruel realization. Now hope was gone. Was this the moment for the scapegoat to earn his name? Had the priests of the *xoanon* Artemis determined that now, in this darkest hour, the time had come for the scapegoat to take all the sins of the troubled city upon his shoulder and, with him, into oblivion? Had these soldiers come to drive him back up the rock, onto the precipice, and over the edge—no longer trespassing, but enacting his destiny—while all Massilia watched and cursed his name?

I held my breath. At last the officer spoke.

"You're not to return to your own house, Scapegoat. I'm to take you directly to the house of the First Timouchos. And I have orders to bring along these two as well." He glared at Davus and me. "Come along!"

Meekly, we obeyed. The soldiers drew their swords and formed a phalanx around us. At a quick pace we headed away from the Sacrifice Rock toward the house of Apollonides.

XVI

As we made our way through the heart of the city, I had cause to be thankful for our armed escort.

The streets were crowded with men and women rushing aimlessly about in panic. Hieronymus in his green robes was quickly recognized. Shouts of "Scapegoat! Scapegoat!" preceded us. At first, the citizens we passed were content to yell curses, shake their fists, and spit on the ground. Then a few of them began to dog our little retinue, running alongside us, waving their arms and screaming hysterically, their faces twisted with hatred. Soon we were surrounded by a roving mob. Urged on by their fellows, a few men, and even some women, dared to rush the moving phalanx. The soldiers shoved them roughly back with their shields, but several of them managed to thrust a hand past the soldiers. They reached for the scapegoat; failing to clutch him, they made obscene gestures. One managed to wriggle his head through. He spat in Hieronymus's face before being thrown back into the crowd.

Finally the commander ordered his men to use their swords if necessary. When the next man rushed the phalanx, there was a flash of steel and a piercing scream. My face was spattered with warm drops. I wiped my cheeks. Beyond the blood on my fingertips, I caught a glimpse of the wounded man as he fell back, howling and clutching his arm.

The mob kept its distance after that, but began to throw things at us, using whatever was at hand—fistfuls of gravel and small rocks, bits of broken paving stones and fragments of roofing tiles, scraps of wood, even household items like small clay pots, which exploded with a loud pop when they struck the soldier's shields and helmets. The rain of objects became so thick that the commander ordered his men into tortoise formation. A roof of shields closed over our heads. A solid wall of shields surrounded us, with swords thrust through the breeches.

It was dark within the tortoise. I was jostled from all sides as we trudged forward. The smell of sweat from the soldiers filled my nostrils. The crashing of hurled debris was like the din of a hail storm.

"Impious fools! Hypocrites! Idiots!" Hieronymus clenched his fists and shouted at the top of his lungs. "The person of the scapegoat is sacred! Harm me now and you only curse yourselves!" His cries were drowned by the clatter and the screams of the mob.

At last we reached our destination. The commander shouted orders. The soldiers contracted into an even tighter formation. We passed through a portal of some sort. Bronze gates clanged shut behind us, muffling the cries of the mob outside. The soldiers broke formation.

We were in a small, graveled courtyard. Relieved to be free of the tortoise and the mob, I turned my eyes upward and for a brief, incongruous moment I was struck by the beauty of the sky above us. It was the hour of twilight. The firmament was dark blue at its zenith, lightening toward the horizon to shades of aquamarine and an improbable orange, streaked with high bands of tenuous, elongated clouds suffused with the blood-red glow of dying sunlight.

I was drawn back to the moment by the clatter of debris hurled against the closed gate behind us. The mob had not dispersed. The soldiers were busy making sure that the crossbar securing the gates was properly in place. Their commander, looking a bit unnerved, mounted the short flight of steps that led up to the porch of a grand-looking house. Its door was open. On the threshold, Apollonides stood with his arms crossed, looking down at us.

"First Timouchos!" barked the officer, saluting. "As you ordered, I've brought the scapegoat, along with the two men who were seen with him trespassing on the Sacrifice Rock."

"You took your time fetching them here."

"I took the most direct route, First Timouchos. Our progress was . . . difficult."

Something—a large wine jug perhaps—crashed against the courtyard gates with a loud explosion.

"I want that mob dispersed at once," said Apollonides.

"First Timouchos, the noise is misleading. They're not as dangerous as you might think. They're completely disorganized. Loud, but not armed—"

"Then they should be easily dispersed."

The officer ground his jaw. "The sight of the scapegoat excited them. Perhaps if we allow them a little time to cool off—"

"At once, I said! Call up archers. Spill some blood if you have to, but clear the streets immediately. Do you understand?"

The officer saluted and backed down the steps. Apollonides turned his attention to us. He glared at Davus and me, then settled his gaze on Hieronymus, who stared sullenly back at him. "You're lucky to still be alive," Apollonides finally said.

"The goddess protects me," answered Hieronymus, his voice steady but hoarse from yelling. "I have a higher purpose."

Apollonides's pale blue eyes flashed. A thin smile spread across the mouth too small for his massive jaw. "Call it what you want.

Your higher purpose will still lead you straight to Hades. When you meet them there, give your parents my regards."

Hieronymus stiffened, and for a moment I thought he might rush up the steps and hurl himself at Apollonides. But Apollonides, a better judge of Hieronymus than I, never flinched.

"Am I under arrest, then?" demanded Hieronymus.

Apollonides snorted. "Don't be ridiculous. I had you brought here for your own safety. You should be thankful for my diligence."

"And my friends? Are they under arrest?"

Apollonides glowered at us. "I'm not sure. I haven't yet made up my mind. Would you believe I've had other things to think about today? In the meantime, you'll all spend the night here—where I can keep an eye on you."

Apollonides withdrew without another word. Slaves escorted us into the house to show us to our quarters. On the way, we passed through the central garden, where evidently a dinner party of considerable size was being prepared. A little army of slaves hurried this way and that, carrying couches, small tables, portable lamps, and stacks of empty serving trays. A celebration feast, I thought; only tonight there would be no cause for celebration.

While Hieronymus was shown to his own private quarters, Davus and I were escorted down the same hallway but in the opposite direction. We descended a short flight of steps. The hallway grew narrower, the ceiling lower, the way more poorly lit, until at last we came to a tiny, windowless room at the very end of the hallway. There were two small sleeping cots and just enough space to walk between them, if I angled my body sideways. A feeble light was cast by a little hanging lamp burning rancid oil. I fell onto my cot and realized, with a long exhalation, how weary I was. But sleep was impossible. Every time I closed my eyes, I saw twisted faces from the mob.

At the sound of footsteps, I sat up. Hieronymus stood in the doorway. He surveyed our accommodations and raised an eyebrow. "Cozy," was all he said.

"I suppose your own quarters are rather larger."

He shrugged. "An anteroom, a bed chamber, and another room with a private balcony. Anything less would be an insult to the goddess!"

By the lamp's flickering light I noticed a shiny object on the little finger of his left hand. It was the ring set with a black stone that he had discovered on the Sacrifice Rock. In the rush of events, I had forgotten about it.

He followed my gaze and wriggled his finger, making the stone flash in the light. "A tight fit, even on my little finger. What do you make of it, Gordianus?"

"A woman's ring, obviously. I don't think I've ever seen a stone quite like it."

"No? I suppose they're more sought after in Massilia than elsewhere, on account of the *xoanon* Artemis. It's a bit of skystone, fallen from the heavens, just as the *xoanon* Artemis fell to earth long ago. Skystones aren't necessarily pretty. Sometimes they're quite ugly, in fact, but this one is rather interesting; not solid black, you see, but with smoky swirls of silver shot through it, and as smooth and shiny as polished marble. Quite valuable, I imagine."

"The sort of ring a Massilian might give to his lover?"

"I suppose, if the man were rich and the lover beautiful enough to wear such fine jewelry." With a bit of effort he twisted it off his finger and handed it to me.

"What was it doing on the Sacrifice Rock?" I asked. "We've seen how difficult it is to get to the summit. No one goes there casually, especially now, with everyone banned from climbing the rock. So how did this ring come to be there?"

Hieronymus pursed his lips. "We do know of two people who were on the rock not long ago. The officer in the light blue cape and the woman who jumped."

"Who was pushed," corrected Davus.

I nodded. "Apollonides dispatched his men to have a look in the vicinity of the Sacrifice Rock, but he explicitly forbade them to climb onto the rock itself. We must assume that the summit of the Sacrifice Rock was never searched. This ring may have been there ever since."

"Perhaps," conceded Hieronymus. "But how did it get there in the first place? It seems unlikely that it could have slipped accidentally from the woman's finger, unless she had very small hands indeed."

"Perhaps she pulled the ring off her finger before she . . . went over the edge," I said.

"Or perhaps the man pulled it off," suggested Davus. "We saw them struggle for a bit, remember? Perhaps he pulled it off her finger, then dropped it when he pushed her—"

"When she *jumped*," insisted Hieronymus.

"In either case, if this ring *did* come from the woman's finger. . . ." I left the thought unfinished. "Do you mind, Hieronymus, if I keep it for a while?"

"You can cast it into the sea for all I care. I've no use for it." He pressed a hand to his belly. "Do you suppose we can expect anything resembling a meal this evening?"

Davus's stomach growled sympathetically.

As if on cue, a young slave appeared in the shadowy hallway behind Hieronymus. "Dinner is served in the garden," he announced.

"A dinner under the stars—delightful!" said Hieronymus, turning to smile at the slave.

By the lamp's feeble glow I saw the boy's look of surprise. His eyes grew wide, then he stepped back and averted his face. "Not . . . not for you," he managed to stutter. "I've come for the two Romans."

"Then where am *I* to eat?" demanded Hieronymus.

"In . . . your rooms," the slave stuttered, his voice hardly more than a whisper, his face turned away from the scapegoat.

"Of course," said Hieronymus dryly. "What was I thinking? The scapegoat dines alone."

The garden was dimly lit. In the few lamps scattered about, the flames burned low. Oil, like food, had become scarce in Massilia.

The light was so uncertain that I had trouble estimating how many people had gathered in the garden; perhaps fifty or more. If this had been intended to be a celebration dinner, whom would the First Timouchos have invited? The most exalted of his fellow Timouchoi; the priests of Artemis; military leaders; perhaps a few important Roman exiles; certainly the Roman military commander. Sure enough, I noticed Domitius reclining on one elbow on a dining couch, sipping from a cup of wine. The slave escorted us to the empty couch next to him.

Domitius peered at us blearily. If anyone should have felt betrayed by the day's events, it was him. In Italy he had disregarded Pompey's advice, made a stand at Corfinium against Caesar, and even before the siege was underway had been handed over to Caesar by his own men. Now, once again trapped in a city besieged by Caesar, he had desperately looked to Pompey for relief—and the ships sent by Pompey had sailed past Massilia and into the sunset.

His speech was slurred. "There you are, troublemaker. I suppose you know you've caused me considerable embarrassment today. A fellow Roman—my personal responsibility—trespassing on sacred ground! What were you thinking, Gordianus?"

"Davus and I wanted to watch the fleet sail out," I said blandly. "The walls were very crowded. The Sacrifice Rock seemed to offer the best vantage point."

"You knew it was forbidden."

"Can a visitor be expected to remember every local custom?"

Domitius took this fiction for what it was worth and snorted cynically. "You can climb up the Sacrifice Rock and take a piss off it for all I care. Better yet, take a leap into the sea. It's probably the only way to get out of this godforsaken place." He held up his empty cup. A slave appeared from the shadows and refilled it. "Only thing they seemed to have stockpiled in adequate amounts—good Italian wine. And slaves to pour it. What a wretched little town this is!" He made no effort to lower his voice. I looked about. Guests were still arriving. The mood of the place was somber and the conversations quiet. Quite a few heads turned our way in response to Domitius's outburst.

"If you're not careful," I said quietly, "your own tongue shall cause you more embarrassment than I ever could."

He laughed bitterly. "I'm a Roman, Gordianus. I have no manners and no fear. That's how we've managed to conquer the world. How some of us have managed to conquer it, anyway. Ah, but here's another glorious loser—Milo! Over here!"

Out of the shadowy crowd Milo appeared, looking as glum and bleary-eyed as Domitius. He dropped onto the couch next to Domitius and snapped his fingers. When the slave brought more wine, I declined; it seemed a night to keep my wits about me.

The garden was a square surrounded by a colonnade. In the center there was a dry fountain with a conventional statue of Artemis. Couches were gathered in U-shapes, alternately facing in or out from the center so that in rows they formed a sort of Greek key pattern of the type one often sees along the hem of a chiton. In this way guests faced in all four directions and there was no true center or focus; the layout also made it possible to overhear conversations from parties that were nearby but faced another direction. Our immediate vicinity seemed to be reserved for Romans. I heard the low murmur of Latin all around. Looking over his shoulder at me from a nearby couch, I saw Gaius Verres, who had the temerity to wink at me.

The guests included both sexes, though men greatly outnumbered women. The women, I noticed, following Massilian custom and in marked contrast to Rome, took no wine.

Apollonides and his retinue were the last to arrive. Everyone stood (some, like Domitius and Milo, not steadily) in deference to the First Timouchos. The grim-faced men surrounding Apollonides I took to be his closet advisors. Also in the party was a young couple. I had heard much about them. Now at last I saw them together: Apollonides's only child, Cydimache, and her husband, Zeno.

The girl wore a voluminous gown made of fine material shot through with gold and silver threads. The colorful veils that hid her face were of some gossamer stuff. On another woman such expensive and elaborate clothing might have made one think of wealth and privilege, but on Cydimache they seemed a sort of costume meant to distract curious onlookers from the misshapen, hunchbacked form within. Even her hands were concealed. Without a single, recognizable human feature for the eye to connect to, one might almost imagine that some bizarre animal had entered our midst beneath those mounds of veils.

She shambled slowly along with an uneven gait. The rest of the party checked their strides so as not to get too far ahead of her. There was something profoundly unsettling about the sight of that little retinue headed by the most powerful man in Massilia, towering, big-jawed Apollonides, held back by the twisted form of Cydimache. The moment seemed supremely strange; I realized that I had never before seen such a misshapen mortal in such a context, finely dressed and dining in a place of honor among the rich and powerful. One only ever sees such wretched creatures wearing rags, sleeping in gutters, and begging in the poorer parts of town. No one knows where they come from; no one can imagine how they continue to exist. Respectable Roman families would never allow such a monster to live, or if they did, would hide it away and never be seen with it in public. But to become a Timouchos required offspring, and Cydimache had been Apollonides's only child; he could not deny her. It might even be, as Milo said, that Apollonides loved her, as any man might love his only daughter. I thought of my own daughter in Rome—Diana, so bright and beautiful—and felt pity for Apollonides.

And what of the young man who walked beside Cydimache, solicitously holding her arm, though his support did nothing to straighten her crooked gait? I had heard that Zeno was handsome, and he was. He had the kind of dark, brooding good looks that one associates with wild young poets. His dark hair was disheveled and his eyes had a haunted look. He had removed his battle armor but still wore his light blue officer's cape. Something in his defeated posture played upon my memory, and I suddenly realized that he must be the officer I had seen that afternoon on the sole returning ship, standing alone on the prow and facing away from the spectators on the city walls.

I noticed something else about him. It was not immediately apparent because the uneven gait of Cydimache was so much more pronounced, but Zeno, too, was limping slightly, favoring his left leg.

XVII

There were no speeches to start the evening, not even a welcome from Apollonides. Had the day turned out differently—had Massilia scored a great victory—everyone would have been happy to listen to speeches and toasts that reiterated to infinity what everyone already knew; boasting and gloating would have been not just permissible but imperative. Instead, what had been planned as a celebration felt more like a funeral, but even at a funeral the guests might have been more cheerful.

I had wondered how Apollonides planned to mount a banquet when the city was facing famine. The ingenuity of his cooks was commendable. I had never seen such exquisitely prepared and presented food served in such tiny portions or in courses spaced so far apart. In any other circumstance it would have been laughable to be served a course consisting of a single olive (and not even a large one) garnished with a small sprig of fennel. This was presented on a tiny silver plate, perhaps intended to trick the eye into perceiving a double image. Milo grunted and quipped, "So what do you think of the new Massilian cuisine, Gordianus? I can't see it catching on in Rome." No one laughed.

The dining couch I shared with Davus was placed in such a way that if I looked past Domitius and Milo I could see the nearby U-shaped array of couches where Apollonides and his party were disposed. Because of the dim lighting, I could hardly see their faces, much less read their expressions, but even their vague silhouettes were a study in dejection. When there was a lull in the murmur of Latin around me, I could overhear their conversation. Increasingly, as more wine was served, I heard one strong, ringing voice above the others. It was the voice of Zeno.

Meanwhile, Domitius and Milo kept up a rancorous, rambling conversation. It turned out that the Roman in charge of the so-called relief fleet was a certain Lucius Nasidius. I didn't know him, but they did, and had strong opinions to express. Neither Domitius nor Milo was surprised that the fellow had hung back from the battle and then turned tail when he saw the day going badly for the Massilians; either of them could have told Pompey never to dispatch a shirker like Nasidius on such a critical mission; this disaster was merely the latest in a unending stream of bad decisions by Pompey; if only one of them had been in charge of that fleet . . . and so on.

Occasionally Domitius or Milo tried to draw me into their exchange. I answered absentmindedly, straining my ears to pick up the conversation from Apollonides's little group. From the bits I was able to overhear, my suspicion was confirmed: Zeno had commanded the ship that sailed back with news of the crushing defeat. As Zeno began to talk about the battle, the murmur of Latin around me died down. Even Domitius and Milo fell silent. They kept their eyes straight ahead, but like everyone else within earshot, they began to eavesdrop.

"They don't fight like ordinary men," Zeno was saying.

"And upon what vast reservoir of experience do you base that observation, son-in-law?" asked Apollonides sharply. "How many battles have you fought in?"

"I fought in this one! And if you'd been there, you'd know what I mean. There was something almost supernatural about them. One always hears talk about the gods overseeing battles, lifting up fallen warriors, urging them on; but I don't think it was the gods out there on the water today, driving the victors. It was Caesar; the inspiration of Caesar. They shout his name to keep up each other's spirits, to shame the laggards, to frighten their enemies. I saw things today I never would have believed, the sort of things you hear in songs. Terrible things. . . ."

In the dim light I saw the veiled form of Cydimache move closer to her husband on the couch they shared, not quite touching him, as if to give comfort simply by drawing near. Did Apollonides, seated across from them, scowl? His gray silhouette sat upright, arms crossed, shoulders stiff, jaw thrust out.

Zeno went on, his words low but clear. Occasionally, when his voice grew thick with emotion, he swallowed and pressed on. "The things I saw today! Blood—fire—death. . . . There were—there were two Romans—identical—they must have been twins. They were on a Roman galley that was trying to draw alongside and board us. The Romans cast grappling hooks at us, but the hooks fell short. They kept trying to close the distance. We kept maneuvering away. Their men outnumbered ours; they'd have overwhelmed us. Our only hope was to draw far enough away to use our catapults against them, or, if we could, swing into ramming position. But the Roman captain kept after us like a hound after a bitch. At one point they drew so close that some of their men jumped aboard. Only a handful—eight or ten—not nearly enough to take command of the ship. Such braveness, almost madness! They did it for glory, you see. If the Romans finally did manage to catch us with grappling hooks and swarm over us, these men could have boasted that they were the first aboard.

"Leading these Romans who jumped on board were two twins. I saw them that close, close enough to see that they were absolutely identical. It was unnerving, like a vision, like some prodigy sent by the gods to confound us. Confusion kills a man faster than anything else in battle. One instant of uncertainty—a blink, a glance from face to face, another blink— and you're dead! They were young, these two, young and handsome, both grinning and yelling and cutting the air with their swords.

"But one of them was careless. He stepped too far ahead of his companions, exposed himself to an attack from the side. One of my men surprised him with a chopping blow—sliced the Roman's right hand clean off, the hand that was clutching his sword. The Roman *never stop grinning!* No, that's not exactly true; his grin turned into something else, but it was still a kind of grin, ghastly, frozen on his face. Blood spurted from his severed wrist. He stared at it, dumbfounded, but still with that mad grin. You'd think that would have been the end of him, but he didn't even stagger. Do you know what he did? He bent over, reached down with his left hand, and picked up the sword that was still in the grip of his severed right hand. It's unbelievable, I know, but I saw it! He managed to get hold of the sword, and then he stood up and continued to fight. He was shielding his brother, protecting him, being completely careless of his own safety. He must have known that it was over for him; he'd never survive the loss of so much blood. He swung both arms recklessly—swung his sword, swung the severed wrist from which blood spurted in great jets.

"My men fell back, horrified, sickened by the spray of blood. I managed to rally them and together we rushed him. The Roman raised his left arm high in the air. His sword was poised to come down on my skull. I thought in that instant I would surely die—but he never managed to bring down his sword. One of my men came up from the side and delivered a two-handed blow that lopped off the Roman's left arm at the elbow. The blood! The sight of him—!"

For a long moment Zeno paused. Everyone in earshot had

fallen silent to listen. Cydimache moved closer to him but did not touch him. Zeno shuddered and gasped, then drew a deep breath and went on.

"His severed left wrist was still gushing blood. His severed right elbow was pouring out gore. Horrible! And still he didn't fall. He stood upright and screamed a single word through his clenched teeth. Do you know what it was? *'Caesar!'* Not the name of his mother. Not the name of his twin. Not the name of a god, but *'Caesar!'* His brother joined him, and then the other Romans, until they were all screaming the name of Caesar as if it were a curse upon us.

"We had them now, you see. Our ship had managed to pull clear from the Roman galley. The Romans on board were stranded. My men had rallied. We greatly outnumbered them. The Romans had no hope. But still the wounded Roman—armless, handless—still he protected his brother. He screamed the name of Caesar and threw himself against us, thrashing this way and that, using his mutilated body itself as a weapon. It was uncanny, monstrous, like something from a nightmare.

"For a moment . . . for a moment I panicked. I thought: This is end of us. This is all it will take. These ten Romans, if they're all like this one, these ten alone will be able to kill us all and seize control of the ship. They're not men, they're demons!

"But they were only men, of course, and they died like men. They might have leaped into the sea to save themselves, tried to swim back to their ship or to some other Roman vessel, but instead they stood their ground and fought. The mutilated Roman finally fell. We stabbed him all over. The wounds hardly bled, he had lost so much blood already. His face was as white as a cloud. He was still grinning that horrible grin when his eyes rolled back in his head and he crumpled to the deck.

"His twin cried 'Caesar!' and threw himself against us, weeping. He was mad with grief, careless. I stabbed him in the belly, then the throat. I was shocked at how easily he died. The rest of the Romans . . . were harder to kill. They took two Massilians for every Roman. Even after they were all dead, and we had thrown their bodies into the sea, they kept on killing us. Their blood itself killed us! The deck was so slippery with the stuff that one of my men—the one who'd landed the first blow that severed the Roman's wrist—fell and broke his neck. He died instantly, flat on his back, his neck twisted, his eyes wide open, staring at the heavens."

Complete silence had fallen over the garden. The guests in the farthest corners had ceased conversing, and the slaves bearing trays beneath the colonnade had stopped to listen. Even the Artemis who stood in the dry fountain seemed to pause and listen, her bow frozen in her hands and her head tilted slightly to one side.

Cydimache moved closer to her husband. Zeno, his head bowed, reached out and laid his hand gently on her cloaked arm, as if she were the one who needed comforting.

Apollonides sat motionless, aware of the sudden, utter silence and of the spell that Zeno's words had cast over everyone. "A bad day for Massilia," he finally said, his voice almost a whisper.

Zeno let out a bitter laugh. "A bad day, father-in-law? Is that all you can say? It's nothing compared to the days to come!"

"Lower your voice, Zeno."

"Why, First Timouchos? Do you imagine there are spies among us?"

"Zeno!"

"The fact is, this is all your fault, you and the others who voted to side with Pompey against Caesar. I warned you! I told you—"

"Quiet, Zeno! That question was argued at the proper place and time. A decision was made—"

"By a group of half-witted old misers who couldn't see the future when it slapped them in the face. We should never have closed our gates to Caesar! When he came to us, seeking our help and promising his protection, we should have opened them wide and welcomed him in."

"No! Massilia has always been loyal to Rome. Nothing has changed that and nothing ever will. Pompey and the Senate are Rome, not Caesar. Caesar is a usurper, a traitor, a—"

"Caesar is the future, father-in-law! When you spurned him, that's what you turned your back on. Now Massilia has no future, thanks to you."

Cydimache laid her hand upon Zeno's arm, either to comfort him or restrain him, or both.

At this gesture of wifely devotion, Apollonides bridled. "Daughter! How can you sit there and listen to this man when he speaks to your father in such a way?"

Cydimache made no answer. I peered at her cloaked figure in the dim light. It seemed to me that she was like an oracle that would not speak—obscure, mysterious, in this world but not entirely of it. I could see nothing at all of her deformed face or body, yet her posture spoke undeniably of torn loyalties and heartbreaking grief—or did I only imagine this, misreading the silhouette of a veiled hunchback?

Zeno extricated himself from her touch—not brusquely, but tenderly—and stood. "All I know, father-in-law, is that while I was out there today, watching our ships go up in flames or crack apart and vanish in the waves, I didn't hear men yelling your name, or Pompey's name, or 'For the Timouchoi!' I heard men crying 'Caesar!' They screamed his name as they killed, and they screamed it as they died. And the men crying 'Caesar!' were the men who won the battle. I expect they shall be crying 'Caesar!' when they bring down the walls of Massilia. 'Caesar!' will be the name we hear as they cut our throats, and 'Caesar!' will be in the ears of our wives and daughters when they're stripped and raped and carried off to be slaves."

This was too much for many of the listeners. There were gasps, grunts, cries of "Shame!" and "Hubris!"

Even in the dim light, I could see that Apollonides trembled with fury. "Go!" he whispered hoarsely.

"Why not?" said Zeno. "I've lost my appetite, even for this pathetic fare. Come, wife."

Apollonides turned his gaze to Cydimache, who seemed to hesitate. At last she rose laboriously to her feet and stood, hunched over, beside her husband. With excruciating slowness, the two of them left the garden, Cydimache shambling along, Zeno limping slightly and holding her arm. Apollonides kept his gaze straight ahead.

In the wake of Zeno's exit, the party became strangely animated. The buzz of low conversation came from every corner. People felt obliged to share their outrage at Zeno, or their agreement with him; or perhaps they felt obliged to babble simply to fill the awkward silence.

"Stay here," I whispered to Davus.

As I stepped past Milo, he pointed over his shoulder and muttered, "You'll find them that way," thinking I was searching for the privies. "Primitive, compared to Roman plumbing," he added.

I took a roundabout way, so that it would not be too obvious that I was following Zeno. There was enough movement among the guests and the serving slaves that I attracted no attention.

They had disappeared through a doorway that opened off one of the colonnades. The doorway led to a long, wide hallway. I walked quickly, glancing into the rooms on either side, seeing no one until I came to the far end of the passage, which opened onto yet another courtyard, this one much smaller and more intimate than the one where the dinner was being held. The courtyard was dark and deserted; or so I thought, until I heard hushed voices. They came from the shadows beneath the opposite colonnade.

I held my breath and listened, but the voices were too low for me to make sense of them. They might have been arguing, and one of them was almost certainly a man's voice; beyond that I could only speculate. At last I cleared my throat and spoke.

"Zeno?"

There was a long pause. Then I heard the voice of Zeno: "Who is it?"

I stepped from the shadows of the colonnade and into the faint starlight of the open courtyard. "My name is Gordianus," I said.

A longer pause. Then: "Do I know you?"

"No. I'm a Roman. A guest of your father-in-law." This was not entirely untrue.

"What do you want?" He emerged from beneath the opposite colonnade and took a few steps toward me. His cape obscured his silhouette, but I thought I saw his right hand move to his waist, as if to reach for a dagger in a scabbard. He took another step toward me.

For a brief moment I was struck by the irony, should my lifeless body be found in this place. How many times had I been called upon to make sense of a corpse discovered in a courtyard, to ferret for clues to the killer's identity, to make sense of the crime? What a jest of the gods if Gordianus the Finder should meet his end as just such a victim as those he had spent his life puzzling over! A slave would find my body, an alarm would be raised, and the First Timouchos's dinner party disrupted. The stab wounds would be noted and the identity of the victim a mystery until someone—Domitius, Milo, Davus, Apollonides himself?—identified me. But from that point it seemed unlikely that anyone would spare much time or effort trying to solve my murder, except perhaps poor Davus.

Unless. . . .

For the briefest of instants, perhaps no longer than the blink of an eye, I entertained a most peculiar fantasy: Meto was still alive and in Massilia, and this was *his* story, not mine. I was the one destined to die, not he; and he was the one destined to grieve for me and search for my killer. I was merely the victim in someone else's story, mistakenly thinking myself to be the protagonist! This fantasy was so powerful that I was wrenched out of the moment, abruptly disengaged from reality, cast into the world where sleepwalkers dwell. It was a foreshadowing of death, such as all men must occasionally feel, especially as they grow older. What is it to be a lemur, after all, but to be written out of the world's story, to become a name spoken in the past tense, to mutely watch from the shadows while others carry on the tale of the living?

I shivered. Perhaps I lurched a bit, for Zeno stepped forward again and said, "Are you unwell?"

"Quite well," I managed to say. "But I couldn't help but notice that you walk with a slight limp."

He stiffened. From guilt, or merely in response to a stranger's rudeness? "A battle wound," he finally answered.

"From today's battle? Or have you had that limp for several days?"

He had drawn so close that even by starlight I could see the frown on his handsome face. "Who are you to ask me such a question?"

"In Rome they call me the Finder. Even here, some of your fellow citizens have heard of me. One of them came to me the other day, a man named Arausio. He was grieving for his daughter. Her name was Rindel."

Beyond Zeno, a figure moved from behind one of the concealing columns. The deep shadows of the colonnade still obscured her, but the misshapen silhouette of Cydimache was unmistakable.

"What do you want?" asked Zeno sharply, whispering. "Why are you telling me this?"

I lowered my voice to match his. "Does the name Arausio mean nothing to you? Or the name Rindel?"

Again he reached toward his dagger. I felt a tremor of fear, but his agitation emboldened me. "Listen to me, Zeno. Arausio thinks he knows what became of his daughter, but he can't be sure—"

"What concern is this of yours, Roman?"

"When a father loses a child, he needs to know the truth. The pain of not knowing gnaws at a man, robs his sleep, poisons every breath. Believe me, I know! Arausio believes that only you can tell him the truth of what happened to his daughter." I glanced at the figure of Cydimache, which remained in the shadows. "If you have nothing to hide, then why have we lowered our voices to keep your wife from hearing?"

"My wife—" Zeno seemed to choke on the word. "My wife has nothing to answer for. If you dare even to speak her name, I swear by Artemis that I'll kill you where you stand!"

He had killed men already that day. I couldn't doubt that he would kill one more. Did I dare to push him any harder? If he saw me reach into the little pouch at my waist, he might misinterpret the movement and draw his dagger; so I moved very slowly and said very softly, "I have something I want to show you, Zeno. It's in this pouch. Here, I'm pulling it out now. Can you see it between my fingers?"

I found myself wishing that the light was stronger, the better for him to see the ring and for me to study his face. Did he recognize the ring or not?

Darkness obscured his face, but I heard him make a strange choking noise between a swallow and a gasp. He drew back. Alarm, or the lameness of his right leg, caused him to stumble. Cydimache lurched forward out of the deep shadows, clutching her robes to her breast; for all she knew, I had struck him a blow.

Zeno looked over his shoulder. "Stay back!" he cried, with a sob in his voice. He turned back to me and drew his dagger. The blade gleamed in the starlight.

His ears were sharper than mine. He suddenly stiffened and lowered his arm. Keeping his eyes on something behind me, he stepped back into the shadows of the colonnade. He slipped an arm around Cydimache, brought his face close to hers, whispered. The two of them withdrew into deeper darkness.

"Father-in-law, here you are!"

I gave a start as Davus stepped up beside me. My heart pounded in my chest. I wasn't sure whether to thank him or curse him. Had he spoiled the moment when Zeno might have weakened, or had he saved my life?

I let out a long sigh and stared at the darkness into which Zeno and Cydimache had vanished.

XVIII

"After tonight, three things are clear," I said, raising a finger to tick the points off one by one. Had there been space in the tiny room I would have paced. Instead, I sat on my narrow bed with my back against the wall, idly tapping the floor with one foot. Davus sat across from me, knocking his cramped knees together.

"First, Zeno recognized this ring." I rolled it between my fingers, studying the strange stone by the feeble lamplight. "His reaction was powerful and immediate."

"Then the ring *did* come from Rindel, and somehow got left on the Sacrifice Rock when Zeno pushed her off," said Davus.

I shook my head. "That doesn't necessarily follow. We don't know for certain that this ring belonged to Rindel; we still don't know for certain that it was Rindel, or even Zeno, we saw on the rock that day; and we don't know, despite your certainty, that the woman we saw was *pushed.*"

"But it must have been Zeno! We saw him limping tonight."

"His limp could have another explanation. He told me it was from a battle wound."

Davus snorted. "I'll wager he had that limp long before he sailed off to battle this morning. That should be simple enough to find out. His fellow officers would know how long he's been limping. Apollonides would know."

"That's easily resolved, then; I'll just interrogate the First Timouchos at my convenience, shall I? But you're right that his lameness isn't something Zeno could hide from his comrades. It would be instructive to know just how long he's exhibited that limp."

I raised another finger and ticked it off. "The second thing we now know for sure is that Zeno truly loves Cydimache. Despite what Domitius told me about her ugliness and deformity, despite Arausio's presumption that Zeno abandoned Rindel and married the First Timouchos's daughter merely to better himself, the two newlyweds share a genuine affection for each other. Did you see them tonight? The way she drew closer to him, to calm him; the way he touched her, casually, almost without thought, yet tenderly. That wasn't an act. I saw a man and woman physically at ease with each other, united by a bond of trust."

Davus snorted. "You could say the same thing about a man and a horse."

"Cydimache is a woman, Davus."

"A woman, a horse—if Zeno is as calculating and ambitious as Arausio thinks, which woman he marries may matter to him no more, and no less, than which beast he takes for transport. All he's looking for is a reliable means to get where he's going, and marrying Cydimache took him straight to the top. But now that he's arrived, he's stuck with her, and he'll have to get her with child if he's to become a Timouchos. So he's forced himself to do the act with her, and for that she's grateful. Why shouldn't she coo and comfort him? And in the process, he's gotten used to her. A man can get used to just about anything in this world—any man who's ever been a slave can tell you that. So Zeno is able to touch her without shuddering—what of it? Especially the way she keeps herself covered; probably she stays bundled like that when he makes love to her, and Zeno just shuts his eyes and thinks of pretty Rindel."

"What! Pictures the girl whom, according to you, he cold-bloodedly pushed off the Sacrifice Rock?"

" 'Cold-blooded'—that's exactly the word for a man like Zeno!"

I shook my head. "No, there's more to this marriage between Zeno and Cydimache than you credit. The way they touched—it reminded me of the way that you and Diana touch, not even realizing it. Yes, exactly the same."

Davus lowered his eyes. A frown pulled at his mouth. With his relentless good nature, it was sometimes easy for me to forget that Davus, too, was far from home, and homesick. He cleared his throat and asked, a little dully, "What was the third thing? You said you knew three things for certain now—that Zeno recognized the ring, that he truly cares for Cydimache . . . and what else?"

"That Zeno is no coward. The tale he told at dinner made my blood run cold. The things he saw today must have been terrifying, yet he kept his wits about him and brought his men safely home. And he didn't hesitate to stand up to his father-in-law. Zeno has nerve. He has courage. I have to ask myself: Is this the sort of fellow who would push a defenseless woman off a cliff?"

Davus crossed his arms, unimpressed. "He would if she was making trouble for him—the kind of trouble a mad, spurned woman might make for an ambitious climber."

"So you saw nothing good in Zeno? No good at all?"

"Not a thing."

"You seem very sure of yourself," I said quietly.

"Why not? I've met Zeno's type before. Haven't you?" Now

it was Davus's turn to tick points off his fingers one by one. "Does he love Cydimache? It certainly profits him to put on a show of pretending to, so he does.

"Is he heroic? Well, if his ship goes down in battle, he'll drown like the rest, so why shouldn't he fight as bravely as the next man?

"Does he have nerve? Undoubtedly. You seem to admire him for talking back to Apollonides in public, but I hardly think you'd like it if I showed that little respect for you, father-in-law.

"Could such a fine fellow kill a woman he once loved, in cold blood? Zeno happens to be good-looking and he comes from a good family, so why shouldn't he be charming and likable? That makes it all the easier for him to get away with something truly outrageous, like pushing a troublesome old lover off a cliff."

Satisfied that he had made his points, Davus tilted back his head, squeezed his eyes shut, stretched his arms over his head, and opened his jaw in a great yawn.

It was time for sleep. I doused the light. The room was so dark that I saw the same blackness whether my eyes were open or shut.

Had I judged Zeno's character so wrongly? I felt weary and confused, like an old hound who can no longer trust his nose and who finds himself, at the end of a long day's wandering, lost in fields far from home.

When I opened my eyes the next morning, I couldn't tell if it was hunger that awakened me or the noise from my stomach, so loud was the growling it made. The windowless room was dim; the only light came from the open doorway and the shadowy hall beyond. Vaguely I heard distant voices, hurried footsteps, and indistinct clattering, the sounds of a great household stirring.

It occurred to me that my preoccupation with Zeno and the incident on the Sacrifice Rock was no more than a distraction, an indulgence to keep my mind off the trouble we were in. Massilia was on the verge of chaos, perhaps complete destruction. It was one thing to pass idle days in the comfort of the scapegoat's house, quite another to face the prospect of house arrest, or worse, in the hands of Apollonides. Rather than twisting my mind around the sins of the First Timouchos's son-in-law, I should probably have spent the previous night doing everything possible to ingratiate myself with Domitius, who might be induced, if I groveled enough, to offer his protection to Davus and me.

That idea was so repugnant that I found myself instead holding up the ring in the dim morning light and peering into the depths of the black skystone.

Davus stirred. His stomach growled even louder than mine, reminding me that our most immediate problem was finding food. It seemed hard to imagine that Apollonides, with all that was on his mind, had bothered to make any provision for feeding two Roman troublemakers who had become his unwanted and unwilling houseguests. We could, I thought, set out in search of the kitchens, though it seemed unlikely that the previous night's grim travesty of a banquet had yielded much in the way of leftovers.

Davus sat up, stretched, and yawned. He stared at the ring in my hand. He blinked. His eyes narrowed. His nose twitched. As he turned and looked toward the doorway, I too caught the unmistakable scent of bread.

The loaf appeared first. The hand that held the flat, round disk was concealed behind it, so that it seemed to levitate, moonlike, of its own accord. It was followed by an arm, and then the smiling face of Hieronymus peering around the corner. "Hungry?" he asked.

"Famished," I admitted. "I left Apollonides's banquet last night hungrier than when I arrived."

"Then his skills as a host exactly match his gifts as a military man and a leader of the people," remarked Hieronymus dryly. "I brought a bit to drink as well," he said, producing a bloated wineskin.

"May the gods bless you!" I said, not thinking.

"Actually, that's the one favor I'm not allowed. But of earthly blessings, my cornucopia is filled to overflowing. Last night, while you starved at Apollonides's banquet, I dined in seclusion on—would you believe it?—not one but *two* roasted quails, with a lovely olive and fish-pickle garnish. I'd have saved some for you, but sitting up on that rock all day and then promenading through the streets was hard work for a humble scapegoat such as I." I remembered the ordeal of yesterday's near-riot and wondered how he could make a joke of it. "And after the quail came the red mullets in almond sauce, the boiled eggs rolled in lemon zest and asafetida, followed by—well, suffice it to say that the priests of Artemis insisted I stuff myself. The worse the battle news, the more they give me to eat. I feel like a goose being fattened for a feast." He patted the round belly that protruded incongruously from his tall, lanky frame. "When I woke this morning, I was still too stuffed to eat another bite—so when they brought me this freshly baked flatbread, I thought of you."

I tore the soft loaf into semicircles and gave half to Davus. I forced myself to take small bites. Davus seemed to inhale his portion without even chewing.

"You're allowed to move freely about the house, then?" I asked.

"No one dares restrain me. The slaves scatter before me like autumn leaves before Boreas. Of course, I do my best to be unobtrusive. I've no intention of barging into meetings of the war council or pestering the starry-eyed newlyweds. Otherwise, when Caesar crashes through the city gates and Cydimache produces a squalling monster, Apollonides will blame both catastrophes on me."

"Will you be going back to your own house?"

There was a ripple in his glib composure, like a wind flaw on water. "I'm afraid not."

"A punishment for trespassing on the Sacrifice Rock?"

"Not exactly. Not a punishment. A repercussion, you might say."

"I don't understand."

"I convinced the priests I had every right to climb up on the rock yesterday; I told them I had heard a summons from Artemis to go and watch for the fleet. Well, they could hardly object to that, could they? I think I managed to talk them into forgiving your trespass as well, Gordianus. They might have briefly impressed the mob by making an example of you and Davus—burning you alive, say, or hanging you upside down and flaying you like venison—but I pointed out to them that in the long term, exacting gruesome punishments against our Roman guests might not be such a good idea, considering that it now appears almost inevitable that Massilia, if the city is allowed to continue to exist at all, shall have a Roman master. If not this year, then next; if not Caesar, then Pompey. Perhaps both shall rule Massilia, one after the other. I pointed out to the priests that you were friends of both men, and that friendship these days means more to a Roman than ties of blood."

"In other words, you saved our lives, Hieronymus."

"It seemed the least I could do. I'm supposed to be a savior, aren't I? My death, in some mystical fashion, supposedly will rescue Massilia from her enemies at the last possible moment. It looks increasingly unlikely that the priests of Artemis will be able to pull off that miracle; and even if they do, I won't be around to see the results! But one thing I can do is stand here in this hole of a room and watch my only two friends, alive and reasonably well, as they devour a flatbread for which I have no use—and that gives me a curious pleasure."

"No bread ever tasted better," I said quietly.

Hieronymus merely shrugged.

"But you said that you won't be returning to your house. If you've placated the priests, why not?"

"Because it's no longer there."

I blinked. "What do you mean?"

"I mean that the scapegoat's house no longer exists. The mob burned it down."

"What!"

"It happened late last night. I suppose, buried down here, you didn't hear the horns blowing the fire alarm. I certainly heard them, up in my room. They woke me from a deep sleep. I was dreaming about my mother; a happy dream, oddly enough. Then the horns woke me. I left my bed and went to the balcony. I saw a red glow in the direction of my house. Apparently a mob gathered there after dark. They demanded that I be brought out and marched at once to the Sacrifice Rock. Apollonides had posted guards at the door, but only a few. They explained that I wasn't there, but the mob didn't believe them. The mob overwhelmed the guards and broke into the house. When they didn't find me, they ransacked the place and then set it afire." He shook his head. "Committing arson in a city under siege is not only a grievous crime, it's incredibly stupid. If the flames had spread out of control, can you imagine the result? People trapped inside the city walls, only a few ships left in the harbor to offer a means of escape, rioting, looting—a fate as terrible as anything Caesar may have in store for us!

"But the guards who had been overwhelmed summoned reinforcements and sounded the fire horns, and Apollonides's men were able to contain the flames. My house was gutted, but those around it were spared. As a result, I find myself homeless once again—what irony!—and the heads of the twenty or so looters whom Apollonides's men managed to capture are mounted on spikes amid the smoking embers. The headless bodies were dumped into the sea."

The last crust of bread turned to ashes in my mouth. "Hieronymus, this is terrible!"

"Yes. We shall no longer be able to sit on my lovely rooftop terrace, watching the clouds over the sea, drinking Falernian wine, and debating fallacies."

"No, I mean—"

"I know what you mean, Gordianus." He sighed. "Worst of all, I dare not leave this house, not even to step outside. If the mob should recognize my litter or my green robes—well, I've no intention of being *thrown* off the Sacrifice Rock." He drew back his shoulders. "When the time comes, I expect a full ceremony—incense, chanting, *et cetera,* as you Latin speakers say. And I shall not be thrown over; I shall jump of my own accord, like that poor girl we saw."

"She was *pushed*," said Davus, his voice barely audible.

Hieronymus ignored him. "So here I am, trapped in the house of Apollonides, the one place in Massilia I least want to be, and the one place where Apollonides least wants me. I suppose the goddess thinks we deserve each other. Perhaps that dour virgin, Artemis, has a sense of humor after all."

He crossed his arms and leaned against the door frame, examining our little cubicle with a sardonic expression. "I'm afraid yesterday's developments have landed you and Davus in considerably reduced circumstances. One lamp, two narrow beds, and a single chamber pot between you. There's not even a door or a curtain to give you privacy."

"It could be worse," I said. "There might be a door—with a lock on it. I'm not sure whether we're free to go or not."

"I suspect, considering the tide of events, that Apollonides has forgotten all about you. His plate is full, if you'll pardon a bad pun. You probably won't cross his mind until the next time you cross his path. These accommodations are Spartan, to say the least, but since you've nowhere better to go, I'd suggest you take advantage of his hospitality for as long as you can. Keep quiet when you're in this room. Find out where to empty that chamber pot. Ingratiate yourself with the household slaves—drop a few hints that you're a friend of Caesar's and therefore worth cultivating, though not such a good friend that you ought to be murdered in your sleep—and otherwise come and go as unobtrusively as you can."

I nodded. "The hardest thing will be finding enough to eat. I heard Milo complaining to Domitius last night about a new reduction in rations. Every portion in every household is to be cut back."

"Except for mine. Don't worry about food, Gordianus. As long as I'm about, I won't let you starve."

"Hieronymus, truly, I don't know how to—"

"Then don't, Gordianus. There's no need. And now I have to leave you. There's some tiresome ceremony or other that the priests of Artemis feel obliged to perform this morning here in the house of the First Timouchos; honoring those lost at sea yesterday, I suppose. For some reason I'm expected to make an appearance, looming in the background." He turned to go, then remembered something and reached into the small pouch he carried. "I almost forgot. Here, take these—two boiled hen's eggs, still in the shell. You can eat them for your lunch."

We had solved the problem of food, at least for the moment. But how were Davus and I to leave the house and get back in? Come and go unobtrusively, Hieronymus had advised—but how? We had entered Apollonides's compound the previous night through a heavily guarded gate. I could hardly expect to pass back and forth through a guarded gate without being vetted by the First Timouchos himself or at least showing some sort of documentation.

I took another bit of Hieronymus's advice and sought out the young slave who had escorted us to the banquet the previous night. The boy took it for granted that we were his master's guests and men of some importance, and that we were also, as was clear from my accent, from somewhere else and thus in need of simple guidance. When I asked him the easiest way to come and go, he didn't hesitate to show me the entrance the slaves used, which was a gate in a section of the wall at the back of the compound between the kitchens and the storehouses. This small gate was manned, not by an armed guard, but by an old slave who had had the job all his life. He was a garrulous, simple fellow, easy to talk to if not very easy to understand, on account of his toothlessness. When I asked him to repeat himself, I pretended it was due not to his mumbling but to my own poor Greek.

The guards at the front gate were something new, the old gatekeeper told me, called up in response to the chaos of the previous night. Ordinarily, the house of the First Timouchos required no more security than the house of any rich man, and probably less; what sneak-thief would dare to steal from the city's foremost citizen?

"Any other day this is the safest house in Massilia!" he insisted. "Still, we can't let in just anyone, can we? So when you come back, knock like this on the gate," he said, tapping his foot three times against the wood. "Or never mind that, just call out your name. I'll remember it—you've got a funny Roman name; never heard it before. Mind you be careful out in the streets. Things are getting strange out there. What kind of errand is so important you have to leave the safety of this house, anyway? Never mind, it's none of my business."

Davus stepped first through the open door into what appeared to be a narrow alley. Following him, I thought of something and turned back. "Gatekeeper," I said, "you must know the First Timouchos's son-in-law."

"Young Zeno? Of course. Uses this gate all the time. Always in a great rush, coming and going. Except when he's with his wife, of course. Then he slows his pace to match hers."

"He goes out with Cydimache?"

"Her physicians insist that she take long walks as often as she can. Zeno goes with her. It's a touching sight the way he hovers over her and dotes on her."

"I noticed last night that he was walking with a slight limp. Has he always been lame?"

"Oh, no. A fit young man. Very fit. Won races at the gymnasium when he was a boy."

"I see. Perhaps he was limping because of a wound he suffered in yesterday's battle."

"No, he's had that limp for a while. It's gotten much better."

"When was he injured?"

"Let me think. Ah, yes, it was the day Caesar's men tried to batter down the walls. A crazy day that was, with everybody running every which way. Zeno must have hurt himself running back and forth along the battlements."

"No doubt," I said. I stepped out to join Davus, who awaited me in the alley with a smug look on his face.

XIX

"The house of Arausio? You're close. Turn down this street to
the left. After a while you'll come to a house with a blue door.
Go down the little alley that runs alongside it, and when that
comes to a dead end, you'll be in what they call the Street of
the Seagulls, on account of the crazy old woman who used to
put out fish for seagulls; some days, when I was a little girl,
they were so thick in the street that you couldn't get past the
nasty creatures. To your right, the street runs up a little hill.
You'll find Arausio's house at the top. I always thought that
house must have a wonderful view of the harbor. . . ."

The speaker was a pale, thin, young woman, whose Greek was
as heavily accented as mine, though with a Gaulish, not Latin,
accent. Her fair hair was pulled back from her gaunt face, tightly
bundled at the nape of her neck with a leather band, and hung
in a tangle down her back, unwashed and badly in need of comb-
ing. She wore no jewelry, but bands of pale flesh around several

fingers showed where she customarily wore rings. Had distress driven her to sell them, or did she fear to wear them in public?

Her voice had a slightly hysterical edge. She seemed glad to have someone to talk to, even two strangers asking for directions. "Those seagulls! When I was a girl, I remember helping my mother carry food home from the market—in a basket just like the one I'm carrying today, perhaps the very same one; this basket is older than I am—and once we took that street, and it was a terrible mistake, because the gulls attacked us. Horrible creatures! They flew at me and knocked me down, stole what they wanted from my basket, and scattered the rest all over the street. Oh, my basket must have been filled with all sorts of food, olives and capers and flatbread, but of course it would have been the fish that attracted them. . . ." I glanced at the straw basket she carried at her side. The handle was of leather, and the Gaulish design featured a spiral pattern around the rim. No seagulls would attack her today for what her basket contained. It was empty.

"Down this street to the left, did you say? Thank you." I gestured for Davus to move on. A glint of madness had entered the woman's eyes.

"There, you see, Davus? I told you it would be a simple thing to find the house of Arausio. Just a matter of asking the locals."

"Yes. You keep asking, and they keep sending us in circles."

"It's these winding streets. Very confusing. Do you suppose that's the house with the blue door?"

"That's not blue, it's green."

"Do you think so?"

"And I don't see an alley running alongside it."

"No, neither do I. . . ."

Davus sucked in a sharp breath. He was justifiably exasperated, I thought, then I realized it was something more than that. "Maybe we should ask *them* for directions," he said.

"Ask whom?"

"Those two fellows following us."

I resisted the urge to look behind. "The same two we saw the other day?"

"I think so. I thought I got a glimpse of them not long after we left the First Timouchos's house. Now I've just seen them again. It can't be coincidence."

"Unless two other lost strangers are wandering the streets of Massilia in circles, looking for the house of Arausio. But who could have sent them? Who wants us followed? Surely not Apollonides. We slept last night under his roof. If he wanted to confine us, he could have locked us in a room. The fact that we're out on the streets today must mean that he's forgotten us, cares nothing about us."

"Unless he intentionally allowed us to leave his house and sent these men to see where we'd go," suggested Davus.

"Why would he do that?"

"Maybe he knows what we're up to."

"But, Davus, even I'm not sure of that."

"Of course you are. We saw Apollonides's son-in-law murder an innocent young woman, and you're trying to find the proof. Things are going quite badly enough for Apollonides these days without the scandal of a murder to taint his household."

"You're assuming that Apollonides knows that Zeno killed Rindel—"

"Perhaps he confronted Zeno. Perhaps Zeno confessed the crime to him!"

"*And* you're assuming that Apollonides knows that I have some interest in the matter."

"You witnessed it. You reported what you saw directly to Apollonides. And if he kept watch on the scapegoat's house, he knows that you had a visit from Arausio. Why else would Rindel's father have come there, except to ask about her murder."

"If I grant that you're right on all counts, then why doesn't Apollonides simply lock me in a room? Or cut off my head and be done with me?"

"Because he wants to see where you go, whom you talk to.

He wants to find out who else suspects the truth, so that he can deal with them as well." Davus tapped his head. "You know how such a man's mind works. Apollonides may be just a mullet compared to sharks like Pompey and Caesar, but he swims in the same sea. He's no less a politician than they are, and his mind works just like theirs. Always scheming, always putting out fires, trying to guess what happens next and who knows what, thinking up ways to turn it all to his advantage. It makes my head hurt, thinking about men like that."

I frowned. "You're saying I'm a hound who imagines he's out foraging on his own, but all the time Apollonides has me on a long leash?"

"Something like that." Davus wrinkled his brow. Too many metaphors had worn him out.

"Tell me, Davus, do you see our two followers now?"

He discreetly glanced over his shoulder. "No."

"Good. Because this must be the house with the blue door, and that must be the alley that runs alongside it. If we disappear around the corner fast enough, we may give them the slip."

The house of Arausio was exactly where the young woman had said it would be. We seemed to have eluded our two followers. Davus kept watch as I knocked on the door, but he saw no sign of them.

Arausio himself answered the door. Meto had once told me that this was the custom among some of the Gaulish tribes, something to do with ancient laws of hospitality, for the head of the household and not a slave to greet visitors. Arausio looked haggard and pale. It had been only two days since I had seen him in the scapegoat's house, yet even in that short space of time he seemed to have lost some vital spark. The ordeal of the siege and his own personal tragedy had worn him down.

When he recognized me, his face momentarily lit up. "Gordianus! I wondered if you were still alive! They say there's nothing left of the scapegoat's house but ashes. I thought you might have. . . ."

"I'm perfectly well. Lucky to be alive, but alive nonetheless."

"And you've come . . . with news? About Rindel?"

"No news; not yet. Only questions."

The light went out in his eyes. "Come inside, then."

It was a well-ordered house, clean and neat, with a few costly ornaments to demonstrate its owner's success—a collection of silver bowls ostentatiously displayed in one corner, a few small pieces of Greek statuary placed on pedestals here and there. Arausio's taste was more refined than I would have expected.

He led us to a room where a woman sat at a loom of some sort; the device was of a Gaulish design I had never seen before, as was the pattern of the garment she was weaving. I realized I knew very little of the Gauls and their ways. Meto had spent years among them, playing his part in Caesar's conquests, learning their various languages and their tribal customs, yet we had seldom talked about such matters. Why had I not been more curious, displayed more interest in his travels? He had always been in a rush, and so had I; there had never been time enough to really talk. Now there never would be.

The woman seated at the loom stopped what she was doing and looked up at me. I drew in a sharp breath. She was beautiful, with piercing blue eyes, and wore her blond hair as Arausio had described Rindel's hair, braided like ropes of spun gold. Was it possible that the missing Rindel had returned? But no, Arausio had been anxious for news of her, and his mood, if his daughter had come back, would have been entirely different.

The woman was not Rindel then, but Rindel's mother. From looking at Arausio's red cheeks and drooping mustache, I had formed no clear picture of the beautiful daughter who could have tempted a youth like Zeno; but if Rindel took after her mother—indeed, if she was half as beautiful—I could well imagine how Zeno might have fallen for her.

"This is my wife," Arausio said. "Her name is Rindel, too; we named our daughter for her." He smiled wanly. "It leads to all sorts of confusion, especially as they look so much alike, and my wife looks half her age. Sometimes, when we're out among strangers, people mistake the two of them for sisters. They think I'm an old man showing off his two beautiful daughters—" His voice caught in his throat.

The woman stood and acknowledged us with a slight nod. Her lips were tightly compressed and her jaw was clenched. Her eyes brimmed with sudden tears. "My husband says that you can help us."

"Perhaps, if finding the truth is of help."

"We want to know what's become of Rindel. We need to know."

"I understand."

"My husband says that you may have seen her . . . at the end."

"We saw a woman on the Sacrifice Rock. Perhaps it was Rindel. When you last saw her, what was she wearing?"

She nodded. "Arausio told me that you wanted to know this, so I've thought about it and looked through her clothes. I can't be sure, but I think she must have been wearing a simple yellow gown, not her best but fairly new."

"And a cloak of some sort? With a hood?"

She frowned. "I don't think so."

"The woman we saw wore such a cloak. It was dark, possibly green—"

"More blue than green," said Davus, interrupting.

The woman nodded. "Rindel owns such a cloak; I'd call the color a gray-green, myself. But I'm almost certain—wait here." She left the room for a moment, then returned, bearing a cloak over her arms. "Here it is. I found it among her clothes. She couldn't have been wearing it, then, not if you saw her. . . ." She lowered her eyes, then raised them. "If the woman you saw was wearing such a cloak, perhaps it wasn't Rindel you saw after all!"

Arausio took her hand and squeezed it, but when she tried to look into his eyes he pulled at his mustache and turned his face away. "Wife, you mustn't raise your hopes. We both know what happened to Rindel. There's no use—"

"Perhaps this will be more conclusive." I held up the ring with the skystone.

The two of them gazed at it curiously but made no comment.

"Did this belong to your daughter?"

"I never gave her such a ring," said Arausio.

"Not all rings given to a beautiful young woman are gifts from her father."

He frowned at the insinuation. "I never saw her wear it."

"Neither did I." His wife shook her head. She seemed fascinated by the stone, unable to take her eyes off it. "Why do you show it to us? Where does it come from?"

"It was found yesterday on the summit of the Sacrifice Rock."

Arausio's face went blank for an instant, then became twisted with rage. "*He* gave it to her! The filthy swine! He thought he could placate her—flatter her, buy her silence—with a ring! She must have thrown it at his feet in disgust. And that's when he—"

His wife put a fist to her lips and sobbed. Arausio put his arms around her and shuddered, his features torn between fury and grief.

I was in no hurry to return to Apollonides's house. We walked aimlessly about the city. Davus saw no sign of our followers.

"What do you think, Davus? If it wasn't Rindel we saw on the Sacrifice Rock, then perhaps it wasn't Zeno, either."

"Oh, no, it was Zeno we saw. And Rindel, too."

"What about the cloak she was wearing?"

He shrugged. "Maybe Rindel owned more than one such cloak, and her mother is confused. Or perhaps Rindel took her mother's cloak, and her mother simply hasn't noticed yet. It's a tiny detail."

"And the ring? Is it as Arausio said—Zeno tried to give her the ring as some sort of consolation, and when she refused it, he decided to put an end to her?"

"Not necessarily." Davus frowned. "I think Zeno must have given her the ring a long time ago, when they first became lovers."

"But her parents never saw it."

"She kept it a secret from them. That's what the ring was, a lovers' secret, shared just between her and Zeno."

"I see. And that's why she made a show of taking it off on the Sacrifice Rock—to spurn him in return?"

"Unless. . . ." Davus furrowed his brow. "This is what I really think happened. It was Zeno who pulled the ring off her finger, against her will. I think that's why he was chasing her in the first place, to take back the ring."

"Why would he do that?"

"Who knows how the mind of such a fellow works? If the ring stood for a promise he'd made to Rindel before he spurned her, then as long as she possessed it, it was a reminder of his own lies and betrayal. Perhaps Rindel threatened to confront Cydimache with it, to flaunt the fact that Zeno really loved her, not his deformed wife."

"So taking the ring from her not only retrieved the tangible evidence of his pledge, it marked a break with the past."

Davus nodded. "Once he'd done that, he found the nerve to push her off the rock and never look back."

I shook my head. "The man you're describing is a complete monster, Davus."

"Yes, he is."

We rounded a corner. I was so lost in thought that I didn't

realize where we were, even when the smell of charred wood was suddenly strong in my nostrils. That smell was mixed with the less pleasant odor of ashes doused with seawater, and another smell, which only gradually I recognized as blood; not fresh blood, but blood spilled hours ago. Suddenly, we stood before the ruins of the scapegoat's house.

The site was littered with broken, charred beams, cracked roofing tiles, pools of black water, and heaps of smoldering ashes. Usually, in the ruins of a great house, one sees remnants of furnishings and decorations—metal lamp stands and marble statues will survive a fire—but in these ruins there were no such artifacts to be seen; before it went up in flames, the scapegoat's house had been picked clean by looters. Instead, poking up from the general debris were remnants of some of the looters themselves. Scattered amid the ruins were poles driven into the mud, and mounted on the sharpened, bloodstained poles were severed heads. I heard Davus murmur quietly and saw that he was moving his lips, counting.

"Eighteen," he whispered. There were as many woman as men among them; some looked hardly older than children.

The looters must have been beheaded on the spot, for at our feet were great pools of blood. Where it lay thin on the paving stones, the blood had dried to purple, almost black. Where it lay thickest, it appeared still moist and dark red. Elsewhere it had mingled with pools of sooty water, staining them deep crimson. Eighteen bodies contain a veritable lake of blood.

I turned my face away. I was ready to return to the house of Apollonides.

Suddenly, there was a sound like a thundercrack, followed by a loud rumbling noise. The earth shook. People in the street stopped in their tracks and fell silent.

The noise was not thunder; the sky above was blue and cloudless.

"Earthquake?" whispered Davus.

I shook my head. I turned to look in the direction of the city's main gate and pointed to a great white plume that rose into the air, billowing and growing higher as we watched.

"Smoke? From a fire?" said Davus.

"Not smoke. Dust. A great cloud of dust. From the rubble."

"Rubble? What's happened?"

"Let's go and see," I said; but with a thrill of intuition that made my heart pound in my chest, I knew exactly what had occurred.

XX

"Apollonides thought he was being so clever to dig that inner moat and fill it with water. He anticipated that Trebonius would attempt to tunnel beneath the section of wall nearest the city gate, and the moat was his solution. It worked, as you and I know all too well. When the sappers broke through, the tunnel was flooded and the men sent to take the gate were horribly drowned."

Davus and I had found a spot a little away from the crowd of spectators who thronged the main market square of Massilia. We were only a few steps from the very spot where we had pulled ourselves out of the water, where I had been abused by the old man Calamitos, and where Hieronymus had come to our rescue. That all seemed very long ago.

The day had begun to wane. The sun was lowering in the cloudless sky, casting long shadows.

Some of the spectators wailed and tore their hair. Some hung their heads and wept. Some stood in stony silence. Some simply stared at this latest, most terrible catastrophe to overtake their city, their eyes wide and their jaws open in disbelief.

A cordon of soldiers kept the crowd away from the frantically working engineers. A path was kept clear for the troops of archers and the teams of laborers who kept arriving from all parts of the city. By the hundreds they converged at this spot. The laborers were dispatched to take orders from the engineers. The archers were sent to the nearest bastion towers, where they scurried up the stairwells to take up posts at the already crowded battlements.

Nothing remained of the moat but a great morass of mud and muck, in which the engineers and their workers stamped about, shouting orders and forming lines to pass broken timbers and bits of rubble toward the gaping breach in the wall.

The breach was narrowest at the top, widest at the bottom. Where the battlement platform had fallen in, a man with long legs might, with luck, be able to jump across. Immediately below that point, the breach widened dramatically and continued to widen until it reached the base of the wall. The pile of debris formed by the collapsing blocks of limestone was considerable, but much too small to contain all the stones that had fallen.

One did not have to be Vitruvius to see what had happened. Over time, the flooded tunnel beneath the wall had created a sinkhole. In a single moment, the sinkhole had given way and had swallowed up the foundation, causing a considerable section of the wall above to collapse. The gaping sinkhole had swallowed much of the resulting debris, so that only a pile of rubble, hardly taller than a man, remained to be seen.

A breach—any breach, no matter how small—in the walls of a city under siege is a disaster. Once a breach is made, it can always be widened. When it becomes wide enough, it can no longer be defended. If the besieger's forces are numerous enough—and those of Trebonius seemed to me more than sufficient—a besieged city with a breached wall must ultimately capitulate.

The great irony was that this breach had not been caused by the besiegers. Trebonius had dug the tunnel, to be sure, but the tunnel itself was much too small to undermine the wall; nor was that its purpose. It was Apollonides who had caused the wall to collapse by flooding the tunnel beneath the foundation. Even so, if after the flooding he had drained the moat and filled the mouth of the tunnel with debris, the sinkhole might have been prevented. But Apollonides had left the moat in place, and in fact had refilled it day by day as the water level continually dropped. He and his engineers had created the sinkhole themselves, and the collapsed foundation was the result.

Apollonides's response was to fill in as much of the breach as he could, as quickly as possible. While the engineers and their workers gathered the scattered debris, archers on the wall stood ready to protect them should Trebonius mount an assault. So far, no assault had materialized, possibly because Apollonides had flown a white flag from the battlements above the breach, a signal that he was willing to parley.

Davus tugged at my elbow and pointed. Two figures had emerged from the mass of soldiers gathered around the breach and were walking toward us. It was the First Timouchos himself with his son-in-law following behind. Both were in full battle armor. Both were covered with mud from the waist down, and from the waist up with white, chalky dust. Apollonides apparently wished to view the breach from a greater distance and walked all the way to the cordon of soldiers, only a few feet away from us, before he stopped and turned back to have a look. Zeno followed after him, badgering him.

"We'll never be able to fill the gap sufficiently," Zeno said, "not with material strong enough to keep out a battering ram. It can't be done. If Trebonius mounts a full-scale assault—"

"He won't!" snapped Apollonides. "Not as long as we fly the white flag. He's held back so far."

"Why should he hurry? He can mount his assault tomorrow or the next day. That breach isn't going away."

"It's a breach, yes, but only a narrow one; narrow enough to be . . . defensible." Apollonides spoke through gritted teeth and kept his eyes on the activity by the wall, refusing to look at Zeno. "Even if Trebonius lined up his entire army to rush the breach, he'd never push enough men through to take the gate. Our archers would pick them off one by one until Roman corpses filled the gap. Any of them who did get through the breach and over the hurdle of debris would be trapped in that lake of mud, like flies in honey, made into even easier targets for our archers."

"And if the breach becomes wider?"

"It won't!"

"Why not? Some of those overhanging blocks on either side look ready to fall at any moment."

"The engineers will shore up the damage. They know what they're doing."

"Just as they knew what they were doing when they filled the moat?"

Apollonides gritted his teeth and made no answer.

Zeno pressed him. "And what happens if Trebonius brings up a battering-ram? The broken edges of the walls on either side will crumble like chalk."

"He won't. I won't let him!"

Zeno laughed derisively. "And how do you intend to stop him?"

Apollonides at last turned to meet his gaze. "You'll see, son-in-law."

"What do you mean?"

Apollonides smiled. He licked a finger and held it aloft. "There's a stiff wind rising—from the south, thank Artemis! We shall use it to our advantage."

"How?"

"Wind carries fire. Fire burns wood. And what are the Romans' ramparts and siege towers and battering-rams made of, but wood?"

Zeno gasped. "What are you planning?"

"Why should I tell you, son-in-law? If it was up to you, we'd have surrendered and thrown the gates open hours ago. I half suspect you of being a spy for the Romans, the way you're always advising me to give up the city to Caesar."

"How dare you! I've fought the Romans as bravely as any Massilian. From the battlements, on the sea—"

"And yet you did manage to come back alive yesterday, when so many did not."

Zeno turned livid with rage. I thought he might strike his father-in-law, but he kept his fists clenched tightly at his sides. "We're flying a white flag of parley. Trebonius has respected it; he's held back from assaulting the breach. As long as you fly that flag, you can't send out men to burn the Romans' siege-works. Caesar will never forgive such treachery."

Beside me, Davus huffed and whispered, "*He's* got some nerve, to talk about treachery!"

"Why do you think I've called up every archer to man the battlements?" said Apollonides. "To protect the engineers re-pairing the breach from a Roman attack, of course; but they'll also provide covering fire to our soldiers when they make their foray against the siegeworks."

"This is madness, father-in-law! The wall is breached. The siege is over. Caesar himself will arrive any day now—"

I pricked up my ears. This was new information.

"We don't know that for a fact," said Apollonides. "A mere rumor—"

"It was Lucius Nasidius who told me so, aboard his ship yes-terday. The commander of the Pompeian fleet—"

"A fleet that sailed away without sustaining a single casualty! A fleet of cowards, with a coward for commander!"

"Even so, Nasidius told me that Caesar is said to be already on his way back from Spain. He heard the news from our own soldiers manning the garrison at Taurois, where the Pompeian ships had anchored for the night. Caesar has defeated Pompey's legions in Spain and taken the survivors into his own army. He's heading back to Massilia at great speed with a huge force of men. He may arrive any day now—tomorrow, even! We can't possibly resist him. It's over, father-in-law."

"Shut up! Do you want the common rabble to overhear you and go spreading these mad rumors?" Apollonides looked over his shoulder, past the cordon of soldiers. His eyes, scanning the crowd, fell on me. For a moment his face went blank, then he yelled at the soldiers nearest to him and pointed at us. "Bring me those two men!"

Davus and I were roughly seized, dragged inside the cordon, and thrust before Apollonides.

"Gordianus! What are you doing, loitering there? Eavesdropping? You *are* a spy, aren't you? In league with my spying son-in-law, no doubt."

Zeno shook with fury.

"An eavesdropper perhaps, First Timouchos, but not a spy," I said, rearranging my tunic where the soldiers had gripped me.

"I should have you and your son-in-law beheaded on the spot, like those looters at the scapegoat's house. Yes, and then catapult your heads over the walls to Trebonius!"

"Don't be stupid, father-in-law!" protested Zeno. "This man is a Roman citizen, acquainted with Caesar himself—and Caesar's mercy is the only hope we have left! Even if this man is a spy, you'd be a fool to kill him now and flaunt his death. You'll only offend Caesar."

"To Hades with Caesar! Look, here comes the assault force."

Marching into the market square, pushing back the crowd with their presence, came a large body of soldiers clad in battle gear, armed with swords and pikes, but also carrying torches and bundles of pitch. The flames of their torches snapped and whipped in the rising wind.

Zeno shook his head. "Father-in-law, don't do this. Not while we're flying a flag of parley. Not before Trebonius can send an officer to negotiate—"

"There is nothing to be negotiated!" snapped Apollonides.

He stepped away from us in order to address the assault force, which now filled the market square in ranked assembly. His voice was ringing, his presence riveting as he strode back and forth with his blue cape snapping in the wind. I could see how he had risen to make himself first among the Timouchoi.

"Brave men of Massilia! For long months we've endured the humiliations and deprivations of a siege unjustly laid against this proud city by a Roman upstart, a criminal renegade. Against his own people he accomplished what even Hannibal could not: He conquered the city of Rome and drove the Senate into exile. And then, compounding his crimes, he dared to replace that ancient body with his own handpicked impostors, so that this false Senate could carry out the shoddy pretense of voting upon his actions and declaring them legal. So long as he prevails, all freedom is dead in Rome—and if he can, he will take away our freedom as well! But he will not prevail. With the true Senate of Rome and all the eastern provinces unified against him, he cannot possibly hope to win in the long run. We in Massilia merely had the misfortune to be the first victims, after the unfortunate citizens of Rome itself, to lie in the path of his insane ambitions.

"Before you, you see a breach in the walls—walls that have never been breached before, that have protected Massilia for hundreds of years. Some look upon this breach as a catastrophe. I look upon it as an opportunity. Because now we finally have the chance to strike back. The breach is not an opening for our attackers but for us! We shall rush out upon them and catch them unawares. We shall burn and destroy their siegeworks. Their battering-rams shall be reduced to firewood. Their ramparts shall become bridges of flame. Their towers shall become bonfire beacons, a warning to their renegade leader to keep his distance!

"The archers on the walls will protect you. But more than that, the righteousness of your cause will shield you. What you do today, you do for Massilia; for your ancestors who founded this proud city over five hundred years ago; for those who kept it, generation after generation, free and strong and independent against the Gauls, against Carthage, against Rome itself; for *xoanon* Artemis, who descended from the heavens and crossed the seas with our forefathers, who watches all that transpires in this city. She watches you today. Her bow is slung on your behalf. Her brother Ares shields you in battle. Those who fall, she scoops up in her loving arms. Those who proudly remain standing, she showers with glory.

"Now go! Go, and do not return until every scrap of wood outside these walls is swallowed up with flames!"

The men let out a great cheer. Even the desolate crowd of spectators seemed to rally and take heart. Beside us, Zeno hung his head.

The engineers stepped back from the breach. Planks had been laid to facilitate the passage of the assault force over the morass of mud and debris. The soldiers disappeared into the breach, yelling battle cries and whipping their torches through the air.

As night fell, the sky beyond the wall became not darker but brighter. A fiery glow emanated from the burning siegeworks outside the city. From the battlements, archers fired their bows nonstop, notching arrow after arrow, pulling back their strings and letting them fly. The buzzing of their shafts mixed with the clattering din of battle from beyond the walls, and the occasional shudder and boom, followed by screams, as some burning structure collapsed upon itself.

Apollonides ascended to the battlements to watch the progress of the foray. He paced back and forth with has arms crossed. From time to time he nodded his head approvingly or pointed to something below and issued a command to a subordinate.

Zeno stayed on the ground. He, too, paced back and forth, but said nothing. From time to time he stared at the breach, or up at the battlements, or at the restless, milling crowd in the square. He crossed his hands behind his back and brooded.

Both of them seemed to have forgotten Davus and me, and we were allowed to remain within the military cordon.

At last Apollonides descended from the battlements and headed back toward us. His carriage was proud and erect. I looked up and saw that the moon had risen. The sky toward the sea was black and spangled with faint stars. The sky above the breached wall was fiery orange. The foray had apparently been a great success.

Who could say what might transpire in the hours to come? Apollonides seemed capable of anything, including the beheading of two hapless Romans, despite the bold defense Zeno had made on my behalf. Why had Zeno done such a thing? Was he really a spy for Caesar, as Apollonides had sneeringly suggested, or merely a pragmatist already preparing for the inevitability of Caesar's conquest? And how had Zeno known that I was acquainted with Caesar? I had spoken to him only once, the night before, and at that time he seemed to have no idea, or pretended to have no idea, of whom I might be. . . .

In the midst of such uncertainty, I might not have another chance to confront Zeno. I pulled out the ring and stepped toward him.

Zeno turned and saw the thing in my hand. He was puzzled for a moment, then gave a start, as he had the night before. He saw his father-in-law approaching. "Put that thing away!"

"Then you *do* know this ring?"

"For Artemis's sake, put it away—before Apollonides sees it!"

"Why should it matter if he does?" I asked—and in that instant, gazing into Zeno's wide-open eyes, I knew the answer. It seemed to me that I must have known all along.

But it was too late. Apollonides had already seen that I held something in my hand and had noticed Zeno's reaction to it. As he approached, he looked from Zeno to the ring. He seemed at first mildly curious, then surprised, then confused. "What is the meaning of this, Gordianus?" he said. "What are you doing with my daughter's ring?"

The wind cut through my thin tunic. I felt a chill, despite the fiery glow in the night sky. Now I understood everything. Or so I thought.

XXI

"I'll ask you again, Finder. What are you doing with Cydima-che's ring?"

"Your daughter's ring . . . ?"

"Yes, of course! Zeno gave it to her on their wedding day. It never leaves her finger."

I made no answer. Apollonides turned to Zeno, who averted his eyes. "Explain this, Zeno. Did *you* give him the ring? Why? As payment to a spy? As bribery? But Cydimache would never allow—"

"Your son-in-law did not give me this ring, First Timouchos. I found it."

"Found it? *Found it?*" There was a note of hysteria in Apol-lonides's voice. I think, by a leap of intuition, he, too, had begun to realize the truth. At our first meeting on the rooftop terrace of the scapegoat's house, when I told him what I had witnessed on the Sacrifice Rock, he had paid only grudging attention, had accused me of lying. The woman who fell from the precipice was of no concern to him. At that moment, how could he have known, how could he have imagined the truth of the matter?

"First Timouchos, I think I can explain; but not here, not in this place. In your house. In the presence of . . . certain others."

I expected more anger and bombast, but instead his voice became quite small. "Others? What others?" All the color drained from his face. In the flickering, reflected glow from the fires outside the city walls, his features looked like those of a lifeless effigy made of wax. His jaw gaped and his brows turned upward until he resembled those heads mounted on spikes in the ruins of the scapegoat's house.

We had no need of torches to light our way as we traversed the city to Apollonides's house. The sullen glow of the burning sie-geworks lit up the sky and cast a fitful illumination over Mas-silia, drenching her open spaces in blood-red light, casting deep, black shadows into her hidden corners and recesses.

Apollonides dispatched soldiers ahead of us to fetch those I had asked him to summon, and ordered more soldiers to form a cordon around us, and after that he said no more. Zeno, too, was silent. Once or twice Davus tried to whisper a question in my ear, but I shook my head and drew away. Our little retinue made its grim way up the winding streets until we arrived at the house of the First Timouchos.

Inside the house, the soldiers who had been dispatched ahead of us stood guard before Zeno and Cydimache's quarters. Outside the room, Arausio and his wife, Rindel, stood huddled together in confusion.

"First Timouchos!" Arausio's voice quavered, "what is the meaning of this? Your soldiers rousted us from our home and brought us here without a word of explanation. Are we under arrest? I see you have the Finder with you. Does he accuse me

of slandering you and your son-in-law? It's not true, First Timouchos! Don't listen to Roman treachery! Have mercy on my
wife, at least—"

"Be quiet, merchant!" said Apollonides. He spoke to Zeno
without looking at him. "Son-in-law, open the door to this
room."

"Open it yourself," said Zeno dully.

"I will not! This is the room where my daughter grew up.
My daughter, who from the first time she saw herself in a mirror
wished me never to enter her presence unannounced, who wished
me never to see her unclothed or unveiled—who wished for even
her slaves never to see her unveiled—whose privacy I have always
scrupulously respected. When you married her, this became the
room she shared with you and you alone. Only once or twice
since Cydimache was a child have I stepped foot inside. I certainly have never forced my way in. I have never even touched
the door. I won't do so now. *You* will open the door."

Zeno stared at the floor, glanced furtively at Arausio and his
wife, bit his lip, then expelled a mirthless laugh. His eyes glittered feverishly. He shook his head and glared at me scornfully,
but also as if he pitied me. "Remember, Finder, this was your
doing. It was you and no one else who brought this about!"

He opened the door to the chamber he shared with his wife.

One by one, we stepped inside—Zeno first, then Apollonides,
then Davus and myself. Last of all came Arausio and his wife.
Their expressions were dumbfounded; for what possible reason
had they had been summoned to the bedchamber shared by the
man who had betrayed their daughter and the monster for whom
he had betrayed her?

The furnishings were luxurious, as I would have expected.
Every surface seemed to be draped with rich fabric. The walls
were covered with sumptuous hangings, the lamps strung with
baubles. The impression was a riot of textures and patterns, as
if the room itself was swathed in layer upon layer of veils.

At the far end of the room, a startled figure turned toward

us, covered with a cowled cloak and heavily veiled as on the previous night at the grim banquet in Apollonides's garden. No wonder, I thought, that Zeno had not wanted her to see the ring of Cydimache when I confronted him in the little courtyard!

For a long moment, no one moved or spoke. "First Timouchos," I said quietly, "do you wish to—"

"No! You do it, Finder. Unveil her." His voice was hoarse, hardly more than a whisper. I felt a sudden, piercing sympathy for him. He had worked out the truth, as I had. He knew what must have happened on the Sacrifice Rock that day; but what father can accept the fact of his child's death without proof, absolute proof, however painful? So it had been for me, unable, finally and without doubt, to accept Meto's death. Without proof, there must always be a glimmer of hope. For a few moments longer, Apollonides could cling to that hope. Once the veil was drawn aside, all doubt would vanish. I saw him steel himself for the moment, a look of utter misery on his face.

I slowly crossed the room. The veiled, hunchbacked figure swayed slightly back and forth as I approached, as if contemplating escape; but escape was impossible. I drew closer and closer, until I was close enough to hear the sound of heavy breathing behind the veil. I raised my hand.

The figure likewise raised a hand and seized my wrist, to stop me from lifting the veil.

I found myself staring, befuddled, at the hand that gripped my wrist. Something was wrong—entirely and completely, terribly wrong. This was not—could not possibly be—the hand of the woman I expected to find behind the veil. Hers would be a smooth, delicate hand, the skin fair and unblemished, even lovelier than that of her mother, who stood trembling with confusion beside her husband at the other end of the room. This hand was coarse, and dark, and bristled with black hairs across the back. This could not possibly be the hand of Rindel, the daughter of Arausio, Zeno's lover!

My heart pounded in my chest. What had I done? How had

I arrived at a conclusion so far from the truth, and drawn all these others along with me?

"Unveil her!" wailed Apollonides, his voice trembling with suspense.

There was no other choice. I prepared myself for the shock, the shame, the terrible mistake of Cydimache unveiled.

But at that moment, Zeno, too, must have seen the hand that restrained me. He expelled a strange, barking laugh fraught with anguish. He cried out, "Beloved! It's no use, anymore. Show yourself!"

What did he mean? I somehow sensed that he was not addressing the veiled one, but someone else in the room. There was a movement behind one of the wall hangings. With a shuddering sob, a slender figure stepped out of concealment and stole across the room, into the astonished arms of Arausio and his wife. They cried out in stunned, joyous surprise as they embraced their daughter. Rindel was even more beautiful than I had imagined.

Apollonides, as confounded as I was, stared from Rindel to the veiled one and demanded, "Unveil her, Gordianus!"

I tried to reach for the veil, but the hand that restrained me was strong—stronger than I expected, far stronger than I was. Suddenly the hand released me and the figure drew back, straightening as if shedding the hunch from its back, growing tall and erect. The coarse, dark, hairy-backed hand reached up to the veil, seized it, and tore it away.

I looked into two eyes I had never thought to see again. The face before me wavered and melted as my tears obscured it. I blinked, wiped my eyes, and stared.

"Meto!" I whispered.

On the upper floor, along the wing of Apollonides's house that faced in the direction of the city's main gate, there were five small rooms all in a row, each opening onto the same hallway. In one of those rooms I sat alone with Apollonides.

The room was dark. Its single window provided a view of the faraway city wall outlined against the flames that now burned low among the Roman siegeworks. In many places the flames had dwindled to embers; the fires had done their work. Against this lingering glow I could see the tiny silhouettes of the Massilian archers who restlessly patrolled the battlements. The breach itself was starkly outlined, a flickering fissure in the midst of the jet-black wall.

Apollonides stared out the window. His face, lit only by the distant, dying firelight, was impossible to read. Finally he spoke. "In all the hours you spent beneath his roof, I suppose Hieronymus must have told you the details of his family history." Alone with Apollonides, after the shock we had both received, this was not the first utterance I expected to hear from his lips.

I nodded. "I'd scarcely known him an hour before he told me about the deaths of his father and mother, and about his own years as an orphan and an outcast."

"His father was a Timouchos."

"Yes, Hieronymus told me. But his father lost his fortune—"

"He didn't lose it; it was stolen from him. Not literally stolen, but taken from him nevertheless, by devious means. His competitors conspired to ruin him, and they succeeded. Hieronymus has never known for sure how it happened or who was behind it; he was too young at the time to understand. So was I."

"What are you trying to tell me, First Timouchos?"

"Don't press me, Finder! Let me proceed at my own pace."

I sighed. In the aftermath of Meto's unveiling, Apollonides had taken charge. His soldiers had driven everyone out of Cydimache's room, up the stairway, and into this wing of the house. We had been dispersed into various small rooms, like prisoners confined to their cells, with soldiers standing guard in the hallway outside. In one room was Zeno, in another, Meto, and in another, Davus. Rindel and her parents were in another room. And in the last room, Apollonides and myself.

"It was my father who was behind it. My father destroyed Hieronymus's father and took his fortune. All that followed— the father's suicide, the mother's suicide, Hieronymus's ruin— came about because of what *my* father did. He never regretted it. And when I grew old enough to examine the family ledgers and eventually discovered the truth, he told me that *I* shouldn't regret it, either. 'Business is business,' he said. 'Success shows the favor of the gods. Failure is a mark of the gods' disfavor.' The very fact that he had succeeded so spectacularly meant that he had nothing to atone for, and neither had I. My father died an old man in his own bed, without regrets.

"But when Cydimache was born . . ." Apollonides sighed. "The first moment I saw her, I thought: this is the gods' pun- ishment for what my father did, that this innocent child should be so hideously disfigured. I should have disposed of her before she drew another breath; any other father would have done so, simply as an act of mercy. But I had my own selfish reasons for letting her live. Over the years she was often sickly, but she survived. She grew, and with every year became . . . even more hideous. She was a constant reminder of my father's sin. And yet . . . I couldn't hate her. Don't the philosophers tell us that to love beauty and hate ugliness is natural and right? Yet against all my expectations, against all reason, I came to love her. So I hated Hieronymus instead. I let myself blame him, not just for his own ruin, but for my daughter's deformity. Can you under- stand that, Finder?"

I said nothing and merely nodded.

"When the priests of Artemis came to the Timouchoi clam- oring for a scapegoat, it was I who arranged for the choice to be Hieronymus. I thought that was very clever of me, to finally rid myself of the pest without having to bloody my own hands, and in a way that would not offend the gods, but in fact would be pleasing to them! It seemed fitting that he should be made to follow his father, be forced to step off the Sacrifice Rock into oblivion and out of my guilty dreams forever. Instead . . . it was my Cydimache who fell from the Sacrifice Rock! Could the gods make their will any more explicit, than to punish me with her death from the very spot where the father of Hieronymus died? My father always told me that the gods loved us. All along, they despised us!"

How strange, I thought, how typical of the gods and their devious sense of humor. I had come to Massilia seeking a lost child who was not lost at all, while Apollonides had lost a child and did not even know it, and we had both discovered the truth in the same instant.

"Finder, when you told me, on Hieronymus's terrace, that you had seen a man and woman on the Sacrifice Rock and that the woman had fallen—how aloof I was, how uncaring, not know-ing . . . it was my Cydimache!" He sucked in a shuddering breath. "Hieronymus said she jumped. Your son-in-law said she was pushed. Which was it, Finder?"

"I don't know."

"But Zeno knows."

I shifted nervously. "Do you intend to torture him, First Ti-mouchos?"

"Why, when I have you to find out the truth for me?"

"Me, First Timouchos?"

"They call you Finder, don't they? Domitius told me all about you; how men are compelled by some strange power to tell you the truth. This was a gift the gods gave you."

"Gift, or curse?"

"What do I care, Finder, so long as you compel Zeno to tell you exactly what happened on the Sacrifice Rock? Do that for me . . . and then you may speak to your son."

XXII

In the small room where Zeno was being held, as in the room where Apollonides had interviewed me, a single window looked out on the distant silhouette of the city wall and the dying fires beyond. But this window, unlike the other, had bars across it. Apollonides had accounted for that when he chose this room for Zeno.

If, indeed, I possessed some unique skill at ferreting out the secrets of others, I had little need to call upon it with Zeno. Or perhaps it was as Apollonides suggested, and the baring of secrets was not so much a skill on my part as a compulsion placed upon others by the gods when I was present. However it was, Zeno was not reluctant to talk. It seemed to me that he desperately needed to talk.

"I should have had you killed, I suppose," was the first thing he said, staring out the window.

I was not quite sure how to answer that.

"I knew that you had witnessed . . . what happened on the

Sacrifice Rock—you and your son-in-law and the scapegoat. I overheard some of the soldiers talking about it, saying they'd been sent to question people in the vicinity of the rock, on account of what the scapegoat and his Roman guests had seen. Later that same night, I passed Apollonides in the front courtyard, and he mentioned it in passing, looked me straight in the eye and told me about some nonsense the scapegoat had reported about seeing an officer in a blue cape and a woman on the Sacrifice Rock. I thought my heart would leap from my mouth. But he wasn't testing me. He had no idea. He had too much on his mind. He never suspected."

"I thought it was Rindel on the rock with you, because Arausio thought so. But it was Cydimache."

"Yes."

"The scapegoat thinks she jumped."

"Does he?"

"Yes. My son-in-law holds a different opinion."

For a long moment, Zeno made no reply. He stared out the window and was so still that he seemed hardly to breathe. "I should never have fallen in love with Rindel," he finally said. "I never meant to. I desired her, of course, but that's not the same thing. It was impossible not to desire her. Any man would. You saw her tonight."

"Very briefly."

"But well enough to see how beautiful she is."

"Very beautiful."

"Extraordinarily beautiful."

"Yes," I admitted.

"But Rindel is a Gaul, and her father is of no account."

"According to Arausio, he's wealthier than your own father."

Zeno wrinkled his nose. "Arausio may have money, but he'll never be a Timouchos. He's not the right sort. If I had married Rindel, I'd never have been anything more than a rich Gaul's son-in-law."

"Would that have been so terrible?"

He snorted derisively. "You're an outsider. You can't understand."

"I suppose not. But if you fell in love with Rindel despite
yourself, I think I can understand that."

"I had almost reconciled myself to . . . marrying her. Then I
saw . . . another opportunity."

"Cydimache?"

"The First Timouchos invited me to a dinner at this accursed
house. It was a great honor; or so I thought, until my friends
began to tease me. 'You fool! Don't you know he's fishing for a
son-in-law?' they said. 'You're not the first prospective suitor
he's invited. All the rest—the monster gobbled up! Mind she
doesn't get her fangs and claws into you! Or worse, drag you off
to her bed!' They all had a hearty laugh at my expense.

"I dreaded that dinner. Sure enough, my place was next to
Cydimache. She wore her veils, of course. I was nervous, at first.
Cydimache said little, but when she spoke, she was actually quite
witty. After a while I thought: This isn't so bad. I began to
relax. I ate and drank. I looked around the garden. I saw the
way they lived. I began to think: Why not?"

"You're hardly the first young man to marry for position," I
said quietly.

"It's not as if I despised Cydimache! I came to care for her . . .
a great deal."

"What about her ugliness? Her deformity?"

"We . . . dealt with that." He smiled ruefully. "Do you know
the image of *xoanon* Artemis? Every Massilian boy is taught to
revere that image, strange as it is. I told Cydimache that she
was my very own *xoanon* Artemis. That pleased her immensely."

"And what about Rindel?"

He sighed. "As soon as I was betrothed to Cydimache, I made
a vow to myself that I would never see Rindel again. No good
could come of trying to explain myself to her; better to make a
clean break, let her think the worst and forget me. I would have
kept that vow, but Rindel wouldn't let me. As long as I stayed

in Apollonides's house, I was safe from her. But once the siege began, my duties took me all over the city. Rindel sought me out. She stalked me like a huntress."

"Artemis with her bow," I murmured.

"In chance moments, when I would find myself alone—there was Rindel, suddenly before me, whispering, beckoning, drawing me into some hidden corner, telling me that she couldn't forget me, that she still wanted me even if I was another woman's husband."

I nodded. "Arausio said she would disappear from his house for long hours. He thought she was taking aimless walks, nursing a broken heart. He thought she was going mad."

"She was hunting for me. And after a while . . . our meetings were no longer by chance. We found a place to meet—a lover's nest. I had forgotten . . . how beautiful she was. Like Artemis, you say? No, Aphrodite incarnate! Making love to her—how can I explain? How can I expect you even to begin to understand?"

I sighed. Like all young men, he imagined that ecstasy was his own invention.

"The last time we met . . . like that . . . was on the day the Romans brought up the battering-ram. With all the confusion in the city, I was late, but Rindel waited for me. It was like never before. The excitement on the battlements—the sense of dread hanging over us—the constant pounding of the battering-ram against the walls; I can't explain. We seemed to make love that day with new bodies, new senses. She was unspeakably beautiful. I wanted to lie in her arms forever. And then . . ."

"Cydimache found you."

"Yes. She suspected. She'd followed me. She found us."

"And then?"

"Cydimache became hysterical. To see the two of them in the same room, side by side—Rindel naked and Cydimache in her veils, but knowing what lay beneath—it seemed hardly possible that two creatures so different could both be made of human flesh. I think Cydimache must have seen the look on my face.

She let out a cry that turned my blood to ice. She ran from the room."

"I thought she was lame."

"I'd never imagined that she could move so fast! Especially considering . . ." He was about to say something, but caught himself. "I threw on my clothes and my armor—I could hardly be seen out in the streets without it—and I followed after her. I thought she would run here, to her father, but then I saw her far away, heading toward the sea. I ran. I caught up with her near the base of the Sacrifice Rock. You saw . . . what happened next."

I nodded slowly. "It was as Hieronymus thought, then: Cydimache meant to throw herself off the rock, and you chased after her, to stop her."

I waited for him to reply, but he only stared silently out the window. "And afterward," I said, "Rindel took the place of Cydimache. A masquerade. Madness—"

"But it worked! In all the confusion of that day, it was a simple thing to sneak Rindel into this house. Once we were alone in Cydimache's room, I dressed her in some of Cydimache's clothes and veils. I showed her how to stoop, how to shamble. I told her to make her voice gruff and to speak as little as possible."

"And Apollonides?"

"Ever since the siege began, he'd had no time for Cydimache. She had a husband, she was no longer his responsibility, and he had a war to fight. Last night's dinner in the garden was the closest that Rindel had ever come to him. She kept quiet. She stayed close to me. Apollonides suspected nothing."

"And what of Rindel's parents?"

"Rindel wanted to send them a message, to let them know that she was alive and well, but I told her it was too dangerous."

"So you let them think she was dead." If only they had let Arausio know the truth, then he would never have come to me; and I would never have pursued the matter, never have heard of

Rindel, never have confronted Zeno with the ring. Their own secrecy had finally been their undoing. "But you couldn't possibly keep up such a pretense forever. You must have realized that."

"In a city under siege, you learn to live from day to day. Even so, time was on our side. Once Caesar takes the city, everything will change. Who knows how things will fall out? One thing is certain: Apollonides will no longer be First Timouchos. He may even lose his head. Whatever happens, Massilia will never be independent again. This is the best we can hope for: that Caesar will disband the Timouchoi and put a Roman general in charge of the city. But he'll need an insider who knows the city, someone loyal to him who can run the bureaucracy, quell sedition—"

"A Massilian lackey. And that would be you?" Just as he had married for position, so, too, was Zeno ready to call Caesar his master.

"Why not? I argued from the beginning that we should open our gates to Caesar, that we never should have resisted him."

I nodded thoughtfully. "My son Meto—how and when did you come to know him?"

He smiled. "I met Meto when he first came to Massilia, just before the siege began. He was passing himself off as a defector from Caesar's inner circle. Right away he must have realized that I was sympathetic to Caesar. I made no secret of it; I objected loudly when the Timouchoi voted to side with Pompey. I was rather scornful of Meto, as a matter of fact. I thought he must be even stupider than my father-in-law. Here was a young Roman who'd risen from nothing to become the companion of Caesar himself, and for some reason he'd thrown it all away and chosen to side with the likes of Milo and Domitius and Pompey. What a fool! The joke was on me, of course. Meto was spying for Caesar all along."

"And he approached you, to turn you into a spy for Caesar as well?"

"Not then; not yet. I had no idea of what he was up to until

Milo exposed him as a spy. Domitius's men chased him over the wall into the sea, and supposedly he drowned. I thought no more about him. The siege went on. And then, the day after the battering-ram attack, the day after . . . Cydimache's death . . . Meto reappeared in Massilia. Or I should say, Massilia saw the reappearance of the ragged soothsayer that had sometimes been Meto's disguise. He sought me out and took a great risk in revealing himself to me. He wanted me to help him infiltrate this house. In return, he promised Caesar's favor. I was already in terrible danger, with Cydimache dead and Rindel taking her place. Helping a Roman spy would put me in even greater danger, and yet it seemed as if the gods had sent Meto to me. In the long run, my only hope was to somehow gain Caesar's favor, and here was the means to do that.

"Once I decided to trust Meto, I told him everything, even about Cydimache and how Rindel had taken her place. It was Meto's masterstroke to sometimes masquerade as Cydimache himself. If Rindel could do it, so could he. The two of them took turns. As Cydimache, Meto could move freely about the house and could even come and go, so long as I escorted him. Your son is a natural actor, Gordianus. Far more convincing than Rindel; she always overdid Cydimache's limp. But Meto was uncanny! And he made the most of the masquerade. If the daughter of the First Timouchos should choose to sit outside the room where the war council met, no one dared to question her. Quite the opposite! Brave soldiers would scurry past her like mice past a cat. They wanted no contact with the veiled monster!"

I shook my head. "A mad risk!"

"But a brilliant one. I've never met a more daring man than your son, Gordianus, or a more fearless one."

"He turned you into a spy, Zeno."

"A spy, perhaps, but not a traitor. In the end, you'll see that it was I who always had the best interests of Massilia at heart, not Apollonides."

"You cast your lot with Caesar. Yet you sailed out to fight against Caesar's fleet—"

"I had no choice. It was my duty to command that ship. I'm not a coward, and I've never betrayed my comrades! I fought as long and hard as any other Massilian that day."

"Did you? Even knowing that if you never returned, your beloved Rindel would be left to fend for herself in Apollonides's house?"

"Rindel wasn't alone; Meto promised to look after her. Had I died that day, Meto would have returned Rindel secretly and safely to her father's house, and Apollonides would never have known the part she played."

"I see. And Meto would have been left to perform the role of your bereaved widow full time, conveniently struck mute with grief, no doubt. So much deceit!" I rubbed my eyes wearily. "Meto revealed himself to you, put his trust in you—yet he never showed himself to *me,* never gave me a sign that he was still alive. Outside Massilia, at the shrine of *xoanon* Artemis—it was Meto I met that day, wasn't it, in his disguise as the soothsayer Rabidus? He deceived me."

Zeno shrugged. "If Meto thought that revealing himself to you posed too great a risk, I think you should defer to his judgment. He's kept himself alive this long, against enormous odds. He knows what he's doing."

"Does he?" I shook my head. I stirred and made ready to leave.

"Haven't you forgotten something, Gordianus?"

"I don't think so."

"You never asked me what happened on the Sacrifice Rock."

"I thought you answered that already. You chased Cydimache to the summit. I suppose she pulled off the ring—the skystone ring you gave her on your wedding day—and threw it down. A gesture of renunciation, before killing herself. Is that right?"

"Yes. Almost."

"What do you mean?"

"She pulled off the ring. She threw it down. I should have

remembered to pick it up later, but it all happened so quickly. Then she lurched toward the precipice."

I frowned. "But there was a bit of a struggle, wasn't there? We all saw that."

"Yes. Her cloak and her veils were loose upon her; it was hard to get hold of her. Even so, I did my best to stop her. I managed to grab her—"

"But she slipped from your grasp."

"Not exactly." His voice abruptly changed timbre, became deeper and slower. It seemed almost as if a third presence had entered the room, as if someone else were speaking through his lips. "Cydimache wanted to die. I'm sure of that. What else could she have intended when she climbed up the rock? She wanted to die, and I tried to save her. You see, she was—she had shown the first signs—no one else knew yet. We hadn't even told her father."

"What are you saying?"

"Cydimache was pregnant with my child."

I drew a sharp breath. No wonder he had tried to stop her! She was carrying the child that would purchase his membership in the Timouchoi.

"I did my best to save her—and she wanted to die—up until the instant I had hold of her. Her veil dropped, and I saw her eyes. She'd changed her mind. She wanted to die; and then, at the last possible instant, *she changed her mind . . .*"

"But it was too late. She was too far over the edge."

"No! Don't you understand? Her veil dropped. I saw her eyes—and her face. That hideous face! She changed her mind, *and so did I.* She wanted to die, then decided to live. And in that same instant . . ."

"You decided . . . not to save her."

"Yes."

"You pushed her."

His voice seemed to come from a deep well. "Yes. I pushed her."

I drew a deep breath. Hieronymus had been right, up to a point. So had Davus.

I had discovered what Apollonides had sent me to discover. My reward would be a reunion with my son in the next room.

Zeno's voice returned to its normal timbre. He ended the conversation as he began it. "I should have had you killed, I suppose. You were a dangerous witness. But early on, Meto explained to me who you were. His father, come to look for him here in Massilia! That complicated matters. You can thank your son that you're still alive. Give him my regards." He flashed a sardonic smile and then turned to gaze out the window.

XXIII

The window in Meto's cell also looked out on the breached wall and also had bars across it. What sort of man, I thought, has a home with prison cells on the upper floor? A man like Apollonides. The kind of man who rises to become first citizen of a city-state.

The fires amid the Roman siegeworks had died even lower, but because of the particular angle of the view from Meto's window, the breach in the wall appeared brightly lit, its jagged edges seeming to glow as if traced with a fiery nimbus. The wall itself and the silhouettes of pacing archers were utterly black.

When Meto had unveiled himself in Cydimache's room, I had not cried out in jubilation, had not embraced him. Why not? Because the moment had been too shocking, I thought. And yet the parents of Rindel, equally stunned, had immediately gathered their daughter into their arms and wept tears of joy.

In Cydimache's room, I had restrained my emotions, I told myself, because the circumstances had been so strange, the presence of others too inhibiting. But now I was alone with Meto. Why did I not rush to embrace him?

Why, for that matter, did he not embrace me and weep for joy? Because he had not feared for me as I had feared for him, I reasoned. He had known my whereabouts from the moment I arrived at the shrine of *xoanon* Artemis outside Massilia. He never thought me lost, never had cause to believe that my life was in immediate danger. But was that true? I easily could have died— by any reasonable expectation *should* have died—in the flooded tunnel. The priests of Artemis might have had me executed for climbing onto the Sacrifice Rock. Apollonides might have had me killed at any time, on a whim. I had been in some degree of danger every moment since I had left Rome, and so had Davus. What did Meto have to say about that? Was he so inured to danger that it counted for nothing, even when it threatened his own father?

He smiled broadly at the sight of me, stepped forward and clapped his hands on my shoulders, but he did not embrace me. Instead, he reached for a great lump of fabric on the floor and picked it up, grinning as he had when he was a boy and had something to show off. He was dressed only in a light tunic, I noticed. The thing in his hands was the costume he had worn in his guise as Cydimache.

"Look at this, Papa. It's really ingenious. I made it myself. Amazing what you can do when you have to rely on your own resources." He held the thing up so that I could see that the sumptuous, voluminous gown and the veils were all sewn together in one piece. "It slips over my head, you see, and everything instantly falls into place, even the hunch on my back—that's just a bit of extra padding. No tucking or tying or bothering with veils coming loose. One minute, I'm Cydimache the hunchback, and the next—" He snapped the garment in the air and turned it inside out. Now it was a ragged cloak with a cowl. "Now I'm Rabidus the soothsayer, who comes and goes as he pleases."

"Very impressive," I said, and coughed. My throat was dry.

"You could use some wine, Papa. Here, I'll poor you a cup. It's good stuff. Falernian, I think."

"I'm surprised Apollonides has supplied you with wine at all, let alone a fine vintage."

"Apollonides may be a fool, but even *he* has begun to realize that it's only a matter of time—hours, maybe—before Massilia belongs to Caesar. It will behoove him to hand me over to Caesar alive and well."

"You're relying on his shrewdness as a politician to keep you alive, then? Apollonides is also a father who's just received a terrible shock."

"And so are you! To Caesar!" Meto clinked his wine cup against mine and grinned, and seemed oblivious of the cruel difference between the shocks that had buffeted Apollonides and me. I had never seen him in such a reckless, giddy mood. It was because Caesar was coming, I thought. Soon Caesar would be here, and Meto's beloved mentor would be very pleased with all that Meto had done on his behalf.

I drank the wine and was glad for its warmth.

Meto paced the room, too excited to be still. "You must have a thousand questions, Papa. Let me think; where to begin?"

"I'm not Caesar, Meto. You don't have to report to me."

He smiled as if I had made a weak joke, then proceeded as if I hadn't spoken. "Let's see; how did I get in and out of Massilia? By swimming, of course. I grew up by the sea; I've always been a strong swimmer. It's really nothing to swim across the harbor here, or even from the harbor all the way out to the islands offshore."

"But the current—"

He shrugged dismissively. "And a single man, swimming at night, especially on a moonless night, can easily get past sentries. I quickly learned which sections of the harbor were least heavily guarded, and the Massilians have been terribly careless about keeping shut the gates that open onto the wharves. So it was no great challenge for me to get in and out of Massilia."

"But when Domitius and his men chased you onto the wall and forced you to jump into the sea—Domitius was certain that you were dead."

He shook his head. "The fall *could* have killed me—if I didn't know how to dive or if I'd struck a rock. But I headed for that particular stretch of wall because I'd scouted it out beforehand and I knew it was the safest place to make a dive. I knew I might have to make a quick escape one day, and I planned ahead accordingly."

"You'd been wounded by a spear."

"Merely grazed."

"They shot arrows at you."

"They missed. Not a decent archer among them!"

"But they saw your body floating off on the current."

"Not my body; my tunic. When I struck the water it inflated with air. I tied it off so that it would float for a while, and at that distance they mistook it for a body. People see what they want to see, and the wise spy takes advantage of that; something Caesar taught me. Meanwhile, I held my breath and swam along the wall toward the harbor. By the time I surfaced, they had no idea of where to look for me. The sun was in their eyes, and they were already looking elsewhere. I took a quick breath and ducked back under the surface. I kept swimming until I crossed the harbor mouth and reached the shore on the far side."

I stared at the dregs in my cup. "Who sent me the anonymous message telling me that you were dead? Was it Domitius?"

He shook his head. "No. I'm almost certain it was Milo. I thought I could win him over to Caesar, but that was a very serious miscalculation on my part. Milo lacks the imagination to see the future; all he can think of is getting back into Pompey's good graces. That's why he almost got me killed. If he could flush out a dangerous spy, that would earn him points with the Great One.

But Milo wanted to capture me alive, and he was never satisfied that Domitius's men had killed me. He suspected—correctly—that I was not only still alive but back in Massilia, and he wanted to flush me out again. How better to do that than to lure my dear father to Massilia, where sooner or later I would surely try to make contact with you. Those were Milo's men following you and Davus whenever you left the scapegoat's house. They weren't interested in you; they were hoping to catch me. Once, they almost did. It was after you left the house of Gaius Verres and paused in the street near that black market."

"Yes, we saw you, dressed in your soothsayer's rags. But then you vanished."

"I had to! Milo's men appeared out of nowhere. They very nearly caught me."

I nodded slowly. "And that was you, as well, waiting at the foot of the Sacrifice Rock on the day of the sea battle."

"Yes." He shook his head disdainfully. "I couldn't believe you had the temerity to climb up there! Did you imagine that no one could see you? I watched you for hours, expecting at any moment to see the priests of Artemis come drag you off. When you finally started to climb down, my only thought was to get to you first and try to hide you somewhere—but once again, I had to flee. Apollonides's troops arrived to whisk you back to his house. Just as well, as that was the safest place for you. Otherwise the mob in the street would have torn you limb from limb, along with the scapegoat."

I was not satisfied. "Surely, Meto, you could have made contact with me at some point. After Domitius told me that you were dead, I went through . . . a very bad time. I didn't leave Hieronymus's house for days. If you couldn't come to me in the flesh, then you might have sent a message. Not even a written message, merely some sign that you were still alive. The anguish I felt—"

"I'm sorry, Papa, but it was simply too dangerous. And frankly, I've been too busy. You have no idea!" He smiled at me indulgently. "That day, when you and Davus stepped inside the temple of *xoanon* Artemis outside the city—where I was accustomed to leave certain secret reports for Trebonius, if you must know—and I heard two voices babbling on and realized it was you, I thought: What in Hades is Papa doing *here?* Well, obviously, you'd come to find me. But there was nothing for you to do here except get in the way. So I tried to warn you off, tried to send you back to Rome."

"While still disguised as the soothsayer!" I snapped, a flash of anger finally creeping into my voice.

"I could hardly have revealed myself to you in front of those two guards. They'd have told everyone in the camp—and who knows what spies the Massilians have among our own men? No one but Trebonius knew of my mission and my disguise. Absolute secrecy was essential."

"You could have revealed yourself to *me*, Meto!"

He sighed. "No, Papa. My only thought was to send you back to Rome where you'd be safe. After I left you on your way to the Roman camp, I doubled back and went directly to Trebonius; he promised me that he'd send you straight home. Even if you managed to thwart him, at the very worst I thought you'd simply spend the rest of the siege in the Roman camp, pestering Trebonius. I never imagined you'd actually find a way to get inside Massilia! And yet, here you are. I have to give you credit for ingenuity. Like father, like son, eh? Perhaps Caesar should use *you* as a secret agent."

At that moment, the very idea filled me with such loathing that the great thundercrack that abruptly shook the room seemed, for a peculiar instant, to be a manifestation of my own fury. But the thunderous booming and the earthshaking vibrations came from outside the room. Meto rushed to the window. "Great Venus!" he muttered.

Billowing clouds of dust, weirdly backlit by the lingering flames, rose from the wall—or more precisely, from the places where sections of the wall had previously stood. The fissure now gaped far wider than before. On either side of the original breach more sinkholes had abruptly given way, swallowing all the rubble piled into the breach, along with the makeshift structures meant to shore up the wall and any of the engineers who were still working there. Then, as we watched, a bastion tower caved in on one side of the growing breach, to the sound of crashing stones and the screams of archers on the collapsing battlements.

Where before there had been a breach that by some supreme effort might have remained defensible, now there gaped an enormous opening in the wall, leaving the main square of the city completely vulnerable. The walls of Massilia were hopelessly breached.

From within the house of Apollonides there were sounds of men shouting and running through the hallways. Abruptly the door opened and the First Timouchos stood staring at us, wearing a stunned expression.

My time alone with Meto was over.

XXIV

His face pale, his hands trembling, Apollonides ordered me to leave Meto's cell. He stepped into the room, followed by several bodyguards, then slammed the door behind him. With the collapse of the wall, my son—Caesar's agent—was the first person Apollonides wanted to talk to.

I wandered down the hall. Around a corner I came upon a group of furiously whispering guards. They scarcely noticed me and made no effort to stop me as I stepped into the main part of the house. I wandered through the hallways until I heard a cry of joy and turned to see Davus, who likewise had been released and apparently forgotten. He laughed for joy and hugged me so hard he squeezed the breath from me.

Tired and confused and at a loss for what to do next, I decided to look for Hieronymus. The door to his quarters stood open. We stepped into the small anteroom, then into the bedchamber beyond. There was another room beyond that, with a balcony looking out on the street. There was no one in any of the rooms, not even a slave. Exhausted, I reclined amid the plush cushions strewn across the scapegoat's bed, thinking to rest for only a moment. I fell fast asleep. Davus stood guard in the anteroom for a while, until exhaustion overcame him as well. He joined me on the bed and he, too, fell asleep.

We woke at dawn in a house where confusion reigned. No one seemed to be in charge. Slaves seemed to come and go as they pleased, with no one to give them orders. But when I tried to enter the wing where Apollonides had questioned me the previous night, two very unhappy guards blocked my way. When I tried to speak, they brandished their swords and shouted me down.

I tried to find Hieronymus again, without success. In the foyer, I saw that the front door of Apollonides's house stood wide open. I stepped onto the porch and saw that the courtyard gates were open as well, with no soldiers standing guard.

The walls of Massilia were hopelessly breached, yet throughout the long night the Romans had held back. Dawn had come, and still Trebonius did not mount an assault.

But overnight, the rumor of Caesar's imminent arrival had spread throughout Massilia. He was expected the next day . . . the next hour . . . the next minute. Fits of panic convulsed the city. Tearful worshippers thronged the temples. I had experienced something similar in Brundisium, but there the people had awaited Caesar as their deliverer. The Massilians awaited him as their destroyer. They knew too well the atrocities he had visited upon their neighbors, the Gauls—villages burned, men executed, women raped, children enslaved.

Chaos ruled the streets. What madness had possessed the sober people of Massilia, famed for their staid academies, their love of order, their bland equanimity? Massilians were said to love money above all else and to exemplify the concomitant virtues— diligence, shrewdness, patience. Yet in the streets that day I saw staggering drunkards, bloody fistfights, a naked corpse hanging from a tree, a man in rich banker's robes chased down and stoned by an angry mob. In the final moments of a great city, some citizens had descended to barbarism and could think only of their last chance at retribution against a neighbor. Massilia was tearing itself apart before Caesar had the chance.

I saw a troop of gladiators marching toward us and gestured to Davus to hide, fearing trouble. But the man commanding the gladiators had already seen us. He ordered his men to halt and strode over to us. It was Domitius, dressed in full battle regalia, his cape thrown back to show the copper disk embossed with a lion's head on his breastplate. Behind the cordon of gladiators, slaves wheeled carts piled high with trunks. Evidently, Domitius was leaving Massilia as he had arrived, with his ragtag band of gladiators, his household slaves, and whatever was left of his six million sesterces. At the siege of Corfinium, rather than fall into Caesar's clutches, he had attempted suicide—and failed. Caesar had forgiven and released him. Now, once again facing the same prospect, Domitius apparently had no stomach for a second suicide attempt and did not trust that Caesar would be as merciful a second time.

I couldn't resist a sardonic jab. "Leaving us so soon, Domitius?"

He glared at me. "I understand that bastard son of yours is alive after all. So Milo was right."

"Yes. But Meto's not a bastard. He was a slave whom I adopted."

"Aren't all slaves bastards by definition?"

"One might say the same about Roman politicians."

His eyes flashed. I glanced nervously at the band of surly gladiators and swallowed dryly, wondering if I had pushed him too far. But in the next instant Domitius barked out a laugh. "Like father, like son, even if yours is adopted. What audacity you Gordianii have! I might almost wish you were on our side."

"What makes you think I'm on Caesar's side?"

"Aren't you?"

I didn't answer. I looked at the carts piled high with trunks. "I suppose you've kept a ship in the harbor?"

"Three ships, actually. Apollonides wanted to conscript them for battle, but I told him I'd have none of that." He wet a finger and held it to the breeze. "The wind's shifted from yesterday; we shall have good sailing. The ship I'll be taking is a long, low beauty, swift as a dolphin."

"She'll have to be, to get past the blockade." I glanced toward the north, where the sky was turning dark. "It look as if Aeolus might be bringing us storm clouds."

"Blockade or no blockade, storm or no storm, nothing shall stop me from getting out of this Hades-on-earth!"

"Caesar will be disappointed. I'm sure he looks forward to your reunion."

"As do I! But not here, not now. Another day, on another battlefield!"

"What about Milo? I don't see him in your retinue."

"Milo is staying right here, where he belongs. If he's lucky, when all this madness is over, Pompey will grant him a generous pardon and invite him back to Rome, where he can grow old and fat fishing on the banks of the Tiber. Until then, Milo must make do with Massilian mullets. No more talk, Gordianus! You've delayed me long enough."

And with that he was off again, barking an order at his glad-iators to quicken their pace.

Dark clouds obscured the sun. Sharp winds blew through the narrow streets of Massilia, carrying the scent of rain. Despite the looming storm, Davus suggested we go to a high place, where we might be able to see the breached section of the wall and scrutinize the activities of Trebonius's army outside.

As we trudged uphill, looking for a good vantage point, we encountered a large crowd gathered outside a temple. Some of the people chanted solemnly with their eyes shut. Some shrieked and spun about madly while others looked on, appalled. I located a spectator who looked reasonably calm and sober and asked him what was happening.

"The scapegoat," he said. "The priests of Artemis are making ready to conduct him to the Sacrifice Rock."

I pushed into the crowd. Davus helped clear the way. At last we came to the steps of the temple, where a black funeral bier lay upon a familiar green-canopied litter. A group of priests were just stepping out of the temple. Their white robes whipped in the wind. Wavering streamers and vortices of smoke rose from their bowls of smoldering incense. Flanked by the priests, a tall figure in green emerged from the temple. His face was hidden behind a green veil, so that from head to toe he was covered in green, like a chrysalis. I tried to step toward him, but a cordon of soldiers barred the way.

I called out his name. Hieronymus turned his head in my direction. He whispered to one of the priests, who frowned but nevertheless approached the soldiers and told them to let me through. I rushed up the steps.

"Hieronymus!" I tried to keep my voice low. "What is this? What's happening?"

"Isn't it obvious?"

"Hieronymus, I can't see your face. That veil—"

"The scapegoat wears a veil on his final day. The gods are watching. The sight of the scapegoat's accursed face could only offend them."

I lowered my voice to a hoarse whisper. "Hieronymus, you mustn't go through with this! If you can postpone the ceremony for only a little while—Caesar is on his way. It may be only hours—minutes—"

"Postpone the ceremony? But why?"

"There's no need for it. The siege is all but over. Your death will change nothing. You can't possibly save the city."

"Not from conquest; but perhaps the city may yet be saved from utter destruction. Who knows what Caesar intends? The sacrifice of the scapegoat may tip the scales and cause Caesar to be merciful."

"Caesar will as do he pleases, no matter what happens to you!"

"Shhh! Don't tell the priests that, or the people of Massilia! For months they've pampered and pleasured me, preparing me to take on all their sins at once. Now they want to see the ceremony carried through to the end."

"But, Hieronymus—"

"Quiet, Gordianus! I'm at peace. Last night Apollonides called me to his private chambers. He told me everything."

"Everything?"

He nodded. "I know that your son Meto is alive. I'm happy for you, Gordianus! Apollonides also confessed to me that it was his father who ruined my father. I had long suspected as much. And . . . he told me about Cydimache. My father jumped from the Sacrifice Rock. Apollonides's daughter was pushed. His line has come to an end. The shades of my parents are appeased."

"And you, Hieronymus?"

"Me?" The wind pressed the veil against his face so that I clearly saw his expression—his lips slightly pursed, one eyebrow sardonically raised. "I'm a Massilian, Gordianus, and above all else, a Massilian respects a contract. When I became the scapegoat, I entered into an agreement with the priests of Artemis and the people of Massilia. I did so with my eyes open. They honored their side of the contract. Now it's my turn. My obligation is to willingly face my sacrifice. Not all scapegoats do so in the end; some have to be drugged, or bound, or even knocked unconscious. Not me! I shall stand tall and meet my destiny proudly."

My voice caught in my throat. I tried to think of words to

persuade him, of something I could do to stop the farce. He laid his hand on my forearm and seized it with a powerful grip.

"Gordianus, I know that you don't take this ceremony seriously, that you don't believe it actually works."

"Do you?"

"Perhaps. Perhaps not. My personal belief hardly matters. But it may be that a scapegoat *can* take on the sins of others and can carry them with him to oblivion, allowing those who survive to start afresh. Since I first met you, Gordianus, I've sensed that you carry a burden of guilt. Some wickedness—some crime you committed—perhaps in trying to save that beloved son of yours? Am I right?"

I made no answer.

"Never mind. I absolve you!" He suddenly released my arm. "There. Whatever burden of sin you may carry has gone out of you and come into me. Do you know, I believe I actually felt something. Truly!"

There was such a thickness in my throat that I could hardly speak. "Hieronymus . . ."

"Now go, Gordianus. This is my moment!"

Two priests of Artemis grabbed my arms, pulled me down the steps, and thrust me back into the crowd beyond the line of soldiers. I looked on helplessly as Hieronymus mounted wooden steps up to the litter and reclined upon the funeral bier, shutting his eyes and crossing his arms as if he were a corpse. The crowd around me surged and wailed. Some screamed curses at the scapegoat. Others shouted blessings. They began to throw objects at the funeral bier, and I started in alarm; but the objects were not rocks and stones but dried flowers and bits of crumpled parchment with names written on them. The priests of Artemis took the green litter onto their shoulders and began to carry it through the street, protected by the cordon of soldiers. Before them and behind them, a retinue of priests clapped hands, chanted, and wafted incense. Shreds of smoke, dried flower petals, and scraps of parchment blew this way and that.

Davus and I followed the procession for a while. We stopped at a point where the street descended sharply and a small clearing on a crest afforded a view of the Sacrifice Rock. In the strange, false twilight that precedes a rainstorm, we watched the procession wind down the hill, gathering more and more spectators. The roar of the crowd, with its mingled curses and blessings, rang out and echoed though the city.

The procession came to a halt at the foot of the Sacrifice Rock. Ringed by the cordon of soldiers, Hieronymus stepped from the funeral bier and began, alone, to climb the rock. The crowd cried out and pelted him with dried flowers and bits of parchment.

More priests awaited him at the summit of the rock, where a green canopy had been pitched. The crowded priests leaned into the stiff wind. Those holding the poles of the canopy were sorely pressed to prevent it from blowing away altogether. Their white robes and the green flaps of the canopy snapped and fluttered. Standing among the priests was Apollonides, his mane of silver hair tossed by the wind and his light blue cape wrapped tightly around him.

Beyond the rock and the wall, mottled patches of shadow and sunlight played across the sea. The wind whipped the green waves into foaming whitecaps.

Hieronymus took his time. He climbed slowly, methodically, almost as if he were savoring the event. Or was he beginning to have second thoughts?

At last he reached the summit. Hieronymus in his green robes stood out, but there was such a crowd of priests beneath the canopy that I had trouble seeing clearly. Tears obscured my vision.

Atop the Sacrifice Rock there was more chanting and a great deal more incense. The capricious wind seemed to play with the smoke, and instead of dispersing it, caused it to whirl about the summit, enveloping the canopy. Priests coughed and waved their hands. They could hardly be expected to control the wind—but surely the scuffle I saw was not a part of the ceremony. . . .

"Davus, I can't see clearly. Tears in my eyes—from the wind. Is Hieronymus—is he *struggling* against them?"

Davus squinted. "He must be! They've all surrounded him— restraining him—pitching back and forth. He's putting up quite a fight. And now—Apollonides—!"

Davus had no need to finish. Blinking away tears, my jaw agape, I saw the final moment clearly. Or did I?

Like Cydimache, Hieronymus must have changed his mind at the last moment. How else to explain the fact that the priests suddenly swarmed around him, restraining him? It was Apollonides who stepped decisively forward and seized the struggling green chrysalis in a fierce embrace. The two of them spun about and rocked back and forth. The priests scrambled back. Apollonides's silver mane whipped in the wind. His cape billowed and wrapped itself around them, until the two figures seemed to meld into a single, writhing creature shrouded in pale blue and chrysalis green.

Together, they staggered toward the precipice. I held my breath. For a brief moment they seemed to be frozen on the very edge of the rock. An instant later, still locked together, they vanished.

Davus gasped. "Apollonides! Hieronymus took Apollonides with him!"

I shook my head, stunned. "Or was it Apollonides who jumped and took Hieronymus along with him?"

XXV

The wind continued to rise. The sky turned black. Thunder boomed and lightning ripped the clouds. Davus and I hurried back to the house of Apollonides. Just as we reached the outer courtyard, rain began to pour down.

We found the house of the First Timouchos as we had left it, with the doors wide open and the slaves in a panic. The wing where I had last seen Meto was still guarded by soldiers, who barred our way and refused to listen to any pleas or threats I could think of.

Where was Meto? What arrangements—for the surrender of the city, for his own survival—had he made with Apollonides, and did those arrangements still mean anything now that Apollonides was gone? If Apollonides had intentionally thrown himself from the Sacrifice Rock, had he first taken revenge on his enemies? Once again I found myself desperately worried about my son.

If he were still alive and well, why did Meto not seek me

out? Of course, I could guess the answer to that: Meto was too busy. With Apollonides gone, others among the Timouchoi would have to negotiate the surrender. In these final hours of Massilia's independence, all Meto's schemes were coming to fruition. Those schemes were his only priority, and in them his father played no part.

Davus, always practical, declared his intention to go scavenging for food. I was light-headed from hunger, but I had no appetite. Bone-weary, I made my way to the rooms that briefly had served as Hieronymus's quarters. In the bedchamber, I collapsed amid the plush cushions where I had slept the previous night. I had no fear of being disturbed. What Massilian would dare to venture into the scapegoat's chambers in the first hours after his death, while his restless lemur might yet stalk the earth?

Rain lashed the house. Amid the crashing of thunder and the howling of the wind arose another noise: wails of lamentation. News of their master's death had reached the slaves who still cowered in the house. One by one they joined in keening for the dead leader of a dying city.

Despite all this, I slept; and for better or worse, Hypnos sent me no dreams.

I awoke with the sensation that someone had been watching me while I slept and had just left the room. The sensation was so powerful that I bolted upright, instantly awake. The room was empty. It must have been Meto, I thought. But why had he not awakened me? Perhaps I had only been dreaming, after all. . . .

A moment later, Davus stepped into the room. "Finally, you're awake! You'll want to hurry out of bed. Something's happening down at the city gates. Something big!"

I rubbed my eyes. "Davus, were you just in this room . . . watching me?"

"No."

"Was someone else just in this room?"

He frowned and put his hands on his hips. "I don't know. I was over in the next room, out on the balcony, watching all the people heading down toward the city gates. Someone might have come in here from the anteroom and the hallway outside, and I wouldn't have seen them . . ."

I blinked. "Is it still raining?"

"No. The storm lasted all night, but now it's over. There's a blue sky and bright sunshine. But what's this?" He let out a cry of delight and rushed to a little tripod table in the corner. "Figs! A whole pile of figs! I couldn't find a scrap of food anywhere last night. I hardly slept at all, I was so hungry. But look at these! They're beautiful. So dark and plump. And the smell! Here, have one. Then we'll head down to the gates."

Davus bit into a fig and laughed with delight. Until I ventured to take a small bite, I hadn't realized just how hungry I was. The sheer pleasure of it overwhelmed me. It was the best fig I had ever tasted.

No starving slave could have been trusted to leave that pile of figs for a sleeping man; the slave would have devoured them. Meto himself must have left them for us, I decided. But why had he not awakened me? Why had he left without a word?

A great crowd had gathered at the city gates. A cordon of soldiers with upright spears held back the throng and kept clear a wide passage from the gates to the center of the market square.

The people around us looked weary, hungry and miserable, but their eyes gleamed with anticipation. For months they had waited, dreaded, hoped. Now, at last, in the next few moments, something would happen. Would they be forgiven and fed by their new master—or cruelly slaughtered? They seemed hardly to care which fate awaited them as long as something put an end to their suspense.

Every crowd makes its own peculiar noise. This one sounded like the a field of tall grass on a breezy day, swaying and hissing in the wind. People spoke constantly, nervously, but never above a whisper. Like fickle winds, hushed rumors of imminent doom and deliverance flitted this way and that through the crowd.

Like everyone else, I found myself staring fixedly at the gates. The great bronze doors stood intact, as did the flanking towers, but only a few steps away gaped the huge breach in the wall, with great piles of rubble strewn about, including the remains of a bastion tower lying on its side. The breach had the strange effect of making the gates look as if they were merely a prop. A theatrical facade may have doors and windows and balconies, but only masquerades as a house or a temple. Just so, the gates of Massilia did not seem really to be gates at all, but only a convincing imitation. What function does a gate possess when the wall nearby has a gap in it large enough to admit a stampeding herd of elephants?

And yet, all eyes were on the gates. When trumpeters atop the flanking towers blasted a fanfare and the great bronze doors parted with a clang, every voice fell silent.

Months ago, the gates had been closed to Caesar. They had remained barred ever since. Now, with a great deal of creaking, they slowly swung outward until they stood wide open. Around me I heard sighs and weeping. The breaching of the wall had been an unimaginable disaster, but for the gates to be opened to the enemy was a disaster of even greater magnitude. Massilia had not merely been bested; the proud city that had stood independent for five hundred years had now surrendered herself to a conqueror.

Roman soldiers marched through the gates. No one could have been surprised, yet the crowd still gave a collective shudder and a gasp. There were scattered screams. Men and women fainted.

The first Romans to pass through the gates fell out of rank and took the places of the Massilian soldiers lining that end of the cordon; the Massilians threw down their spears and tramped out of the gates, giving themselves up. The next rank of marching Romans took the places of the Massilians farther up the cordon, and so on. This ceremonial replacement continued in an orderly fashion until not a Massilian soldier was left. Romans now made up the cordon that held back the crowd, and the broad passage from the gateway to the center of the square was littered with discarded spears.

There was another blast from the trumpets. Trebonius came riding in on horseback, accompanied by his officers. Among them I recognized the engineer Vitruvius, who kept looking over his shoulder and peering at the breach in the wall, more interested in Massilia's failed ramparts than in her conquered people.

A few people cheered halfheartedly. Their uncertainty prompted scattered laughter. The mood of the crowd was tense. Trebonius scowled.

If the gates of Massilia seemed an overwrought theatrical facade, then Caesar's arrival was like that of a deus ex machina. Had he been lifted down from the sky by a crane, literally like a god at the climax of a drama, the effect on the crowd could hardly have been more stunning. A white charger cantered through the gates, and upon it sat a figure wearing a golden breastplate that gleamed in the sunlight. His bright crimson cape was thrown behind him. His balding head was bare and his red-crested helmet was tucked under one arm, as if to demonstrate that he was unafraid to show his face to men and gods alike; for though the gods might have turned a blind eye to Massilia in the preceding months, who could doubt that they were watching now?

Caesar reached the clearing at the center of the marketplace, then slowly turned his charger in a full circle, surveying the crowd. In the utter silence, the clatter of the charger's hooves against the paving stones echoed loudly.

Davus and I had worked our way through the crowd to a place just outside the cordon of soldiers at the center, close enough to see Caesar's face clearly. His lips were tightly pressed together, not quite smiling. His bright eyes were wide open. His long chin, high cheekbones, and balding pate (about which, according to Meto, he was so sensitive) gave him an austere, ascetic appearance. Somehow he managed to look both grim and pleased at the same time. It was an appropriate expression for the god to wear at the end of a drama, when he appears from nowhere to pronounce the judgment of heaven and restore order to chaos.

Caesar spoke at what seemed to be a normal, almost conversational pitch, but from long training in the Forum and on the battlefield his voice reached every corner of the market square. "People of Massilia," he began, "for many years we were the best of friends, you and I. Just as Massilia has ever been the ally of Rome, so you were my ally. Yet when I came to you some months ago, you shut your gates to me. You severed all ties to me. You pledged your allegiance to another.

"Today, you see the fruits of that decision. Your harbor is desolate. Your fathers and mothers are sick from pestilence. Your children weep from hunger. Your walls have fallen and your gates stand open against your will. When I asked for it, had you given me your friendship and your support, I would have rewarded you generously; my arrival today would be an occasion of mutual thanksgiving. Instead, it has come to this. I must take what I require, and my terms will not be those of an ally with an ally.

"When I last passed by, my situation was uncertain. Ahead, I faced the prospect of a long campaign in Spain. Behind me, in my absence, I had no assurance that events in Rome would unfold to my liking. The circumstances were such that you might have negotiated with me to your advantage; oh, yes, I know how you Massilians love to drive a hard bargain! Whatever agreements I might have made with you then, I would have honored, upon my dignity as a Roman. But it was not to be; you closed your gates to me and declared yourself my enemy.

"Now, upon my return, the circumstances are quite different. The forces that opposed me in Spain have been vanquished. From the East comes word that Pompey and his misguided supporters are more confused and paralyzed with uncertainty than ever. And upon my arrival in camp this morning, extraordinary news arrived simultaneously by messenger from Rome. To deal with the current crisis, the Senate has voted to appoint a dictator. I am honored to say that the praetor Marcus Lepidus has nominated me for that distinguished post, and upon my return to Rome, I intend to accept the people's mandate to restore order to the city and her provinces.

"What, then, shall I do about Massilia? When you might have welcomed me, you spurned me; more than that, you harbored my enemies and declared me your foe. When your walls were breached, my general Trebonius respected your flag of parley and restrained his men from storming the city—yet you dared to send an incendiary force against my siegeworks! A more vengeful man than myself might seize upon this occasion to make an example of such a treacherous city. If Massilia were to meet the same terrible fate as Troy or Carthage, who would dare to argue that I had dealt with her unjustly?

"But I am not a vengeful man, and I see cause for mercy. At the last moment, the leaders of your city saw reason. They ordered your soldiers to lay down their arms. They opened the gates to me. They have put in my hand the key to your treasury, so that Massilia may contribute her full share to my campaign to restore order. I see no reason why Massilia and Rome cannot once again be friends, although that friendship from now on must necessarily be on terms very different than before. When I leave for Rome, as I must do almost at once, I shall leave behind a garrison of two legions to make certain that the order I have established here will prevail.

"I have made up my mind, then, to show mercy to Massilia.

I made this decision not in return for services rendered, however belatedly, and certainly not out of respect for those misguided leaders who delivered Massilia to this sorry pass. No, I was swayed to show mercy because of the deep and abiding veneration I feel for the ancient fame of this city. That which Artemis has protected for five hundred years, I will not obliterate in a moment. On this day, Massilia might have been destroyed. Instead, she shall be reborn."

Where the cheering started from, I couldn't tell. I suspected it originated with a cue from Trebonius to the cordon of Roman soldiers, and was then gradually picked up by the crowd, who at first murmured uncertain acclamations, then cried out more and more unrestrainedly. Caesar had, after all, spared them from death. They and their children would live. The future of Massilia—a vassal now to Rome—would not be what they had expected and hoped for, but for the simple fact that Massilia had a future, they were thankful. The long struggle was over; and if nothing else, they had survived. For that, they cheered, louder and louder, more and more wildly.

Perhaps, I thought grimly, the scapegoat's sacrifice had worked after all, even despite his apparent last-minute change of heart. Massilia had been spared.

As the cheering went on and grew even louder, a slight commotion nearby indicated that a procession of some sort was making its way through the crowd, toward Caesar. I craned my neck in the direction of the movement and saw, bobbing above the crowd, a golden eagle with red pennants streaming behind. It was the eagle standard of Catilina.

Caesar saw the procession approaching and beckoned to the soldiers to make an opening. The standard entered the clearing, borne aloft, as I knew it would be, by Meto. My son was dressed now in his finest battle armor. He smiled broadly and gazed up at Caesar with unabashed adoration.

Caesar's face remained stern, but his eyes glittered as he

looked upon the eagle standard. He glanced down only briefly to acknowledge Meto's worshipful gaze.

The others in the little procession did not enter the clearing but stood at its edge, outside the cordon of soldiers. Among them I saw Gaius Verres, who crossed his arms and tilted his head at a rakish angle, smiling smugly. Beside Verres I saw Publicius and Minucius and a great many other men in togas, whom I took to be their fellow Catilinarians in exile. At the sight of Caesar extending his hand to accept the eagle standard from Meto, they practically swooned. They threw their arms in the air, cried out, dropped to their knees, and wept with joy.

Wanting a better look at Meto, I had gradually drawn closer to the clearing until, like the Catilinarians, I stood just outside the cordon of soldiers. It was not Meto who noticed me—his gaze was for Caesar only—but the imperator himself. When Caesar at last took his eyes from the eagle to survey the cheering crowd, his gaze came to rest on me. We had met only a few times and always briefly, yet he recognized me at once. His lips curved almost into a smile. When he leaned over to hand his helmet to Meto, I saw him speak into Meto's ear.

Meto stepped back. Looking dazed, he peered in my direction. It took him a moment to find me. When he did, he stepped toward the cordon and told the soldiers to let me through. The soldiers looked to Caesar, who discreetly nodded.

I stepped reluctantly into the clearing. Before me, Caesar sat astride his white charger, holding aloft the eagle standard that had once belonged to Marius. What did this moment mean to him? Now Caesar was conqueror of Gaul and Spain; now he had transcended even his mentor, for Marius had never become dictator of Rome. Nearby, the acclamations of the Catilinarians had become even wilder and more ecstatic. Here at the very center of the uproar, the cheering of the crowd was thunderous.

A curious revelation had come to me when I decided to enter

Massilia by tunnel: with age I seemed to have grown not less impulsive, but more so, not more cautious, but less. Was it because, from accumulated experience, I no longer needed to tortuously think a thing through before I acted? Or had I simply lost all patience with slow reason and fearsome hesitation, and come full circle to act as a child acts—as gods act—from pure, spontaneous willfulness?

I had not planned beforehand to do what I did in that clearing. I had not even imagined such a moment.

Meto stepped toward me. He was holding Caesar's helmet with one hand. With the other he was stroking the red horsehair plume, as one might stroke a cat. He grinned, shook his head, and raised his eyebrows. "It's all a bit overwhelming, isn't it, Papa?"

I simply stared at him, resisting a sudden impulse to knock the helmet from his hand.

"Papa, when all this is over . . . when I finally come home—"

"Home, Meto? Where is that?" I found myself shouting, simply to be heard. My heart pounded in my chest.

He wrinkled his brow. "Your house in Rome, of course."

"No! My home is not your home, Meto. Not now. Not ever again."

He laughed nervously. "Papa, what in Hades are you—?"

" 'When all this is over,' you say. And when will that be, Meto? Never! And why should you want it to be over? You thrive on it! Trickery, lying, betrayals—for you, they're not means to some glorious end. They're an end in themselves."

"Papa, I'm not sure—"

"First you became a soldier, and you thrived on it, killing Gauls for the glory of Caesar. Burning villages, enslaving children, leaving widows to starve—it always sickened me, though I never spoke against it. Now you've found a new calling, spying for Caesar, destroying others by deceit. It sickens me even more." I had raised my voice so much that even Caesar overheard. Atop his charger, he glanced down at the two of us with a puzzled frown. Meto's face was ashen.

"Papa, I don't understand."

"Nor do I. Is this how I raised you? Did I pass nothing of myself on to you?"

"But, Papa, I learned everything from you."

"No! What matters most to me? Uncovering the truth! I do it even when there's no point to it, even when it brings only pain. I do it because I must. But you, Meto? What does truth mean to you? You can't abide it, any more than I can abide deceit! We're complete opposites. No wonder you've found your place at the side of a man like Caesar."

Meto lowered his voice. "Papa, we'll talk about this later."

"There is no later! This is our last conversation, Meto."

"Papa, you're upset because I . . . I wasn't as forthcoming . . . as I might have been."

"Don't talk to me like a politician! You deceived me. First, you let me believe that you were part of a plot to kill Caesar—"

"That was regrettable, Papa, but I had no choice—"

"Then you flaunted your disguise as the soothsayer in my face! You let me think that you were dead!"

Meto trembled. "When this is over . . . when we're able to talk—"

"No! Never again!"

"But, Papa, I'm your son!"

"No, you are not." Speaking the words made me feel cold and hollow inside, but I couldn't stop them from spilling out. "From this moment, you are not my son, Meto. I disown you. Here, before your beloved imperator—excuse me, your *dictator*—I disown you. I renounce all concern for you. I take back from you my name. If you need a father, let Caesar adopt you!"

Meto looked as if he had been struck in the forehead with a mallet. If I had wished merely to stun him, I had succeeded. But the look on his face gave me no pleasure; I couldn't stand to look at him. Caesar, knowing that something was wrong, called to Meto to come to him, but Meto stood unmoving and unheeding.

The crowd continued to cheer. The cheering had taken on a life of its own; people cheered simply for the sake of cheering, as a means to let out all the pent-up emotions inside them. The sound they made was like a roaring waterfall that showed no signs of running dry.

I pushed my way past the soldiers and through the mass of jubilant Catilinarians. Verres threw back his head, laughing. Publicius and Minucius attempted to seize me and swing me about in a joyful dance, but I pulled free and plunged blindly into the crowd. Davus was nearby; I did not see him but sensed his presence, knew that he was staying close to me but keeping out of my way, wondering, no doubt, what in Hades had just happened. How often had I silently ridiculed Davus for his guilelessness and his simple nature? Yet at that moment, how much more like a son he felt to me than the man I was leaving behind!

XXVI

"Go ahead, say it. You think I made a terrible mistake, don't you?"

Davus frowned but said nothing. We stood side by side at the ship's rail, looking back at Massilia as it dwindled in the distance. Viewed from the sea, the narrow city within its high walls looked cramped and tiny.

Salt spray stung my nostrils. Gulls followed close behind us, flapping their wings and cawing shrilly. Sailors called back and forth as they lifted oars and hoisted sail. As we threaded a course between the rugged headlands and the islands offshore, Massilia disappeared from view.

The ship was one of the three that Domitius had held in reserve for his escape. Driven by the storm, Domitius himself—always the rabbit eluding the trap—had succeeded in slipping past the blockade, but his two companion ships had been turned back. Now they were Caesar's ships. This one Caesar was dispatching back to Rome, loaded with treasure and with lieutenants charged with making preparations for his triumphant return.

It was Trebonius who approached me and offered places for Davus and me on the first ship out. It seemed that Caesar's bountiful generosity extended even to me, despite my actions in the market square. Perhaps Caesar was fulfilling a promise to Meto to see me safely home. More likely, he simply wanted to get me out of the way as quickly as possible, before my unwanted presence could dampen even further the morale of one of his most valued men.

I saw no reason not to accept. The sooner I could leave Massilia, the better, and I had no desire to retrace the long, landward route back to Rome, especially if it meant sharing the road with Caesar's legions.

What would become of the proud city now? One thing was certain: Massilia would never be independent again. What Rome takes, she keeps; freedom is a gift she never gives back. The Timouchoi would be reduced to a mere ceremonial body or disbanded altogether; all power now would come from Rome and Rome's dictator. I could easily imagine Zeno presiding over the city as Caesar's puppet, obediently taking orders from a Roman governor.

As for the Roman exiles in Massilia, Caesar, exercising a dictator's largesse, had pardoned them wholesale. Publicius and Minucius and their fellows would be going back to Rome. But Caesar had specified two notable exceptions. Despite his guardianship of the eagle standard, Verres would remain in exile. So would Milo.

I sighed, and hefted the heavy, bulging purse tied at my waist. If nothing else, I was leaving Massilia a richer man than I had arrived. Even as I was boarding the ship, Arausio had sought me out and had insisted on paying me generously for my efforts to discover the truth about his daughter. Rindel was safely back in her father's house. Apollonides had released her and her parents just as he had allowed Davus and me to go free. The final scene on the Sacrifice Rock had posed yet another puzzle: Did Apollonides intend to revenge himself on Rindel, and had he been prevented only because Hieronymus pulled him, unwilling, to his death? Or did Apollonides intentionally throw himself from the rock, and before his suicide, had he made up his mind to be merciful to Rindel? Having lost his own daughter, perhaps he had no desire to inflict the same grief on Arausio.

For the time being, Rindel was locked in her room, where she would remain, Arausio declared, no matter how much she wept and tore her hair, declaring her love for Zeno. "What grief our children cause us!" he had muttered as he left me. I had not contradicted him.

Apollonides had lost his Cydimache. Arausio had lost his Rindel, and then, to his delight and consternation, had found her again. I had lost Meto, found him, and lost him again forever. I had acted rightly, I told myself. What I did, I had to do. Why, then, did I feel a nagging doubt? I professed to hate all deceit. Was I deceiving myself?

In our wake, the green waves churned and folded in on themselves. Somewhere in their depths was whatever remained of Cydimache and her unborn child, and Apollonides . . . and Hieronymus! He had been so dignified on the temple steps, so sure of himself, so fearless. What had gone wrong? There had been a struggle—but had Hieronymus struggled to save himself, or to take Apollonides with him? It seemed unfair that I should have resolved the circumstance of one death from the Sacrifice Rock, only to be leaving Massilia with the circumstance of two more deaths unresolved.

The voice, coming from behind me, raised hackles on the back of my neck: "Did you enjoy the figs I left for you?"

Davus and I spun around together. For a moment I was speechless; no breath would come. "Hieronymus!" I finally cried.

Davus laughed, then gasped. "But . . . we saw you—"

"You saw me go tumbling with Apollonides off the Sacrifice Rock?"

"Yes!" I cried. "I saw you. So did Davus."

Hieronymus raised an eyebrow. "Never trust your eyes, Gordianus. That bit of confusion between Cydimache and Rindel should have taught you that."

I reached out and gripped his arms to satisfy myself that he was real. "But, Hieronymus, what happened? What *did* we see?"

"Everything went according to Apollonides's plan; overseeing the sacrifice was his last official act as First Timouchos. I was kept in the dark; I didn't know what Apollonides had in mind until I was actually atop the Sacrifice Rock. I expected to die. I was prepared to do so. But when I reached the summit, what should I see, lying in the hollow of the rock surrounded by priests, but another figure swathed in green from head to toe—my double!

"Apollonides ordered me to stay back. The priests swarmed around me. In the blink of an eye, they had me out of my green robes and into white ones, so that I looked like another priest. It was all very confusing. Clouds of incense swirled around us. Apollonides hissed at me to keep quiet and pressed a very substantial bag of coins into my hands—loot from his final raid on the treasury, no doubt. If I wished to keep breathing, he said, I was to keep my mouth shut, show myself to no one, and leave Massilia on the first ship out; your son Meto would handle the arrangements.

"I stood there, dumbfounded. Meanwhile, the priests had lifted the other fellow in green to his feet. They were trying to push him toward the precipice. His arms must have been bound beneath his robes, but he still managed to put up a struggle, thrashing this way and that. I suppose he was gagged as well, because he didn't utter a sound, not even when Apollonides threw his arms around him and the two of them staggered and pitched and finally plunged over the edge."

Davus frowned. "But who was it? Who was the man in green?"

"Who else?" I said quietly. "Zeno."

Hieronymus nodded. "It must have been. Once Apollonides decided to end his own life—and who could be surprised at that, after the shock of Cydimache's death and the shame of losing the city—he was determined to take Zeno with him. What more fitting place for both of them to meet their ends than there on the Sacrifice Rock? Because Zeno took my place, the priests agreed to spare me. It's a lucky scapegoat who has a scapegoat to take his place!

"I spent the night at the Temple of Artemis. You'd be amazed at how much food the priests still have, hoarded away. That's where the figs came from. The next morning, while everyone was gathering at the gates, I thought I'd steal into Apollonides's house and collect a few personal items from my rooms while I had the chance. I expected to find the house deserted, and it was, except for you two. You were sleeping like a child, Gordianus. I didn't dare awaken you. No one could know I was still alive, not even you."

"Deceived yet again, for my own good," I muttered.

"But I left you the figs!" said Hieronymus. "It seemed the least I could do." He sighed, stepped to the rail, and gazed back in the direction of Massilia. "I shall never return. I've never been anywhere else. Is Rome as wonderful as everyone says?"

"Wonderful?" I asked quietly. By the time we returned, the Senate would have acted on the proposal put forward by the praetor Lepidus. When Caesar arrived, resplendent in glory, he would enter not as a mere proconsul or imperator, but as dictator of Rome, the first since Sulla.

Hieronymus put his arms around Davus and me. "Wonderful, yes! Because when I arrive there, I shall already have two great friends!"

He grinned, happy to be alive. For his sake, I managed a halfhearted smile. Together, we three watched the waves and the gulls circling overheard. The day was bright and clear, but it seemed to me that my eyes were scarcely of more use than those of a blind man. The sunlit world around me was full of shadows. Those I thought dead had returned to life. The one I had known best in all the world, I did not know at all. The truth of a moment clearly seen could never be surely known, for everything of real importance happened inside the heads of others, where no man can see. I could not see clearly even inside myself! Was it the world that wore a mask of deceit, or was I the veiled one, unable to see beyond the veil of my own illusions?

After a while, we left the ship's stern and walked to the prow. "Look!" cried Davus. "Dolphins!"

Chattering like giddy children, the dolphins leaped and dove through the waves alongside the ship, like a vanguard escorting us home. Massilia and the dead past lay behind us. Rome and the uncertain future lay ahead.

AUTHOR'S NOTE

Massilia is the Latin name for the city the founding Greeks called Massalia and which the modern French call Marseille. Our knowledge of the ancient city comes from an array of scattered, tantalizing references. From Aristotle and Cicero we learn something of the city's government; Strabo explains the hierarchy of the Timouchoi. Servius's commentary on *The Aeneid* cites a lost fragment of *The Satyricon,* which refers to the tradition of the scapegoat. Valerius Maximus relates some curious customs, such as the fact that the Massilians facilitated suicide so long as it was officially approved. From Plutarch's *Life of Marius* comes the tale of the vineyard fenced with the bones of slain Gauls. Lucian's *Toxaris, or Friendship* recites the strange tale of Cydimache, which I have freely adapted. My method has been to gather these intriguing tidbits and to assemble them around the crucial moment of Massilian history, the siege of the city by Julius Caesar in 49 B.C.

About the siege itself, our information is less scattered and more concrete, but naggingly inexact. Caesar's self-serving (and therefore not entirely reliable) *The Civil War* is our prime source. Lucan's epic *Pharsalia* vividly describes the razing of the ancient forest and the bloody sea battles, but Lucan is a poet, not a historian. Cassius Dio gives the background of the siege, and Vitruvius sketches a few details. The British historian T. Rice Holmes, in a feat of ratiocination worthy of his kinsman Sherlock, assembled all the data and put forward a credible reconstruction of events in *The Roman Republic and the Founder of the Empire* (1923). But as Holmes himself ruefully acknowledges, "The history of the siege presents many difficulties and its chronology is obscure."

Until very recently, comprehensive studies of ancient Massilia were to be found only in French, in Michel Clerc's two-volume *Massalia* (1927, 1929) and J.-P. Clébert's two-volume *Provence Antique* (1966, 1970). This changed in 1998 with the publication of A. Trevor Hodge's witty and astute *Ancient Greek France*. (Noting the city's position, before the siege, as Rome's window onto Gaul, Hodge points out that "Massilia was an ideal centre for gathering intelligence, more or less in the way Berlin was in the old days of the Cold War.") An older but still useful volume is *The Romans on the Riviera and the Rhone* by W. H. Hall (1898).

Nan Robkin pointed me to the research of A. Trevor Hodge long before his book was published. Claudine Chalmers supplied me with relevant pages from the *Guide de la Provence Mystérieuse*. Claude Cueni linked me to images of ancient Massilia from the Musée des Docks Romains and the Musée d'Histoire in Marseille. Penni Kimmel read the first draft. Thanks, as always, to

Rick Solomon; to my editor, Keith Kahla; and to my agent, Alan Nevins.

The fates of various historical figures in *Last Seen in Massilia*—including Milo, Domitius, and Trebonius (not to mention Caesar)—may yet be dealt with in future volumes of the *Roma Sub Rosa*. But as it seems unlikely that Gordianus will cross paths again with Gaius Verres, I will note that the notorious art connoisseur came to a bad end. Six years after the siege, still an exile in Massilia, Verres was put to death in the same round of proscriptions, ordered by Marc Antony, that proved fatal to his old nemesis, Cicero. Verres's crime? Antony coveted one of his ill-gotten works of art.